Home at Last

Other books in the Chicory Inn series

Home to Chicory Lane
Two Roads Home
Another Way Home
Close to Home

Deborah Raney

Abingdon Press
Nashville

HOME AT LAST

Published in association with The Steve Laube Literary Agency

Macro Editor: Jamie Chavez

Library of Congress Cataloging-in-Publication Data

Names: Raney, Deborah, author. | Raney, Deborah. Chicory Inn novel.
Title: Home at last / Deborah Raney.
Description: Nashville : Abingdon Press, [2017] | Series: A Chicory Inn novel
Identifiers: LCCN 2016041059 (print) | LCCN 2016044551 (ebook) | ISBN 9781426770487 (pbk.) | ISBN 9781501837456 (e-book)
Subjects: LCSH: Interethnic dating—Fiction. | Man-woman relationships—Fiction. | Missouri—Fiction.
Classification: LCC PS3568.A562 H65 2017 (print) | LCC PS3568.A562 (ebook) | DDC 813/.54—dc23
LC record available at https://lccn.loc.gov/2016041059

16 17 18 19 20 21 22 23—10 9 8 7 6 5 4 3 2 1

MANUFACTURED IN THE UNITED STATES OF AMERICA

In memory of my precious grandparents
who carried on—then handed down—
a legacy of faith and love.
We intend to keep it going.

Acknowledgments

It seems like only yesterday that I was signing the contract for this five-book series. I could hardly imagine a day when the first book would be finished, let alone a day when I'd be writing "the end" on the final book! But here I am, and I must admit I shed a few tears saying good-bye to the Whitman family. We authors are strange that way. Our characters truly do become like family to us.

And once again, I'm struck with awe at how many people it takes to make a book become a reality. And how many people I owe such deep gratitude.

It would take an entire book to thank everyone who contributed to this series, whether through help with research, critiquing and editing, or the all-important "author support," which my dear friends and family do so well.

As always, my agent, Steve Laube, deserves a huge thank-you. We've been traveling this road together for over thirteen years now, and I can't say enough how much I appreciate you, Steve.

My critique partner and dear, dear friend, Tamera Alexander, has been walking with me even longer—ever since she offered to critique my novella at the very first ACFW conference in Kansas City in 2002. Tammy was published a few years later, quickly became one of my favorite writers on the planet, and has been running circles around me ever since! You are a gift from God, Tammy.

My original editor, Ramona Richards, shared my vision for this series about an ordinary yet extraordinary family simply living out their faith and learning to hang tight to God through the ups and downs of life. She and Jamie Chavez have given me such tremendous editorial direction throughout these past four years. I'm so grateful for you both.

The team at Abingdon Press has been wonderful to work with, and I am grateful and honored to be one of your authors.

To my dear Club Deb and my precious friends who know me better than anyone—and still somehow love me: Courtney, Mary, Roxy, Sharon, Terry. I can never express how much your friendship means to me.

So many friends, family, acquaintances, and complete strangers help in the research stage of a novel. I'm especially grateful to Noah and Julia Collins, Veronica Brayboy, and others who shared their experiences with me.

To my own big, loving family—my precious mom and dad, my wonderful spunky mother-in-law, my brother and sisters, my kids and in-laws of all varieties: thank you all for loving me, believing in me, offering support and encouragement. Daddy, I think you single-handedly sold (and gave away!) more books than most of the bookstores! Vicky, thank you for reading galleys for me when my deadlines didn't allow.

And as always, to the man who makes this earthly life So. Much. Fun. The love of my life, the man of my dreams, my best friend and garage-sale buddy, the father of my children, and the "papa" in Papa and Mimi. There simply are no words, babe, to say how much I love and respect you. But give me a few more years, and maybe I'll come up with something.

Finally, to my Lord and Savior, Jesus, the Christ, how very grateful and humbled I am that You have written my name in heaven.

For he himself is our peace, who has made the two groups one and has destroyed the barrier, the dividing wall of hostility, by setting aside in his flesh the law with its commands and regulations. His purpose was to create in himself one new humanity out of the two, thus making peace, and in one body to reconcile both of them to God through the cross, by which he put to death their hostility. He came and preached peace to you who were far away and peace to those who were near. For through him we both have access to the Father by one Spirit.

Consequently, you are no longer foreigners and strangers, but fellow citizens with God's people and also members of his household, built on the foundation of the apostles and prophets, with Christ Jesus himself as the chief cornerstone. In him the whole building is joined together and rises to become a holy temple in the Lord. And in him you too are being built together to become a dwelling in which God lives by his Spirit.

—Ephesians 2:14-22

1

A thin layer of snow and ice covered the narrowing road, and Link Whitman tapped the brakes to slow his pickup. Police in the little berg of Langhorne, Missouri, were famous for doling out speeding tickets, and Link already had two on his record—which gave new meaning to the *premium* in insurance premiums.

Running his fingers through unruly curls that could stand a good cut, he leaned to check his reflection in the truck's rearview mirror. His sisters would have given him a hard time if they'd seen.

Who you primping for, Linkie? Must be a girl!

He grinned to himself, hearing their high-pitched voices as clearly as if his sisters were in the seat behind him.

He loved his sisters, but they could annoy the tar out of him too. And ever since Bree had gotten engaged, the Whitman women had upped the ante big-time. After Bree and Drew's wedding next month, he'd be the last Whitman standing, and the pressure was on. All his siblings had kids too, and no doubt Bree would want to start a family right away. Yep, he was a slacker, and his sisters would remind him at every opportunity. Mom would do worse. She'd already tried to set him up with some great-niece of a friend of a friend of a friend.

No thank you. He could find his own woman. And he'd do it when he was good and ready.

He gave a little snort. Who was he kidding? He'd been good and ready for a long time. But he wasn't going to settle for the first pretty thing that came along. He had standards. Standards too high, according to his sisters.

Well, they'd be happy to know he was on a mission today. A mission involving a woman. He didn't think Mom suspected anything when he'd jumped at the chance to make a bakery run for her this morning. But a certain girl who worked there had caught his eye.

He'd actually met Shayla first at the homeless shelter in Cape Girardeau. He and some buddies from work had done a couple of volunteer projects there last summer, getting the shelter's Internet and office computers set up. He'd pulled into the parking lot at the same time as Shayla and had helped her carry in a stack of boxes from the bakery.

Listening to her snarky banter with the other volunteers and a crazy client they were dealing with, he'd fallen in love with her a little bit that day. Then more than a little, once he got up the courage to talk to her the following week. And the week after that. And the one after that. The shelter's computers had never run so seamlessly. And since he was volunteering his time, he felt only slightly guilty for making excuses to keep "tweaking" their system on the days he knew Shayla would be delivering. And he *had* made things work better each time he was there. But if someone—say his sisters, *or Shayla*—wanted to make a case against him for stalking her, they wouldn't have to look too far for evidence.

He didn't care. The more he'd gotten to know Shayla, the more he liked what he saw. Not that she was making it easy. Over bad coffee, compliments of the shelter, they'd practically solved the problems of homelessness, world hunger, and the recent city council elections. They'd also agreed on best doughnut—sour cream cruller—and which houseplants were the easiest to kill—maidenhair fern and fiddle-leaf fig, which Shayla knew from experience and Link could discuss semi-intelligently thanks to his sisters. But he had yet to learn anything really personal about the mysterious Shayla. Unless you counted that she hated her hair—

thick, wild curls that weren't quite an Afro, but close...and cute as all get out, in his opinion. Which she hadn't asked for and he hadn't given.

He'd flirted with her the last couple of times he'd been in the bakery. And if he knew anything at all about women, it seemed the feeling might be mutual. *Shayla*. He was still working on getting her last name. His mission today: get that name and talk her into a real date. Just coffee. He didn't want to scare her off.

His cell phone chirped from his pocket, and he fished it out. Mom. He tapped the brakes again and answered. "Hey, Mom. What's up?"

"Have you already left the bakery?"

"Nope. Just got into town."

"Oh, good." She breathed a relieved sigh into the phone. "Could you also see if they have any cinnamon rolls? Or maybe a coffee cake? Anything that would feed four guests in the morning? We got a last-minute reservation and I have too many other irons in the fire to be baking."

"Sure. But don't you feel guilty putting the Chicory Inn's reputation on the line like that?" he teased.

"Not one bit. And don't you go trying to change things."

"Don't worry, I'll bail you out. It'll cost you though."

"Ha ha." She tried to sound irked, but Link heard the smile beneath her tone.

"I'm here now," he said as the Coffee's On Bakery came into view. "See you in about twenty minutes."

"You'd better *not* show up here in twenty minutes. There is no way you can do all that and get back here in twenty minutes, and I happen to know you don't need another speeding ticket."

"What? How did you find—"

Something—a dog? a coyote?—darted into the street in front of him, a blur of brown against the dirty snow paving the street.

He slammed on the brakes, spewing a word his mom would not appreciate.

"Link? What happened? Link?"

His brakes squealed as the pickup skidded, and he held his breath as two tons of steel careened directly toward the anim—Wait! That wasn't a dog. It was a *kid*!

The brake pedal was already pressed to the floor, but he pushed harder then gave the pedal a frantic pump, his pulse screaming in his ears. *Please, God! No!*

Somehow his cell phone had ended up in the passenger seat, and he could hear his mother's distant frantic cries. But he had bigger things to worry about. The kid stood frozen in the middle of the street staring up at him through the windshield, mouth agape, her wild curly hair blowing in the wind. She needed to move! Now!

The pickup was in a slow-motion, sideways skid now. There was no time to lose! Adrenaline gushing, he slammed the gear-shift into park, threw open his door, and half ran, half slid toward the girl. He scooped her to his chest and rolled with her out of the path of the front fender.

Heart slamming, he watched the truck come to a full stop, tires grinding against the curb. When he could finally catch a breath, he scrambled to his feet with the girl in his arms. She scarcely weighed more than a feather, but she started screaming like a banshee, kicking at his knees with her little brown boots. Sharp-toed boots. *Ouch!* And while she might be a featherweight, fear had given her the strength of a cornered doe.

"Oww!" He grabbed her legs with his free hand and tried to hold them still while also remaining upright—no easy feat considering the ice.

About that time, a woman came flying out of the bakery, wailing. She stepped off the curb—and instantly bit the dust. Link watched, open-mouthed, as she rolled over and scrambled on all fours on the icy street, looking frantically to where Link was trying to stay on his own feet on a thin sheet of sleet and ice. With this little spitfire still flailing in his arms.

"Stay there!" he yelled, his breath forming puffs of steam in the cold November air. The next vehicle to come by might not see her, and she definitely wasn't taking time to look both ways before crossing the street.

"Portia! Baby? Are you okay?"

He knew that voice. It was Shayla! Her gaze didn't leave the child in Link's arms.

He shifted the little girl to face outward so Shayla could see she was in one piece—despite the blood-curdling screams pouring from the tiny creature. Tucking the girl under one arm like a football—or more like one of those crazy bouncy balls his nephews had—he half skated across the street.

He helped her to her feet with his free hand and started to transfer the little girl to her arms when Shayla began pounding her fists on his chest.

"You could have killed her! You could have *killed* her!"

He stumbled backward, trying to fend off the mama bear's blows while baby bear continued to thrash in his arms. "Hey, stop! She's okay. She's going to be okay!"

Seeming oblivious to the fact that he held the little girl, Shayla continued screaming at him, then, without warning, she wilted into a puddle at his feet.

He didn't think she'd recognized him yet. She was, understandably, a little out of her mind. It seemed a petty thought considering what had just happened, but he hadn't known she had a kid. *Did that change things?* Not that it mattered now. Nearly running over a woman's daughter probably wasn't his best pick-up line.

Shayla wept gulping sobs that might have scared him a little more if he hadn't been raised with three drama queens for sisters. Not that Shayla didn't have cause to be upset, but her little girl was obviously fine.

He set the child down on the sidewalk next to her, keeping tight hold on the fur collar of the kid's coat so she didn't escape again. "Hey?" He knelt beside Shayla. "You okay?"

Without looking up, she waved him away, then pulled the little girl onto her lap.

"It's cold out here," Link said. She was in shirtsleeves except for the bib apron that bore the Coffee's On logo. "And that sidewalk is a sheet of ice. Why don't we get you both inside?" He offered his hand.

But she batted it away. "I can get myself inside. I think you've *helped* enough for one day." She sniffed and looked up at him, topaz-colored eyes blazing. Slowly, recognition dawned in them. "It . . . it's you." Her creamy brown complexion went rosy.

"Yes. It's Link." He offered his hand again.

But she ignored it. "Go on about your business. We're fine." She pushed the little girl's corkscrew curls off her forehead and inspected her for injury. The child's hair and skin were a paler shade of brown than Shayla's—almost a muddy blonde—and her eyes were a striking blue-gray. Even so, she was the spitting image of Shayla. The little girl whimpered, but she didn't appear to be bleeding or otherwise harmed. A miracle.

Watching them together, the sequence of events replayed in his mind, and he shuddered, feeling a little weak in the knees himself. "That *was* a close one."

Shayla pierced him with a look. "Yeah, well . . . You might want to think about slowing down next time. You could have killed her."

"So you said." *About fifteen times.* He narrowed his eyes. "And you might want to think about watching your kid closer next time." He turned toward the street, half wishing he'd held his tongue. But *seriously*? She was going to blame *him*? He'd quite possibly saved the kid's life. She should be thanking him.

"Hey!"

He turned back at the strident chord in her voice, preparing to get chewed out again.

But she only said, "You're coming for the order for the B&B, right? The Chicory Inn?"

He eyed her. "Yes." *Wanna make something of it?*

"Your order's ready." She pointed a thumb over her shoulder. "Inside."

"Oh." He curbed the urge to roll his eyes. "Thanks. My mom would've killed me if I forgot." He winced inwardly. *Nice choice of words, Whitman. Way to remind her you nearly ran over her daughter* and *that you're running errands for your mommy.*

Shayla struggled to her feet, testing the sidewalk beneath her before lifting the girl into her arms. "Come on in. I'll ring you up."

Did he hear a hint of truce in her tone? "You're sure I'm allowed in your store? After all, I did almost kill your daughter." He couldn't help it. The sarcasm came second nature.

She opened her mouth to say something, but instead, hitched her daughter higher on one hip and opened the door to the bakery.

Shaking his head, Link followed her inside.

The heady scents of coffee, warm cinnamon rolls, and maple icing wafted over them, and Link couldn't keep from inhaling deeply. The mingling of aromas had a calming effect on him.

Shayla set the little girl down at a child's table near the cash register. The stack of coloring books and buckets of crayons and markers on the table looked like a scene from one of his sisters' homes, and the little girl was instantly distracted.

Flecks of ice sparkled in Shayla's wild Afro. She looked gorgeous as ever, even if her complexion now seemed more gray than the creamy mahogany shade he remembered. Behind the counter, she consulted an order pad. "You had two dozen Parker House and a loaf of rye, right?"

"Yes. I guess. Whatever Mom ordered." He didn't have a clue and couldn't remember right now if his life depended on it. No doubt, his mother—He took in a sharp breath. *Mom!* He'd left her on the phone thinking he'd been in an accident. She'd be frantic.

He reached into his pocket then remembered his cell was still in the truck. At least he hoped it was. "Hang on a sec, would you? My phone . . . Be right back."

She barely nodded and went on wrapping the bread.

He risked ruffling the little girl's hair as he went by. She flinched at his touch, but at least she didn't start screaming. Shoot, his ears were *still* ringing.

He jogged out to the pickup and did a quick walk around, inspecting it much the way Shayla had inspected her daughter. The truck was caked with dirty slush and mud, and the back right tire was scuffed where it had met the curb, but otherwise, no worse for the wear. He considered reparking since the truck had parallel parked itself across two angled parking spaces, but there were plenty of open spots on the street, and he didn't want Shayla to think he was leaving.

After calling his mother and giving her a carefully edited version of the morning's events, he tucked his cell in his pocket and trotted back into the shop.

A white bag with the bakery's logo stamped on the side sat waiting on the counter, a receipt stapled to the side.

He looked at it. It seemed a little high, but he retrieved his wallet from his back pocket and extracted a twenty-dollar bill.

She made change and handed it to him without a word, seeming a little dazed. Well, he was too. He bent to peer into her eyes. "You sure you're okay?"

"I'm fine." She wiped her hands on her apron and came around the counter, peeking at the table where her little girl was bent over a coloring book.

He held up the bag of rolls. "Thanks." He almost felt like he should apologize, even though he'd done nothing wrong, but under the circumstances, he decided it would be best not to press the issue. No sense getting her riled all over again.

He headed out the front door, but halfway to the truck, he remembered the extra cinnamon rolls his mom had requested before all the excitement. Or was it coffee cake? He hurried back inside. "Sorry, I almost forgot! My mom wanted—"

Behind the counter, Shayla stood with her face buried in the skirt of her flour-dusted apron, her shoulders heaving.

Link's heart stopped for the second time that day. "What's wrong?" He looked around for the little girl. She was still coloring, seeming perfectly fine and oblivious to her mother's tears.

Shayla quickly turned away, dabbing at her face with the hem of the apron. But not before Link saw the tears blazing shiny trails down her smooth cheeks. When she faced him again, her forehead and cheeks were smudged with flour. "What do you need?"

"Are you sure? Is everything okay?"

"It's fine." Her lips firmed. "What else do you need?"

Her tears rattled him now, and he stuttered. "My mom . . . um . . . she wanted something to serve for breakfast at the inn. She mentioned coffee cake, I think."

Shayla walked to the end of the pastry case and pointed to a ring-shaped confection with crumbly stuff on top. "We have this one. Or a pumpkin loaf."

"Okay. I'll take two of those rings." He hesitated, watching her closely. "You *sure* you're okay?"

She ignored his question and went to work boxing the coffee cakes. "That'll be sixteen forty-seven."

"Um . . ." He waited for her to look up from the register. "You have flour"—he smiled and brushed his own cheek—"on your face. From your apron, I think."

She wheeled away, rubbing at her cheeks as if they were on fire.

He laughed. "At least you've got some color in your cheeks now." *Stupid* thing to say. "You were looking pretty pale—earlier, I mean." *Stupider* thing to say. "You got it." He pointed to her face. "It's all off now. I just thought you'd want to know. Before your next customer comes in."

She glared at him. "That'll be sixteen forty-seven," she said again.

"Oh. Sorry." He filed through his wallet. He only had a ten, plus the change she'd given him earlier. He handed her his credit card.

She ran it and slid the receipt across the counter for him to sign. He scribbled his name and handed it back.

"Thank you." She couldn't quite meet his eyes and seemed anxious to get rid of him. Nothing like last time when he'd flirted, and she'd flirted back, offering him a sample of a new sticky bun recipe they were testing.

Those warm, gold-flecked eyes flashed at him. Only today they flashed defiance, not the intense interest he thought he remembered from before.

The back door opened and a tall black man stepped through. He nodded in Link's direction. "Mornin'." He looked at Shayla then back at Link. "Everything okay here, baby?" He came and put a protective arm on her back, his hand cradling her neck.

Great. He'd been flirting with a married woman. He squelched a sigh. And now she'd probably tell her husband that he'd almost killed their daughter. He'd checked for a wedding ring the first time he met her. He was positive there'd never been one. But then, it probably wasn't a good idea to wear a ring when you worked in a bread-dough factory. That'd teach him to assume.

"Everything's fine." Shayla looked over to where Portia was coloring, then wriggled out from under the man's embrace. She tucked a wayward curl behind her ear. But a second later, she crumpled back into the guy's arms.

He leveled a glare in Link's direction. "What'd you do?" he growled, taking a step toward him, even with Shayla draped over him like a coat.

"No!" Shayla pulled the man's arm. "It's okay."

Link took a step back, scrambling to explain. "Your little girl ran out into the street. I...almost hit her. With my truck."

"That true?" The man looked down at Shayla, then cut his glare toward the table where the child sat. His countenance visibly softened when his gaze landed on her. When Shayla didn't answer, he tipped her face upward, as if he might read the truth in her expression.

She cast her eyes down, but nodded. "She's okay, Daddy. She wasn't hurt."

The man narrowed his eyes at Link. "What happened?"

Link swallowed. "Like I said, she ran out in front of me. I couldn't get stopped on the ice. Truck skidded pretty good, but it didn't even graze her. It was close though. She's a lucky little girl."

He wanted Shayla to come to his defense—to tell the guy that he'd bailed out of his truck and rolled to safety with the little girl in his arms. He was pretty sure Shayla had seen that part, despite her accusations. But he kept it to himself, suddenly more eager to get the heck out of Dodge than to stand here and paint himself as a hero.

The man looked to Shayla as if for confirmation. Link saw nothing in her eyes, but apparently the guy was satisfied Link hadn't tried to kill anyone.

"I'll be going now. If... if you have any other questions or"—he shrugged—"whatever, Shayla knows where to contact me."

He gathered the cake boxes and strode to the front of the store, feeling foolish. And confused. She'd called the guy "Daddy." His sisters called their husbands that sometimes when they were talking about their kids. And the guy didn't look old enough to be her father, but a little too old to be her husband. Not that that meant anything these days. Of course even if the man *was* her father, she could still have a husband. She had a kid after all.

He climbed in the truck, jabbed the key into the ignition, and revved the engine. She probably *was* married. He sure hadn't known that when he'd flirted with her. And in his defense, she had never given him one single back-off-buddy-I'm-married signal. Not one.

If she had, he would have run hard and fast in the opposite direction.

2

Thanks, honey. That's perfect." Audrey Whitman lifted the coffee cakes from the bakery boxes Link had delivered, then quickly covered them with a clean tea towel—that is, hid them from Grant. Her husband was not to be trusted around fresh bakery fare. "I was starting to think you'd forgotten."

Link shook his head. "Nope. Just took longer than I expected. Here's your change from the twenty, but I had to put the coffee cakes on my credit card." He laid a wad of wrinkled bills on the kitchen counter, then deposited a few coins on top. "Here're your receipts."

"No, you keep the change. That's your gas money. Hang tight, and I'll pay you for the rest." She smoothed the receipt out with the palm of her hand. "Sixteen dollars? For two little coffee cakes?" She shook her head. "I'm in the wrong business."

"If you don't need anything else, Mom, I'm going to head out." He seemed distracted. "I'm pulling an extra shift tonight."

"Sure. You go on. I'm set. Thanks again. See you Tuesday."

"Not sure about Tuesday. I'll let you know." Link inched toward the door, seeming a little too eager to get away.

She wondered if he had a date. *From her lips to God's ears.* "Oh, hey! You said you slid on the ice? What happened?"

Link stopped with his hand on the door like a kid caught with his hand in the cookie jar.

"You didn't smash up your truck, did you?"

"No. No damage. Just scared the snot out of me."

"Yeah, so I heard. Except snot's *not* what I heard." She gave him the look. The one her kids used to call "Mom's stink-eye." Probably still did. She knew her kids weren't angels, and she appreciated that they cleaned up their mouths around her and Grant—and the grandchildren, she *hoped*. But as she'd always told them when they were kids, what slipped out in a moment of crisis was a good indicator of what was in their hearts. She hoped Link had taken note. But he was a grown man—twenty-nine!—and she wasn't going to hassle him about his mouth now. That was between him and God. Still, she couldn't help but think that a good woman would smooth out her boy's rough edges.

With a sheepish grin that made him look like a little boy again, Link opened the door. "Tell Dad hi. See you later." He gave a little wave and exited before she could say more than "drive safe."

Hmm. She knew her son, and something was definitely up.

Oh, that it was a girlfriend!

The roads were still slick and Link drove with a newfound caution. The more he thought about the close call this morning, the heavier his gut felt. In the blink of an eye, his life—and the lives of so many others—could have changed in horrific ways. He truly didn't think what happened had been his fault. He hadn't been speeding. He was sure of that. And yes, he'd been pulling double shifts for several weeks now, but he wasn't sleep deprived. Still, he *had* been distracted—on the phone with Mom, thinking about work…about flirting with the pretty girl at the bakery. *Shayla*.

He threw up a prayer of thanks that things had turned out the way they had. That the little girl was safe. Although her existence sure did throw a wrench in things. Even if Shayla was available, a single mom wasn't exactly on his list of things to look for in a woman. But probably a hazard of dating at his—according to his sisters—*ripe old* age. He remembered his mother saying something about her and Dad not being surprised if he ended up with a woman who'd been married before. He rolled his eyes. They all acted like he was fifty or something. Never mind that some days he *felt* like fifty.

Part of it was work. He didn't really mind his job, but it wasn't where he'd envisioned himself at this point in life. He'd been with Carson Tech since one month after graduating from Southeast Missouri State. It was just a job. An entry level job—testing electrical wiring—that really had nothing to do with his business major. It was merely supposed to be something to pay the bills until he found a "real" job.

Yet here he was, six years later—no, almost seven now. Man, where had the time gone? He'd gotten a couple of raises over the years and had managed to put away some savings. But that was only because his apartment was a hole in the wall studio in a not-so-great part of town.

He pulled up to the apartment and parked along the curb, praying he didn't have to scrape the windshields before he went in to work tonight. Flipping on the lights inside his studio, he tried to view the place with objective eyes.

No way around it: he'd be embarrassed for any woman to see where he lived. Not to mention, walking in the front door was essentially walking into his bedroom. Despite his sisters' attempts to convince him to fix the place up, he hadn't done more than move in some of Mom and Dad's castoff furniture and buy some matching dishes off Craigslist.

He'd been able to pick up some extra shifts this fall, hoping to save enough to afford a better place after the first of the year. But in the back of his mind, he knew what he really needed was to find another job. Not just because of the money. But because he was afraid if he didn't get out of Carson Tech now, he'd be retiring from here. And he wanted more than that out of life. A lot more.

He shrugged out of his jacket, flipped on the TV, and navigated to the sports channel. He could save a hundred bucks a month if he canceled cable. He rarely watched it now that he was working overtime anyway. An involuntary sigh escaped him, and he went to the fridge for an almost empty carton of orange juice. Drinking from the carton, he kicked off his shoes and settled on the futon.

Settled. That was his problem. He'd settled for a life that was comfortable and easy, but he didn't like being *settled* at twenty-nine. And it got worse every year. His friends from high school and college were all either married with kids, or off living in some exotic spot in the world. There were a few slackers like him, but fewer every year. And in truth, it might not have bothered him that much if it didn't bother his family.

Of course his little brother—God rest his soul—had set the bar high. He had beat Link to the altar when he got married at twenty-one. To Bree Cordel, who set the bar even higher. Tim had been a Marine by the time he was twenty-two. Then dead—a hero—two years later. Tough act to follow. It seemed strange that his brother, who'd been only a year younger than Link their whole lives, was now almost five years younger—forever twenty-four in Link's mind and memories.

The TV droned on. Scores of games he didn't really care about. And even though he was only working the seven-to-eleven shift tonight, he needed to catch some shut-eye before heading in. He put his feet up and closed his eyes.

The truck started sliding. He slammed on the brakes but nothing happened. He slammed harder. Nothing! The little girl stood there in the middle of the road just looking at him. Staring. Like she wasn't even afraid.

"Porsche!" It was Shayla's voice. He was sure of it.

He pushed the brakes harder, but it was like stepping on a dry sponge.

"Porsche!"

Why was she yelling that? He wouldn't mind having a Porsche, but he drove a Dodge Ram. With a hundred seventy thousand miles on it. And if he couldn't get the beast to stop, he was going to hit that little girl!

Stop!

Link bolted upright on the futon. He broke into a cold sweat, his heart racing. He'd almost hit her! Another split second and...

No. It was only a dream. *A nightmare.* She was fine. He'd seen her with his own eyes. Everybody was fine. But it had been too close. Way too close.

Thank you, Lord. He took a deep breath and got to his feet, trying to shake off the terror of the dream. The TV said it was 2:27.

Porsche. Where had that come from?

Thinking back, he was pretty sure Shayla had screamed that word. In real life. Maybe it was the little girl's name. He'd heard stranger names, although he didn't even want to think about why somebody would name their kid after a sports car. Tim had teased him once that he was named "Link" because he'd been conceived in the back of the '75 Lincoln Continental Mom and Dad owned the first few years they were married. He didn't think it was true, but . . . *Eww.* Thanks a lot for nothing, bro. Hope you're happy for putting that image in my mind for the rest of my adult life.

Porsche. Maybe it was just part of his crazy nightmare. Some dream interpreter would probably say it represented his deep, dark desire to drive a fast sports car away from life as he knew it—or some other wacko mumbo jumbo.

He looked at the clock again. The bakery in Langhorne would still be open. He probably should call and make sure everything was okay. He could almost hear his dad's voice. It would be the right thing to do. Dad was always all about doing the right thing.

He grabbed his jacket and his keys off the counter. If he hurried, he had time to do one better: he'd go and see for himself if everyone was really okay.

3

The bells on the door jangled, and Shayla Michaels looked up to see who had the nerve to show up five minutes before closing time. She'd just sent her part-time college help home early, and she was eager to call it a day.

Her breath caught. It was the guy from this morning—Link. She pretended not to see him and busied herself boxing up the day's unsold pastries for the homeless shelter in Cape Girardeau—ironically where she'd first met him. They'd been on a first-name-only basis, but thanks to Google, she now knew his name was Link Whitman. And his parents ran the Chicory Inn up the road a few miles off Chicory Lane.

He strode toward the counter now, but she didn't look up until she could see his reflection in the display case. "Yes?" Her trembling voice betrayed her, but probably not for the reason he thought. "May I help you?"

"I just came by to check on your daughter. I'm Link Whitman. I've never properly introduced myself." He stripped off his gloves and extended his right hand.

She held up her own plastic-gloved hand. "Sorry. I'm working with food."

"Oh. No problem." He withdrew his hand. "I understand. Is she doing okay? Your daughter?"

"She's not my—Like I told you this morning, she's fine."

His mouth tilted in a sheepish smile. "Maybe the question is, how are *you* holding up?"

She couldn't help but stare at the steel gray-blue of his eyes. From that first day at the shelter, his eyes had reminded her of Portia's eyes. "I'm fine." If she said anything else, she might dissolve into tears again. He'd already caught her losing it once today. That was plenty.

"Listen..." He shifted from one foot to the other, then back again. "I'm really sorry about what happened. I know that must have scared you to death. I don't have kids, but I've seen my sisters freak out about a lot less with their own kids." He looked at the floor. "I honestly don't think I was driving too fast or anything, but—well, if it was my fault, I'm really sorry. I've had nightmares about it."

She tilted her head and eyed him. "It just happened this morning. How could you be having nightmares?"

"Well, night*mare*. I'm working extra shifts lately. So sleeping at odd hours. Like this afternoon. And I had a wild dream, a nightmare. I'm not lying to you."

"Never said you were."

"That's where I'm headed now. Work." He nodded to where his truck was parked out front. "But I wanted to be sure your daughter was okay first. I could tell your husband was upset and I just—"

"My husband? What in the world are you talking about?" She hadn't meant for it to come out quite so shrill.

"The guy in here this morning." One side of his mouth tipped up. "Sorry. That wasn't your husband?"

She couldn't help laughing. "That's my *dad*."

"Oh."

If she didn't know better, she'd have thought he looked relieved. *Don't go getting any ideas, Shayla Jean. You've got no business—*

"Sorry. He... he doesn't look old enough."

"Yeah, well... Listen, you need anything from the bakery?" She pointed to the empty case. "This stuff is all going to the shelter in Cape, so if you want anything, speak now."

"Or what? Forever hold my peace?"

She smiled before she could stop herself. "Something like that." The warmth that slid into his eyes somehow worked its way inside her as well, and she remembered how he'd made her feel when they were flirting.

"No," he said quietly. "I don't need anything. Other than... I just wanted to see how you were doing. And to check on your daughter."

"Oh. She's not my daughter." Not that it was any of his business.

"What? What in the world are you talking about?" His voice went as shrill as hers had seconds earlier.

They both laughed at his parroting of her words. But he looked confused. "That wasn't your little girl this morning?"

"Portia is my brother's child," Shayla offered.

"*Porsche*! I knew it!"

"What?" She propped her hands on her hips. "Somebody better start talking some sense here pretty quick."

He grinned. "That's your daughter's—I mean, your *niece's* name? Porsche. Like the car?"

"It's Portia." She spelled it for him. "And what do you mean 'I knew it'?" She mimicked his crowing.

"In my dream—my nightmare—you were yelling that. *Porsche*. Over and over."

Now he was dreaming about *her*?

"I guess you were yelling that in real life too. Portia. Her name, I mean—it sounds like the car. You know—Porsche?"

"I know what a Porsche is."

He shrugged. "I don't remember much, but I remember you yelling her name. The whole thing is kind of a blur."

She rolled her eyes. "Tell me about it. But yes, I'm sure I yelled her name. Scared the potatoes out of me."

He laughed. "Yeah, me too. I just keep thinking about what could have happened. It could have been so much worse—"

"No." She waved a hand at him. "I don't even want to go there. I'm just trying to forget it happened."

"So what did your brother say when he heard about it?"

Oh boy. Here it came. She swallowed and averted her gaze. "My brother?"

"You didn't tell him yet?"

"Oh." She looked at the floor. "He doesn't know. He's... out of town."

"Well, I'll vouch for you, if you need me to. There wasn't anything anybody could have done. It was just... one of those things. So, you were babysitting?"

She stared at him. He was awfully nosy. Good looking as all get out. But nosy. "Something like that," she said.

He gave her a look that asked for more.

She checked the clock above the cash register. "I really need to close up shop."

He followed her gaze. "Oh, right. Sorry. And I need to get to work. Can I give you a lift home?"

"Not unless you want to carry me up those stairs?" She nodded toward the open staircase that hugged the back wall of the store.

"Seriously? You live here?"

"Last time I checked." She probably shouldn't have told him that. Daddy had left for Bowling Green—to see Jerry—at noon and wouldn't be home till late. Portia was upstairs watching TV. They were essentially alone. Not that she was scared of Link Whitman. She'd had enough dealings with the Whitman family to know they were good people. The grandmother used to live here in Langhorne before they'd put her in a home, and one of the sisters still lived here. The one with the adorable twins.

"There's an apartment upstairs, huh? I never knew that. So you guys own the bakery?"

"Us and the bank." He didn't need to know that the apartment was essentially a warren of bedrooms. They'd never had a kitchen upstairs, but had always used the bakery's kitchen to prepare their meals, which they ate in the dining room or in the little alcove at the bottom of the back kitchen stairs. And when they'd taken Portia in two years ago, they converted the sitting room upstairs to a third bedroom and playroom. Shayla had a small sofa in her room, but she actually preferred the sunny seating area at the back of the bakery with its comfy leather couches and the collection of green plants she babied. Customers gravitated to the cozy nook during the day, but when the bakery closed at three each afternoon, it was all hers.

"Yeah, I get that," Link said. "Kind of like my truck . . . me and the bank." He glanced out the front window to where his pickup was parked.

She smiled and went on packing up the day-old pastries.

"My mom really likes your stuff—your baked goods, I mean. Says if she ever got tired of baking for her guests, she'd just let you do it."

She felt herself flush. "It's mostly my dad who does the baking. I'm learning a little, but he does most of it. I just man the counter. And wash dishes. And sweep floors."

"And box up stuff for the homeless shelter." He looked pointedly at the tower of boxes she'd formed atop the empty display case. "That's really nice of you to do that."

She shrugged. "Better than putting it in the Dumpster. Or eating it." She patted her belly and was rewarded with his laughter. It was his laugh that had attracted her to him the first time they'd met at the shelter in Cape that day. She'd loved talking to him there. Just shooting the breeze, but he always made her laugh. She'd been disappointed when the shelter director told her the IT work was finished.

Link slipped his cell phone from his jeans pocket and checked the time. "I'd better get going or I'll be late. I just wanted to make sure everybody was okay." He started toward the front door.

But watching his broad shoulders, she felt an urgency rising inside her, as if she might not get another chance to say what she needed to say. "Hey." She peeled off the plastic gloves and tossed them into the trash, coming around to the other side of the counter where he'd been standing. "Link!" It came out too loud.

But he wheeled around, curiosity written in his expression. "Yeah?"

"I feel bad about what I said this morning. I know it wasn't really your fault."

A hint of mischief came to his eyes. "Do you feel bad about beating the snot out of me?"

She made a show of covering her face with her hands. "I was hoping you wouldn't remember that part." She peeked at him from between her fingers.

"Oh, I remember all right." He winced. "Got the bruises to prove it. On top of the bruises your niece gave me."

"You're not serious..." She knew her eyes must be as round as the doughnuts she'd just boxed up. "I'm so sorry. I was a little out of my head. Seriously, I feel awful. I didn't know I hit you that hard. You don't really have bruises?" She was pretty sure he was exaggerating.

But what if he wasn't? What if he filed assault and battery charges against her? Had anyone witnessed what happened? But surely, someone from a family like the Whitmans wouldn't do such a thing. Still, people could be pretty sue-happy these days.

She didn't remember anyone else being in the store at the time or on the street, but surely someone had heard his brakes squeal and come by to see what was going on. She'd wondered if they should have called the police to report what happened. But she could already imagine her father shaking his head adamantly at the idea. No police. It had been that way for men like him—black men—forever, but after what happened with Jerry, Daddy's disdain—fear even—of the police had risen to a new level. And the whole thing with Ferguson a while back hadn't helped matters any. It seemed like her father was on edge all the time these days. For no reason. But then, a lot of things had happened "for no reason," so she couldn't really blame him.

A new thought struck her. What if the Chicory Inn quit ordering from the bakery? And told other people in town to do the same? Her stupid mistake might cost them.

"Quit looking like that." Link touched her wrist briefly. "I'm just giving you a hard time. I'm fine. Wouldn't be much of a man if I couldn't take your wimpy punches."

"Hey!" She laughed nervously, but she'd never been so relieved to be teased. And so happy to see his smile reappear. "Don't make me show you how hard I *can* hit if I really need to."

He put up both hands in surrender but laughed as he did. "Don't worry. I have no intention of getting you riled up again."

"Smart move, Whitman." Seeing him like this, she remembered how he'd made her feel when he flirted with her the other times he'd come in.

His smile faded. "Seriously, though. Don't think anything of it. Like I said, I know my sisters would have reacted the same if one of their kids—or a niece or nephew," he added quickly, "was in danger. All's forgiven. You forgive me?"

She gave him a knowing smile. "For saving Portia's life, you mean?"

"Well, I didn't want to say anything, but now that you mention it . . ."

"You don't have to look so smug."

He cocked his head, studying her. "Would you want to go out with me?"

Wow. That was fast. "Out?"

"As in, on a date? Out on a date?"

"You don't waste any time, do you?"

"It just seemed like the thing to do."

She gave him a skeptical look. "What's that supposed to mean? I'm not a charity case."

"What? Who said anything about charity?"

"You're not just asking me because you think you owe it to me because you almost killed Portia."

"Wait a minute, wait a minute. Two minutes ago I saved her life. How'd we get back to 'almost killed her'?"

She was pretty certain he was still flirting, but she wasn't sure where this was going. Or if he was serious about asking her out.

Only one way to find out. "Are you seriously asking me out on a date?"

"Dead serious."

"Why?"

"Do I have to have a motive?"

"Men usually do."

"Um, would it be the wrong answer if I said I thought you were really pretty, and I like talking to you?"

She couldn't hide the smile that came. Or the surprise. "That would be a good answer, I guess."

"That would be the truth."

"Well, alrighty then. When were you thinking this date would happen?"

"Can you do Sunday? I'm working some overtime until after Christmas, so Sunday night's about the only time I'm free the rest of the year. Unless you want to do an early breakfast."

"You mean like three a.m.? Because I have to be down here to work at four."

"Oh." Link's eyes got big. "Then Sunday's it, I guess. That work?"

She frowned. Daddy wasn't going to like this. At all. "I'll have to see about a babysitter."

"You babysit on Sundays too?"

She forgot she hadn't explained the situation. "Portia lives with us. My brother's . . . not exactly in the picture right now."

"Oh. What about Portia's mother?"

"Not in the picture either."

"Oh. Wow . . . I'm sorry."

She shrugged. And considered just telling him everything right off the bat. Let him reject her before he wasted any time or money on a date. But there was something different about him. She wasn't sure what, but she wasn't willing to let him go so easily. "It is what it is," she said finally.

"We could take her with us—Portia. If that's okay with you. And if it's okay with your dad . . . or whoever you have to check with."

For some crazy reason, that made her smile. "I have to check with me, myself, and I. I'm pretty much it where Portia's concerned." She tilted her head, studying him. "You sure you want to take a five-year-old with us on a date?"

"Sure. Why not?"

"I'm not sure you're counting the cost here. She can be a little feisty."

"You haven't been to a Whitman family dinner yet. Eight little rug rats running around screaming their heads off, coloring on the walls, climbing the curtains, wiping their sticky fingers—and runny noses—on everything"—he made a face—"every Tuesday. I sometimes sit right there at the kids' table. And live to tell the tale."

She laughed. "Okay, okay. You convinced me." But he'd said *yet. You haven't been to a Whitman family dinner* yet. Somehow she couldn't picture herself and Portia at a table with the Whitman family. Just like she'd never been able to picture herself at a table with her mother's family. Or wanted to. And for good reason.

She'd been out to the inn before, delivering baked goods. It was a fancy house. And Mrs. Whitman—Link's mother—was a fancy lady. The kind that wore makeup and earrings around the house.

Shayla shook off the comparison. She'd cross that bridge when she came to it. If she ever did. She frowned. "You don't really sit at the kids' table?"

He shrugged a shoulder. "Guess you'll just have to find out for yourself someday."

4

Link walked backwards to the curb, watching Shayla Michaels move around inside the bakery. When he finally turned and approached his pickup, he caught his reflection in the window in the last inkling of daylight—and realized he was smiling.

A rare occurrence recently, according to his biggest sister. His smile widened, imagining how Corinne would chide him if he referred to her as "biggest" to her face. "*Oldest* sister, buddy. Use your words," she'd say. And then, of course, he'd have to give her a hard time about how ancient she really was at the ripe old age of thirty-three.

He loved all his sisters, and most of the time he didn't mind the way they mother-henned him to death. Even Landyn, who was his little sis, somehow managed to boss him around.

Mom always said—only half joking—that Link's poor wife would pay for all the damage his sisters had done to him with their coddling. But he wasn't too concerned.

What he *was* concerned about was the fact that he'd somehow ended up asking a girl for a date! A girl with a kid . . . even if it wasn't her own. And a girl who was about as far as she could possibly be from the list he'd written out when he was sixteen or seventeen: "The Woman I Want to Marry." The list had been some youth group exercise, if he remembered right. He wasn't even sure why he'd participated. He couldn't have cared less about being married back then. All through college even.

It wasn't until his two older sisters started settling down with their husbands, and then Tim married Bree, and Link started thinking marriage looked like a pretty good deal. He'd just never met the right woman.

His sisters accused him of being too picky. He hadn't gotten any less picky as the years went by, but even so, Shayla wasn't anything like the elusive—imaginary—woman on his list. Not only because she wasn't blonde and blue-eyed, but because Shayla had no doubt been raised very differently than he had. A whole 'nother culture.

He checked the thought. That wasn't fair. He was making assumptions based mostly on the color of her skin. But he also knew enough after their conversation just now to guess that they might not be on the same page on a lot of things.

Not that he wanted to end up with a female carbon copy of himself. But if that list—the one that had silently guided him for over a dozen years now—held any weight, Shayla wasn't even on the radar. Actually, if the list held any weight, he'd be marrying a carbon copy of his sisters.

He climbed into the pickup and backed out. Slowly, remembering the events of this morning. The ice had melted from the streets, but he knew he'd drive a lot more carefully for a long time to come.

He thought about Shayla and how different she'd seemed this afternoon compared to this morning when she'd looked like she wanted to kill him. There was something about her that drew him. And had from the first time he'd ever spoken to her. He didn't think it was his imagination that she felt it too. There was definitely a spark there.

He pulled into the parking lot at work and tried to shift gears and quit thinking about the events of the day. That was one thing he liked about his job: it required a measure of concentration that kept him from dwelling on any problems he might have.

Not that he had anything to complain about. He'd had a lot of good things happen in his lifetime, and he'd lived long enough to recognize that not everyone was blessed with the kind of life he enjoyed. Still, he couldn't shake the feeling that there was something missing in his life. Something the rest of his family had because they *had* families. He wasn't necessarily lonely. He had plenty of friends, and he spent more time than most people with his family. There were a lot of them and they were a noisy bunch.

No, it wasn't loneliness exactly. It was that thing about not having any one person in the world you loved above all others—and who loved you above all others. Whenever he heard that Scripture verse in Genesis where God said, "it is not good for man to be alone." He got that.

"Hey, Whitman."

Link waved across the parking lot at Isaiah Ruiz, one of his favorite guys on the evening crew. "Hey, Izz. Hold up."

He jogged to catch up with his friend, glad for a change of subject. It was not good for man to think too hard about being alone.

From her uncomfortable vantage point on her hands and knees on the guest room carpet, Audrey looked up at her husband. "What on earth could they have spilled that refuses to come out? It's almost like paint. Or the world's largest lipstick."

"Well, don't kill yourself trying to get it out. We have scraps of that carpet. It won't be that big of a deal to cut a patch out and replace it." Grant tossed a pillowcase onto the pile of dirty linens, then began stripping off the rest of the bedding.

"Not those, Grant! Put that sham back on. I don't wash the decorative pillows."

"You don't?"

"Not every time. We'd be replacing them twice a year if I washed these every time."

He acknowledged her with a grunt and struggled to put the sham back on the feather pillow.

The kids would all be here Tuesday night for the every-other-weekly family dinner and she had a hundred things to get done before then. And a full house of guests every night until then. In fact, tonight's guests would be arriving any minute now.

She threw down the brush she'd been scrubbing with and struggled to her feet. "Here. Give me that." She took the pillow and sham from him. Maybe a little too roughly. She picked two dog hairs from the fabric. "Did somebody let Huck up here?"

When Grant didn't answer she shook out the pillow sham and muttered between clenched teeth. "Why is that stupid dog shedding so much? It's November. Isn't he supposed to be *growing* a coat, not shedding one?"

She looked at Grant, half expecting him to answer her question.

But he only shrugged. "Don't look at me. *I'm* not shedding."

"Ha ha." He was not going to humor her out of this.

"Hey, I'm just trying to help. What else do you need me to do?"

"It would take me longer to give you the list than to just do it myself."

"Not exaggerating or anything, are we?" He threw her that look that pushed all her buttons.

"You want to know what you can do to help? You can call the kids and tell them not to come Tuesday."

He stared at her as if trying to figure out whether she was serious or not.

"I can't do everything, Grant! I've got two rooms to get ready and I haven't even started thinking about what I'm going to make for dinner Tuesday. Never mind getting the house ready."

"You don't have to serve a gourmet meal, you know. The kids would be fine with peanut butter and jelly."

"I am *not* going to serve peanut butter and jelly to my family!" Was he nuts?

"Okay, pizza then. We can call and order it and have Link pick it up on his way out."

"I doubt he's coming. At least not in time for dinner. He said he was picking up extra shifts until after Christmas."

"Then Dallas and Danae can pick it up. You don't have to knock yourself out every week."

"Really? That's funny because you were the one who came up with this bright idea."

"What bright idea? Do you mean our Tuesday night family dinners?"

Great, stick the knife of guilt in and turn it. But the edge that had come into his voice told her she'd better back off. Grant was a good, kind man, but if she pushed him to a certain point, he kicked into defensive mode and quit being rational.

Well, she was tired of always having to be the rational one. And this innkeeping business was going to be the death of her. If she kept things up with the inn, her family—her kids and grandkids—got the short shrift. If she did right by her family, their guests at the inn got less than pristine lodging—and coffee cake from a bakery. Granted, a good bakery, but when the inn's website advertised "homemade" it didn't seem right.

She willed herself to temper her words. "I can't do it all, Grant. I just can't. I can barely keep up with the day-to-day stuff, and with Christmas barreling down on us, I don't see how I can possibly—"

"What do you want me to do about it?" His glare demanded an answer.

"I never said I wanted you to do anything about it. I'm not looking for you to *fix* it. I'm just trying to tell you why I'm struggling." Tears of frustration pressed against the back of her eyelids, and she turned away so he wouldn't see them, pretending to straighten the embroidered runner on top of the dresser.

"I've told you before I can help out more with the food and cleanup and—"

"That's not the point!" She whirled to face him, not caring now if he saw her tears. "You are not hearing me!"

"What? I'm listening." He held out his arms as if there was something in that stance that would prove to her that he understood.

But he didn't. He was clueless. Recent history told her exactly how it would go down: Grant would force her to give him a list. He'd tell her half the things on the list weren't even important.

Then he'd do two little errands for her, and that was supposed to fix everything.

She pressed her hands together and worked to even her tone. "I need to not have Tuesday night dinners for a while. At least not until after the holiday—"

"What?" He started shaking his head before she'd even finished her sentence. "We already cut back to every other week. That is *not* something I'm willing to give up altogether, Audrey. We can do carryout pizza. Or cut back on bookings if that will help but—"

"We can't afford to cut back on bookings. If anything, we need to start booking on Tuesday nights." Her voice cranked up an octave.

"We've been doing just fine without that income."

She flashed him a look meant to convey a rather snarky, "Seriously?" She took a breath, willing herself to remain calm, then chose her words carefully. "You must have a different definition of 'just fine' than I do."

"The bills are paid. We're not starving. The cars run. Both of them."

"And we'll *never* retire." In the last month alone, they'd spent an extra six hundred dollars on household repairs.

Grant studied her, gauging, she knew, how close she was to a meltdown.

He apparently thought one was imminent because he tossed aside the throw pillows he'd been holding and drew her into his arms. "Talk to me, babe. Why are you freaking out like this?"

She stiffened, not quite ready for the "easy" solution she knew he was likely to offer—simply to not face the real issues. She wriggled out of his embrace, but reached up to kiss his cheek. "I'm not mad at you. I'm just mad at the situation. We'll talk about it later. I don't have time right now."

His jaw tensed. "Okay. I'm making an executive decision. We'll iron things out later. But I'm ordering ahead for Tuesday: six large pizzas. And tonight, you are going to go take a much-deserved soak in the tub." He grasped her shoulders and directed her toward the door.

She released a hot breath of frustration and let him steer her into the hall. "I'll take you up on the pizza, and I'll take a rain check on the bath."

She felt him hesitate behind her, but to his credit he didn't try to argue. Instead, he said, "Don't worry about the dishwasher. I'll take care of that."

"As you always do." She turned, appropriately chastened, but not ready to let him think he'd solved her problems so easily. "And I know you'll help me Tuesday with the babies and with cleaning up afterward. And I appreciate that. I truly do. I'm just . . . feeling a little overwhelmed with everything right now. I'll be fine."

He patted her shoulders and kissed the back of her neck. "I know you will."

She wished "being fine" were as easy as simply speaking the words. But lately it felt like her dream-come-true was snuffing the life out of her.

5

Shayla scooted the little vanity bench back, lifted the hem of her long skirt, and bent to slather lotion on her ashy ankles and feet before slipping into the new sandals she'd found at the Goodwill. Six dollars, which had meant leaving behind a little dress Portia had begged for. But the dress was raggedy, and Portia truly didn't need more clothes. Besides—Shayla finished fastening the strap—she'd wanted these sandals. Especially when she'd seen the exact pair in a store downtown for almost a hundred dollars.

Sometimes she resented that her budget dictated shopping at secondhand stores, but if she could get past the embarrassment of living on the verge of being a poverty statistic, she rather enjoyed the challenge of finding something the original owner had paid a pretty penny for and worn twice—and likely taken a healthy tax credit for as she dropped it off at a donation center in her fifty-thousand-dollar SUV, all proud and smug because she'd helped the poor.

Cut it out, Shayla Jean. She was thinking like Jeremiah. Jerry had let the chip on his shoulder drag him down. Down and under.

She pushed the memories away. Her brother was a topic sure to elicit tears if she pondered too long on it. And she wasn't going to let anything ruin this date with Link Whitman.

A *date.* When was the last time she'd been on a real, live date? She couldn't remember. Probably Danny Sherwood. That loser was enough to make any woman swear off dating. The man had what Mama had called Roman hands and Russian fingers. Mercy!

Somehow she didn't think she'd have that problem with Link Whitman. He was the very definition of a gentleman.

"What's so funny, Shay?"

Shayla looked up to see her own smiling face in the mirror, and Portia's reflection behind her. "Nothing, sweetie. Now go get your shoes on. Mr. Link will be here in a few minutes and we don't want to make him wait."

"Hows come Mr. Link is takin' us to a movie?"

"How come?" She pushed off the bench and inspected her niece's hair. "Well, I guess because he wants to. He likes us. And he thinks you're a cutie." She licked her forefinger and thumb and smoothed a wayward wisp of Portia's hair. With her fawn-colored hair and blue eyes, this child was going to be a stunner when she grew up.

Portia tilted her head and gave a knowing grin. "Is he your boyfriend?"

"Mr. Link? No. And don't you go saying that in front of him either. He's a friend. Just a friend."

"Yeah, but he's a boy."

"Go get your shoes on."

"And he's your friend. So that's boy friend."

"Hush, girl."

"Can I wear my sandals?"

"No, it's too cold."

"No fair! You're wearin' sandals." Portia put her hands where her hips would have been if she had any meat on her bones.

"When you're a big girl, then you can wear sandals in November."

"I *am* a big girl. Big Daddy said so."

Shayla knelt and got on eye level with the child, making her voice stern. "You do not sass. Do you understand me? You're a big girl, but you're not a grown-up yet."

"You're not the boss of me."

"I most certainly am the boss of you." Shayla grabbed Portia by her bony shoulder—a little harder than necessary.

"Ouch!"

"Do you want to go to the movie with me and Link or not?" Portia loved movies, but Shayla wouldn't put it past the little snot to refuse, just to be obstinate. And if she did, Shayla would have no recourse but to tell Link she was sorry, but they'd be staying home.

But apparently the movie won out. Portia only pouted and hung her head.

Shayla sighed and rose. If she'd learned anything from her sweet mama, it was that you couldn't let a child win when it came to minding. Portia was a sweet girl, but she could push the limits with the best of them. She was what Mama had called a strong-willed child. Portia took after her dad that way. Except Shayla felt sure Mama would have worked the will out of Jeremiah if she'd lived long enough. But Daddy had gone easy on Jerry—on both of them—after Mama died. Shayla had been old enough and meek enough that Mama's discipline had already "took."

But her brother was a different story. And look where it landed him. Impulsively, she pulled Portia into her arms. Poor baby. At least Shayla had known a mother's loving care until she was grown. This baby was growing up without mother *or* father in her life.

Sometimes it terrified Shayla that she was trying to fill not just Tara's shoes for Portia, but Jerry's and Mama's too. She sighed. If she thought about it too long, she felt every one of her thirty-three years.

"Come on, girlie. Mr. Link will be here any minute. We don't want to make him wait." She checked her hair in the mirror. She'd spent half the afternoon straightening it, oiling and blow-drying, and flat-ironing it to within an inch of its life. But the humidity was already winning, and she could almost see her hair frizz before her eyes. Why couldn't she have inherited her mother's hair? Straight blonde hair that hung almost to her waist. Until she'd lost it all to the chemo.

"Is Mr. Link gonna kiss you?" Portia looked up at her with a sly grin.

She froze. "Girl! What would make you even *think* such a thing?"

"That's what people do on dates."

"Who told you that?"

Portia shrugged her shoulders. "I don't know. I just know it."

"You know no such thing!" She felt her heart race. This whole evening could be a disaster in the making. "Get your jacket on. And don't you say one word about that to Mr. Link. In fact, you just keep your lip buttoned tonight."

Portia giggled. "My lip don't have buttons. You're funny."

"It's *doesn't*. Your lip *doesn't* have buttons."

"I know it doesn't. That's what I said!"

She gave a little growl. "Never mind. Just go get your jacket."

She heard a car outside and her heart accelerated. "Lord, what have I done?" she whispered.

Link wiped his palms on his jeans and reached to open the door. Finding it locked, he knocked on the wood framing the paned glass.

A light came on at the back of the bakery, and he saw movement near the open staircase at the rear of the store. A minute later, Shayla, with Portia trailing behind, unlocked the door and peeked out. "Hi there. We're ready." She held up a car booster seat. "Do we need this?"

He looked at Portia. "If she's big enough for a booster seat, I've got them in the backseat of my truck—for my nieces and nephews," he explained. "I wasn't sure if she still needed a regular car seat."

"No. She's big enough for a booster. Thanks." Shayla stepped outside and locked the door behind her.

"You look nice." Link grinned at her, then peeked around her shoulder at Portia. "You look nice too, young lady."

Portia stuck out her lower lip in a pout. "Shay won't let me wear sandals."

"Well, it's kind of cold for sandals, don't you think?"

"Careful, there." Shayla looked down at her own feet, which were shod in a pair of strappy open-toed shoes that his sisters would have declared "darling."

"Oops," he said, feigning a wince. "Double standard?"

"Always," she said.

He looked at her again. "You look really nice."

"So you said." She dipped her head, looking embarrassed by his compliment.

"I've never seen you with your hair down."

She smoothed a hand self-consciously over the shiny, dark brown hair that framed her heart-shaped face. "The inspector kind of frowns on that during business hours."

"Oh, yeah. I guess I can see that. Well, it looks great." The truth was, he preferred her hair curly and a little wild. But she would have looked good bald, so he wasn't lying. "*You* look great. Really great."

"Okay, okay, I get the picture."

"What? You don't like a compliment?" This woman was a puzzle. His sisters ate up stuff like that.

"Sorry. No, I like a compliment fine. Thank you." She tapped her niece's shoulder. "Portia, what do you tell Mr. Link? He said you look nice."

She smiled up at him. "I know. Big Daddy says I'm bee-yu-ti-ful."

"Portia Beth!" Laughing, Shayla shook her head. "We're working on manners."

"That means please and thank-yous," the little girl told him.

"That's right." Shayla gave her a stern look. "Now would you *please* tell Mr. Link *thank you* for the compliment?"

"Thank you." Portia suddenly turned shy.

"You're welcome." He opened the passenger-side door of his truck, tipped back the seat, and put down the built-in booster. "Hop in, young lady." He lifted her into the back. She couldn't have weighed twenty-five pounds.

She scrambled into the booster. He stepped back and let Shayla buckle her in. She waited for Link to put the seat back in place before climbing into the passenger seat. "Wow, it's roomy in here."

"I've had four rug rats back there at a time. My nieces and nephews," he explained. "Not sure that was even legal, but we did get 'em all buckled into car seats. Even if a couple of them had to share a seatbelt."

She gave him a look that made him regret bringing that up. Added to him almost running over Portia, Shayla was going to think he was an accident waiting to happen.

"How many do you have?"

"Six nieces, two nephews. So far."

"Wow. That's a houseful. Or a truck full."

"You all in?" When he was sure she was clear of the door, he closed it and jogged around to the driver's side.

"Everybody ready?" He caught Portia's eyes in the rearview mirror and wriggled his eyebrows at her. She giggled but quickly looked away.

"Ready." Shayla shifted in her seat to angle toward him. Probably to make sure he didn't run over somebody.

Checking the street, he pulled out and drove slowly through town toward the highway.

"So. You like living in Langhorne?"

Shayla shrugged. "It's okay, I guess."

"You guys moved here because of the bakery?"

Another shrug. "I guess you could say that. Sort of..."

"What do you mean?"

"My dad wanted to get us out of Cape Girardeau. Get my brother into a smaller school. So my parents bought the bakery."

"Oh, so did you go to high school in Langhorne?" He didn't remember her.

"No. It was after I'd graduated." She eyed him as though trying to decide if she wanted to continue. "Are you just making small talk, or are you asking because you really want to know?"

He laughed, even though he sensed she wasn't exactly making a joke. "A little of both, I guess. I really want to know. But yes, I'm making small talk. Isn't that what you're supposed to do on a first date?"

"How would I know?"

"Don't tell me you've never been on a date before."

"I won't tell you that because it wouldn't be true. But...it's been a long time. I'm talking a *really* long time."

"I find that hard to believe."

She glanced behind them to the backseat. "It may come as a surprise to you, but not every guy is thrilled about having a five-year-old along on dates."

"Yeah, I guess I can see that."

"So you're not thrilled either." It wasn't a question.

He grinned. "Maybe *thrilled* isn't the exact word I'd use, but I don't mind. Not at all. She's a sweetie."

"You're a good man, Link Whitman."

"Well, let me back up a little."

She tilted her head, looking extremely cute.

"I reserve the right to have you to myself once in a while. One of these days."

"You're assuming I'd say yes to a second date." Her topaz eyes flashed. "Let's get through this one first."

He laughed out loud. "Point taken. Let's concentrate on making this one something you'd like to repeat."

"Yes, let's."

Link couldn't quite read her smug expression. But he had to admit that her air of mystery was one of the things he liked most about her.

6

Shayla helped Portia out of the truck and held her hand as they crossed the busy parking lot to the movie theater.

"I gotta go! I gotta go potty!" Portia held herself, wriggling.

Link waved them off. "You take her. I'll get the tickets. Meet you in front of the restrooms."

When they came out, he ruffled Portia's hair. She squealed and ducked out from under his hand, but Shayla could tell she liked it. Liked Link. A thread of caution tugged at her spine.

"Do you want popcorn?" Link asked.

"This girl can't watch a movie without popcorn," Shayla said. "But I'll get it. You want anything?"

He eyed her, then fished in his back pocket for his wallet. "I'm a little old-fashioned, okay? This is a date. I'm buying the popcorn."

She shrugged, somehow fully relieved of guilt that he was paying for everything. "Portia and I will share."

He stepped into the line at the concessions counter and herded them close with an arm lightly around each. Despite how much she liked the way it felt, Shayla couldn't let herself lean in the way she might have if Portia hadn't been with them. She tried not to resent her niece for that fact. But at the same time, she couldn't let Portia get too attached to Link Whitman. He might be gone next week. And Portia'd had enough heartbreak. So had she.

While Link ordered their snacks, a group of teenage boys roughhoused in the line next to theirs, punching each other hard in the shoulders, not caring who they bumped into. The ringleader had a tall, yellow-dyed Mohawk, his eyebrow pierced with a silver spike identical to the one in his lip—newly installed, judging by the way he kept working his tongue over it. She turned away, pretending she didn't see them.

"Man, look how dirty that kid is. That's what happens when you mix where you shouldn't mix."

She wheeled to see the ringleader pointing at Portia. Shayla pulled her close, turning her back to the thug and shielding Portia from their view. It had been a long time—since she was a little girl—but the script hadn't changed. Mama and Daddy had taught her and Jerry that some people—both black and white—didn't think races should mix. "That's like saying tall people shouldn't marry short people," Mama had said. "But there's no accounting for ignorance."

"Just ignore them," was Daddy's mantra.

But sometimes Mama couldn't seem to resist muttering an argument. Shayla had never understood that like she did now. But she held her tongue, hearing Daddy's voice louder than Mama's in her head. It helped that Mohawk weighed probably two hundred pounds.

Link left the concession stand in time to see Mohawk pretend to spit on the carpet near Shay's feet. She instinctively jumped away, pulling Portia with her.

"What's going on?" Link thrust two tubs of popcorn at Shayla, shooting her a questioning look.

"It's nothing." She started to walk toward the hallway where their movie was showing.

"Didn't sound like nothing."

"Apple doesn't fall far from the tree apparently," one of Mohawk's sidekicks muttered.

He was rewarded with guffaws from his buddies.

"A little soap and water might be in order . . ." Mohawk raised his voice. "Don't you think?"

Shayla pulled Portia closer and tugged on Link's sleeve. "Come on. Let's go."

But he didn't look at her and instead glared at the gang, his hands in tight fists at his side.

"Come on," she said, panic rising in her throat.

Ignoring her, Link took a step toward the kid with the Mohawk. "You need to apologize."

"For what?" he challenged.

"For what you said."

Mohawk only made himself taller, standing with legs apart, and crossing his arms in front of him like Mr. Clean. He flexed his muscles comically.

"Just forget it, Link." Shayla shifted the popcorn in her arms and tugged on his shirt sleeve. "It's not worth it."

"Apologize," Link told the kid again.

Mohawk's buddies flanked him, copying his stance. People were watching now and Shay's breath came in shallow huffs. This would not end well. "Link, come on." Her voice rose.

"What's wrong, Shay?" Portia looked up, her tiny brow furrowed. "What did that guy with the funny hair say?"

"Nothing, sweetie. Come on. Let's go find our seats." She couldn't stay here and let Portia get caught in the middle, but everything in her wanted to scream for Link to let it go.

She hurried away, but before they reached the ticket-taker, she realized Link still had the tickets in his shirt pocket. "Come on, sweetie, we'll wait over here." She guided Portia to a spot where she couldn't see over the concession stand to where Link stood. Shayla could just see the yellow Mohawk quivering and hear their raised voices.

Link glared at the guy. "Does it make you feel like a man to pick on a five-year-old?"

"Wasn't her I was picking on." The guy sneered.

"Well, if it was either of those ladies, you owe an apology. And if it was me, you still owe an apology."

"You gonna make me?"

"As a matter of fact, I am." He took a step closer, straightening until he was half a head taller than the guy.

Shayla saw fear in the punk's face. His so-called buddies had slinked away, apparently not willing to defend him. But that didn't mean they wouldn't help him get even later. She shot up a prayer that Link would just let it go.

Instead, he took another step closer and got in the kid's face. He lowered his voice, but Shayla could read his lips. "I want to hear an apology."

"Yeah, and people in hell want ice water."

"Real original." Link gripped the guy's bicep. To a bystander, it could have looked like a friendly grasp, but Mohawk's expression said otherwise.

Link's jaw tensed. He spoke through clenched teeth, and Shayla couldn't hear what he said.

But Mohawk's eyes widened. He looked at the ground and muttered, "Yeah, whatever."

"What's that?" Link said, tightening his grip.

"Sorry." The guy shrugged and jerked away from Link. "Now get your freakin' hands off me."

"Happy to. Enjoy your movie." Link gave guy's bicep a pat and walked away.

A minute later, he appeared at Shayla's side looking pleased with himself. "Okay, let's go watch a movie."

"What did you do?"

"I just taught the guy a few manners is all."

She stopped and put a hand on her hip. "This isn't funny, Link."

"I wasn't laughing."

"You're being smug."

"I kind of think I have a right to be smug."

"You shouldn't have gotten involved."

"I just squeezed an apology out of him is all."

She scoffed. "Yeah, well, you have that luxury. We don't."

He stopped, cocking his head. "What do you mean? We? Who's we?"

She gave him a look meant to say, "Seriously?" She didn't think Link was that naive, but maybe he was. Sometimes the nicest people were the most clueless. "You know what?" she finally said. "Let's just go watch a movie. Forget about it."

She felt a tug on her jacket and looked down to see Portia's huge blue eyes looking up at her. "Why did that guy with the crazy hair say I was dirty?"

Shayla felt sick knowing Portia had heard him. She shot Link a look, working to keep the anger from her voice. "He probably just meant because you got your hands dirty. From the popcorn."

"No, 'cause I didn't have any popcorn yet."

Busted. "I know, but . . . Maybe he thought you did."

"That don't make no sense." She gave an exaggerated frown that made Shayla and Link both laugh.

But you couldn't pull anything over on this little girl. Shayla herded Portia closer to the fancy-wallpapered wall of the corridor and squatted down in front of her. She felt Link behind her. "Don't you worry about anything that guy said, baby. He's just a dumb teenager who doesn't know what he's talking about. Come on. Let's go see our movie!" She forced false cheer into her voice.

The film—even though the theater was full of noisy kids—was an entertaining one, and Portia was glued to the screen, seeming to have forgotten all about the disgusting creature with the Mohawk. But Shayla felt Link's eyes on her more than once during the movie.

After the feel-good ending, Shayla could almost forget what had happened earlier. At least until Portia said she wanted to go to the bathroom.

"Again?" she said. "The movie was only an hour and a half long."

"I don't gotta pee. I wanna wash my hands."

"You can wash them when we get home."

"No, they're dirty. I need to wash them now."

It struck Shayla then what was going on. She didn't really want to press it in front of Link, but she didn't want to let it go for Portia's sake either. "Why do you need to wash your hands, sweetie?"

Portia held her hands out and inspected them, turning them over to reveal her pale colored palms. "I just do. They're dirty. 'Cause of the popcorn."

Shayla looked up at Link and motioned for him to give them a moment. He took a step back and watched people streaming in for the next showing. But she got the distinct impression that he was listening to her and Portia.

She knelt in front of her niece. "We can go wash your hands if you want to, but they are perfectly fine. They aren't dirty and they never were. Well, except maybe that time you played in the mud with Josie."

That earned her the giggle she'd been going for.

"Maybe I can wait till we get home," Portia said.

"Good plan." She rose and touched Link's shoulder. "Okay. We're ready."

Portia skipped ahead of them, singing a song from the movie.

"Everything okay?" Link's brow wrinkled with genuine concern. "What did I miss?"

She gave him a short version of the exchange, not sure if he'd heard everything that had transpired before he picked a fight with the yellow-haired kid and his gang. "She wanted to go wash her hands."

"Oh, man. That loser," Link said under his breath.

"So what really happened? Earlier. What did you say to him?"

"I just told him he needed to grow up. And to pick on somebody his own size . . . if he could find a Neanderthal anywhere in the county."

"You didn't?" She held her breath.

"Well, I might not have said that last part loud enough for him to hear. But he got the picture."

She rolled her eyes. "Well, I appreciate the thought, but I really wish you would have just let things be. We don't need any trouble."

He straightened and lifted his chin, and she could almost see his defenses rise. He opened his mouth but just as quickly closed it as if deciding better of what he'd been going to say. "You hungry?" he said instead.

"Sure."

Portia was waiting for them by the door. Two clean-cut black teens slammed through the doors nearly knocking her over.

One of them stuck out a hand to keep her from falling, but looking embarrassed, he yelled at Portia. "Hey, move it, kid! Not a good place to stand."

Shayla hurried to her, looking daggers at the kid.

He ducked his head and rushed away.

But Portia just shook her head matter-of-factly. "It's okay. He's just a dumb teenager who doesn't know what he's talking about."

Shayla looked at Link and they both lost it. They laughed all the way to Link's truck with Portia asking over and over, "What's so funny?" Which only made them laugh harder.

Link sat at a table in the back of the bakery, listening to murmurs and giggles drifting down from upstairs. Shayla was tucking Portia into bed. It sounded like they had a routine a lot like his sisters' kids—brushing teeth, reading stories, saying prayers. He had to keep reminding himself that Portia wasn't Shayla's daughter.

He heard one last round of goodnights, then saw the light at the top of the stairway click off, and Shayla came trotting down the stairs.

"Whew. She's down." She slumped into the chair across from him. "You want something to eat?"

He patted his belly. "No way. I'm still stuffed." They'd gone for burgers at Culver's after the movie and he'd overdone it with a large chocolate shake.

"Something to drink? Coffee?"

"Maybe some water."

"Sure." She scooted the chair back and went to the sink behind the pastry counter.

"Thanks," he said, when she set glasses of ice water on the table. "Hey, I'm sorry about that jerk at the theater."

She shook her head. "There's one born every minute. You learn to ignore them."

"Maybe you shouldn't. Maybe you ought to let him have it."

"Oh, yeah. That would go over real well."

"Because you're a girl?" *Or because you're a* black *girl?* The question hung between them, unspoken.

Shayla answered it anyway. "Not *just* because I'm a girl. Besides, how would that help Portia if I'm always walking around with a big ol' chip on my shoulder? She doesn't need to go through her whole life expecting the worst of people."

"Even when people are at their worst?"

"Those kind of people don't deserve one moment of my attention or emotion. And for sure not a moment of Portia's. There're always going to be people like that in the world. Doesn't mean we have to let them ruin ours."

"Well, you're a bigger man than I am."

"Excuse me?"

He grinned. "You know what I mean. Anyway, despite that yellow-headed idiot, I had fun tonight."

She nodded. "Me too. And thank you. For including Portia."

He shook his head. "She's a character."

Shayla giggled. "That's one way to put it."

"Do you know...how long you'll have her?" As soon as the words were out, he knew it sounded like he was trying to gauge when Shayla would be rid of the "brat." He hadn't meant it like that at all. "You said her parents aren't in the picture? You mean... like *ever*?"

She took a long drink of water. "I don't know about ever but not for a long time." She eyed him, as if she were trying to decide whether she could trust him. "My brother's in jail. Prison. Eight years before he'll be eligible for parole. Drugs. He's not exactly father material. At least not now."

"I'm sorry. That's got to be hard."

She shrugged. "It is what it is."

"What about Portia's mother?"

"She passed away."

"Really?" Link knew his face showed his shock, but he was curious why Shayla hadn't said anything before. That seemed like the kind of thing you didn't just forget to mention. "I'm so sorry. That's got to be tough. Portia seems really . . . well-adjusted. I wouldn't have expected that." He felt like he was saying all the wrong things.

But Shayla didn't blanch. "Daddy and I have tried to keep things stable in her life."

"Of course. I didn't mean—"

She waved him off. "I know. It's an awkward situation. People don't know what to say."

"It's not that." He hesitated and hoped he'd managed to look sheepish. "Well, I guess it is that." He held up a hand. "I'm really not meaning to be nosy. I just wondered."

"She's probably going to be part of our lives—my dad's and mine—for a long time. I don't blame you if that scares you off. You wouldn't be the first."

Did it scare him? If he was honest, yes. A little. He'd had enough experience with nieces and nephews that he wasn't uncomfortable around kids. He wanted kids of his own someday. He hadn't really considered that he might get them "ready-made." He released a sigh. "I'm still thinking about that, I guess. Just trying to be honest."

"I get that."

Except he wanted to ask her out again. He knew that. "Do I have to decide before you'll go out with me again? I'd really like to ask you out again." He was diving into the deep end. Sink or swim.

She tilted her head in that winsome way she had. "I don't suppose you'd be content to just be a friend for a while?"

"Is this your way of saying you like me but . . . not in that way?" The disappointment hurt more than he expected.

But her smile gave him quick relief. "No. I'm not saying that. I'm saying—" She pushed her chair back from the table and grabbed a bar rag from the bakery counter. She rubbed it in circles on the table until Link thought the finish might come off. Finally, she straightened and looked at him hard, a nervous half-grin on her lips. "Why are we having this conversation? Tonight was only our first date. Can't we just take it one step at a time?"

He shrugged. "Hey, that's all I'm asking for—the next step. Will you go out with me next week?"

She scrubbed the table with a vengeance. "Let me see if I can find a sitter for Portia. Are you thinking Sunday night again?"

"You can bring her if you want."

"You don't understand. If we take her out with us again"—she motioned between them—"then it's a 'thing' with her. And if we never see you again after that . . ."

"Okay. I get that. You'll let me know? If you can get a sitter?"

"Can I text you?"

He shrugged. "Sure. You have my number?"

She nodded.

He rose. "How about next Saturday night? Does that work for you?"

"Unless you want to do breakfast. Like really early breakfast."

"Saturday?"

"Any day."

He grinned. "I figured you got free breakfast here." He eyed the case of pastries. "Man, if *I* lived here, I'd never eat anywhere else."

"Yeah, and you'd weigh four hundred pounds."

"At least." He wanted to see her again. Soon. "How about I'll come by some day this week and we'll figure out a time then."

"It's a free country." But her smile said she wouldn't mind if he did.

7

Come on, baby girl. It's time to get you to school. Run get your backpack now." Daddy scraped his chair back and grabbed his jacket off the hook by the door.

Shayla gave Portia's skinny butt a playful pat. "Hustle now, girl. You don't want to be late."

Portia dashed upstairs while Shayla cleared off the table. She took a clean apron off the hook behind the stairway, slipped it over her head, and tied it behind her back.

The bells on the front door jangled as someone tried to get in.

"Unlock that, Shay, will you? We're running behind."

She ran to flip the sign in the front window to Yes We're Open, and unlocked the front door. "Good morning. Come on in. Sorry we had you locked out."

"Oh, no problem. I'm a little early." The woman stomped the snow off her feet on the front mat, then pushed back the hood of her down jacket. "It's cold out there!"

Shayla closed the door behind her, making sure it remained unlocked. "I haven't been out yet, but I saw the forecast. Looks like we're in for a few days like this."

The customer slipped off her coat and folded it over her arm. She sniffed, then inhaled deeply. "It smells heavenly in here! I'll take one of everything." Laughing, she finger-combed her long blonde curls, and turned to face Shayla.

Recognition hit her. This was Link's sister—the one who lived here in Langhorne. She and her husband sometimes brought their little towheaded twins in for doughnuts.

Shayla's stomach fluttered with foolish nerves. "May I help you?" She wondered if Link's sister knew he'd gone out with her. And Portia.

Link's sister put out a hand. "I'm Landyn Spencer."

Shayla shook her hand, feeling immediately intimidated—and a little confused—by Link's sister's professional demeanor. People didn't usually formally introduce themselves before ordering a latte and a doughnut.

"Hello." She tried to mirror Landyn's tone. "I'm Shayla Michaels. What can I get for you this morning?" For a brief moment, panic inched up her spine. What if Landyn had come on the sly to warn her to stay away from Link?

"Oh. Sorry. I should have explained." Landyn's poise slipped a notch. "I'm meeting my sister-in-law here so we can sample some of your pastries. We're trying to decide on cakes and pastries for her wedding reception in December."

Shayla grinned. "That sounds like one of those tough-job-but-somebody-has-to-do-it problems." It was a joke she heard at least twice a week, but it still got a smile from Link's sister. Who was drop-dead gorgeous. With hair the color Shayla's mom's had been. Except Mama's hair had been straight as a stick.

Landyn laughed. "I'd better have a cup of coffee to go with that tough job."

Shayla smiled. "Just black, or can I make you a latte?" She reached for the coffee pot. Link's sister had the figure of a black coffee gal.

"Better just do black. Keep the palate clean. And go ahead and pour one for my sister-in-law too if you don't mind."

"Of course." Shayla grabbed two cups and the coffee pot and took them to the best table in the bakery where the sun would warm them and make the dishes and glasses sparkle. It was where she sat herself if there was ever a lull early in the afternoon.

Portia's patter sounded on the stairway and Shayla heard her niece chattering to Big Daddy as he helped her into her coat. The back door closed behind them, but it was only quiet for a moment before the bells on the front door jangled again, and another woman about Shayla's age entered. The woman blinked while her eyes adjusted to the dimmer light.

"You made it!" Link's sister went to her, and the two women embraced. They were both so beautiful and stylish.

"You didn't think I was going to miss doughnuts, did you?" the sister-in-law said.

Shayla recognized her. She'd been in here before for breakfast. With a man. Probably her fiancé. A twinge of envy pinched her. And tried to quash the hope that glimmered briefly. Hope that tempted her to believe she had a prayer of ever being part of a family like Link's.

No, not part of a family *like* Link's. But rather part of *his* very family—the Whitmans. It was the kind of family she'd always dreamed of having—and that she'd been blessed to have once upon a time.

And then Mom got sick. And everything had gone downhill from there. Worse than downhill. But she didn't want to dwell on that now.

Landyn and her sister-in-law got settled at the table near the window, and while they talked excitedly, Shayla fetched menus. She carried them to the table, then remembering what Landyn had said, she stopped. "Would you rather I bring a sampler? You can choose from the menu, or I can just bring you an assortment of our favorites if you'd prefer."

Landyn gave the other woman a questioning glance. "Your call. Oh! And by the way, this is my sister-in-law, Bree Whitman—soon to be Brooks."

"Congratulations." She smiled and started in on her canned spiel. "I'm Shayla Michaels. If you choose to go with Coffee's On, I'll be your contact." That part felt a bit disingenuous, given that she was essentially the *only* contact. Daddy was the chef and baker, but she ran the cash register whenever their part-time help wasn't there and did most everything else, including being chief janitor and dishwasher. She also handled the few catering jobs they took on.

"Oh, we're definitely going with you. Drew—my fiancé—gave strict orders."

"That's great. We appreciate your business. So a sample platter for you two ladies? Complimentary, of course."

"Oh, you don't have to do that," Bree said. "We'll be happy to pay for it."

"Oh, no. It's part of our package. And"—she laughed and lifted a brow—"you'll pay for it. Just not today."

The women laughed with her, and Shayla heard Link's voice in his sister's laughter.

"Well, bring it on then!" Landyn clutched her upturned fork like a hungry longshoreman.

Shayla hurried to prepare a small platter of the pastries and brought them back to the table. "I think I left these such that you'll be able to tell which is which, but I did cut them into smaller bites so you can taste several. Most people order a variety, but if there's anything you taste that you'd prefer not to be in your order, we can certainly accommodate that." She always felt so *prissy* when she spoke that way. But she'd learned that people responded better when she spoke in a professional tone. White people anyway.

Landyn and Bree dove into the plate and made appreciative sounds as they tasted each pastry. Shayla couldn't help but smile at their swooning *oohs* and *aahs*. And feel a little proud that they'd chosen Coffee's On to cater Bree's wedding. Never mind theirs was the closest location. And probably the best price. Still, a lot of people went to Cape or even St. Louis for their catering needs—especially for a once-in-a-lifetime event like a wedding. So she was happy. And grateful. The bakery did fine and they managed to pay the bills each month, but they were by no means getting rich.

And the older Portia got, the more it cost to take care of her medical and dental needs, let alone the pretty clothes she liked so much—and changed three times a day if Shayla let her.

"Shayla?"

She turned at the sound of the voice. Both women were eyeing her with questioning looks.

"I'm sorry. What was that?" She had to quit daydreaming when she was supposed to be concentrating.

Landyn smiled.

Was her expression condescending? Shayla couldn't tell.

"We were just wondering about the cake. Are these the only sizes you have available?" Link's sister tapped the catering menu with a manicured nail.

"Those are our most popular, but we can probably make just about anything you request. There might be a small surcharge if we have to order odd-sized pans, but it's very reasonable. What did you have in mind?" She turned to include the bride-to-be in her question even though Link's sister seemed to have taken on the role of wedding planner.

Bree pulled a sheet of paper from her leather bag and showed her a tall stacked hearts cake that Shayla had admired on Pinterest just a few nights ago.

"Oh, sure. We can do something like that." She flipped the menu over and showed them the pricing for a similar cake. "Does that sound about right?"

Bree nodded. "That's very reasonable. Could you do it in pink? A very very pale rose shade though. I'm not sure my groom would be too happy if it came out bubblegum pink." She dug in her purse again and came up with a swatch of fabric. "This is what my dress will be."

"Ah, champagne pink."

"Is that what it's called? This is . . . not my first wedding." Bree glanced at Landyn with a mournful expression that caused Shayla to remember how these two women were related. Bree had been married to Link's brother—his *only* brother. Shayla had forgotten his name—or maybe she'd never known it—but he'd been killed in Afghanistan. Four or five years ago, she thought. She silently chastised herself. She had a bad habit of forgetting that other people's families had tragedies too. She wasn't the only one. And yet, somehow the Whitmans' felt easier. Yes it was tragic, but it was honorable. There was no shame attached.

"Anyway," Bree said, "I won't be wearing white, and things will be a little more informal than the typical wedding you probably cater."

"We've done all kinds, so no worries. You just tell us exactly what you want, and we'll make it happen. I know the last thing you need to worry about is whether the food and the cake will be perfect. That's what we're here for."

"Thank you." Bree gave her an appreciative smile. "I think we're ready to place our order then."

"Sure." Shayla pulled a chair out from their table. "May I?"

"Of course." Landyn patted the seat of the chair.

Shayla took a pad from her pocket. "Now what's the date of the wedding?"

Bree smiled. "December 13. I hope people don't think that's too close to Christmas, but it just worked better for us."

"No, that's perfect! December weddings are so special." It came out with more . . . *emotion* than she'd intended. She'd always dreamed of a winter wedding and a gown with white fur trim. But they didn't need to know that, nor would they care. But the sisters seemed pleased with her reaction. Nevertheless, she tempered her voice and tried to regain a professional tone. "That's on a Saturday. The first weekend in December is when the holiday orders really ramp up."

Landyn frowned. "Is that a problem?"

"Oh, not at all. You've given us plenty of notice." She helped them finalize a light supper for seventy-five guests and a variety of other cakes to serve alongside the stacked-hearts wedding cake.

Twenty minutes later, as they gathered their things and prepared to leave, Landyn pointed at the doorway to the storage room. "I love the way you have that burlap curtain hanging in the door."

Shayla looked behind her, wondering for a minute if Landyn was being sarcastic. She didn't seem like the type to gush over burlap curtains. But she seemed genuinely enthralled with Shayla's spur-of-the-moment solution to hiding the clutter of the room where they stored the coffee beans and other supplies. She laughed. "It's just a coffee sack. That's what our whole beans from the roaster come in."

"How clever!" Bree exclaimed.

Landyn's eyes sparkled. "Bree, wouldn't that make perfect curtains for Chase's studio?"

"Oh, it would!" Her sister-in-law gave a little clap. "I could see those in a kitchen even."

In unison, the women turned questioning eyes on Shayla. "Would you ever consider selling a couple of those sacks?" Landyn asked.

"Oh. We usually just throw them out. You'd be—"

"Oh, no!" Landyn clasped her throat comically. "Don't throw them away!"

Shayla cringed. "Sorry. I never thought about reusing them except when I hung that curtain up. It was just going to be temporary. But it's kind of growing on me." She *was* pleased with the way the makeshift curtain turned out and had already decided to leave it up.

"I saw a coffee shop in St. Louis where the whole place was decorated with a burlap theme. I bet those were coffee bags too." Bree looked around the bakery. "They'd be cute as curtains at the windows."

"In here?" Shayla wasn't sure whether they were talking to her.

"Yes," Bree said. "You could put them on rods with curtain clips..."

"Or for a bulletin board." Landyn touched Shayla's arm. "Don't you dare throw any more away!"

She laughed nervously. "Who knew I was throwing out such valuable treasures all this time?"

"I'm serious, I'd be happy to pay whatever you think is fair for a couple of them."

"Oh, you're welcome to just take them." Shayla waved her off. "I don't have any empty right now, but maybe check back in a week?"

"I definitely will."

Shayla walked them to the door and waved as they each climbed into their cars and drove off in opposite directions.

She liked these women, Link's sister and sister-in-law. It had been such fun to talk decorating and parties with them. It made her miss the friendships she'd enjoyed once upon a time. The truth was, most of her friends had drifted away after Mama got sick. And the few who'd hung in through that awful time bailed when the whole thing with Jerry happened.

She'd allowed the customers who came in to the bakery to fill the spot her friends had once filled. But it wasn't the same. She missed having someone to confide in. Someone whose history you knew and who knew yours—and loved you anyway, warts and all.

Sometimes she worried that she'd forgotten how to be a friend. Watching Link's sisters, old insecurities had crept out like cockroaches in the dark. Had Landyn and Bree only been putting on an act with their friendliness toward her? Were they, even now, laughing on their phones together about the crazy "bag lady" who hung old coffee sacks in doorways?

Mama would have said, "Take people at face value, Shay. Expect the best of them and you'll usually get it." Her mother could always reassure her.

Now, for the first time in a while, Shayla became aware of the depth of that awful ache—that empty place inside that only a mother—*her* mother—could fill.

And there would be no filling it this side of heaven.

8

Where have you been hiding yourself, son?" Grant handed Link a stack of salad plates as the two of them emptied the dishwasher.

Audrey kept on dicing onion for the salad in quick, rhythmic motions, but she cringed inwardly at Grant's question. He was being far too obvious. Link would be onto him and then they'd never get any answers.

"It's called a job, Pops. You should try it."

"Link!" She forced a laugh, knowing he was only teasing. But these days Grant could be sensitive to the subject of retirement. It seemed certain people had gotten the idea Grant had retired and *she* was running the inn. Which was preposterous. There was no way she could do this without him. Not to mention the poor man had earned a retirement after all the months of back-breaking renovation, and more recently, building CeeCee's cottage. A house Grant's mother would probably never inhabit, given how settled in she'd become at the assisted living facility. Thankfully, CeeCee's cottage already stood to earn them some much-needed extra income since they'd started booking it as a "deluxe private suite." She only hoped the cottage would be ready in time for the first reservation.

Link put his hands on his father's shoulders and shook him playfully before taking the stack of plates from him. "Just kidding, Dad."

"Sure you were." Grant chuckled and wriggled out from under Link's grip. "And I was just kidding about you being welcome to stay for supper."

Audrey smiled to herself. All was well.

"I'm glad you could come for a little while. The kids have missed you."

"Yeah, well, like I said, I can't stay long. I have to be in to work by eight."

"Well, take some of the leftovers with you when you go," Grant said over his shoulder. "And don't think I didn't notice you dodging my question."

Audrey shot Link an apologetic wince. Grant wasn't going to let this go. And as much as they tried not to pry into their children's business, she was equally curious about what was going on in their son's life. She knew Link had been working extra shifts, and that probably meant he needed more sleep, but even so, he certainly made himself scarce these days. And whenever they asked how things were going, he was strangely reticent. She was starting to suspect it might involve a girl, though it'd been so long since Link had a girlfriend they'd begun to worry he'd given up altogether.

"I wasn't dodging, Mom." Link set the plates on the table. "And yes, it may involve a woman."

She stared at him, jaw agape. "I never said—"

"You didn't have to say it. I can read you like an open book."

"Smarty pants." She punched his arm. "So spill. A woman, you say?"

He gave her that grin that would melt the heart of any young woman. "I said it *may* involve a woman."

"What's that supposed to mean?"

"I'll let you know the minute there's anything to tell."

Audrey gave a frustrated growl, which earned Link's charming laughter.

She knew it would be futile to press him further, but she was thrilled at the prospect of a girlfriend for her son. She supposed they'd find out soon enough, as he'd said, but the suspense would likely kill her.

Link looked pointedly around the kitchen. Danae and Dallas were picking up the pizza, and they hadn't arrived yet so the counters were empty. "So what's for supper, Mom?"

Changing the subject again. A trick as old as history. Grinning, she shot him a look of disdain. "I'll let you know the minute there's anything to tell."

Grant's snicker charmed her every bit as much as Link's had.

"You're sure you don't mind?" Shayla cringed. Surely Link would tire of taking Portia with them on every date.

"I don't mind. But I hope—" The wind gusted on the sidewalk in front of the bakery, and Link trapped a passing leaf under the toe of his shoe. He crushed it to a fine gold powder. "You're not just using her as a shield, are you? I won't bite. I promise. I'll be a perfect gentleman."

"A shield?" She ignored that last part about being a gentleman. "As if I could get Portia to hold still long enough to be a shield."

That made him laugh—a sound she'd grown to love. She did not want to scare the man away. Yet maybe it would be best if she forgot all about him.

"I truly don't mind, Shayla. But sometimes I would like to have time with just you."

Sunday would only be their third date, if you counted Link hanging out at the park with her and Portia before he went in to work Monday evening. Still, her heart lifted at his "sometimes." That meant he saw this as an ongoing thing.

She glanced back through the glass, squinting to see beyond the reflection of the cars parked in front. She really needed to get back inside. Her college help was watching the counter, but this was ten a.m.—coffee break time for most of the town, and the bakery was busy. It wouldn't be in Link's favor if her dad caught him bugging her during work hours.

She was surprised Link had stopped by unannounced, especially after working back-to-back shifts. It was only Wednesday, but he said he wanted to make sure they were still on for a movie Sunday. He could have easily called her instead, but he apparently wanted to *see* her. Which made her smile.

But already there were complications. At least that's how he obviously saw things. Portia had tagged along with them on their very first date, and now Shayla was asking Link to let a five-year-old join them again. But he was wrong if he thought it was because she felt the need of protection from him. Not hardly. If anything, it was on her father's account she needed Portia along. But she couldn't tell Link that.

"For one thing, it's hard to find a PG movie to see—Shayla? Earth to Shay..."

"Oh—" Link's use of her nickname pulled her from her reverie—and warmed her in a way she hadn't felt for a long time. "I know." She gave him a wry smile. "I'm sorry."

"Would it help if I paid for a sitter?"

"No. You're not going to pay for my babysitter." She hadn't meant to sound so harsh.

He cocked his head. "You sound like she's your sole responsibility. Won't your dad watch her sometimes?"

"He does. Sometimes." *Hardly ever.* She'd been Mom's designated caregiver all those years. And now she had Portia to take care of. The only relief she ever got—the only time Daddy was willing to watch Portia—was when she had an event to cater. Daddy always managed to get away for his Tuesday night prayer meetings in Cape. But somehow there was never time for her to get away, unless she took Portia, of course.

When would it ever be *her* turn? Immediately the guilt came. She'd loved her mother. It had been her privilege to take care of Mom. And in Daddy's defense, he'd had to keep the bakery running. And he did pay her a fair wage, and didn't charge her rent, so she'd managed to put a little savings aside.

And as for Portia, she was precious. And innocent.

Sometimes Shayla let herself daydream that her little niece was her own daughter. At the rate she was going, it might be the closest she ever got to being a mother.

She took a step backward and reached for the bakery door. She didn't like the direction her thoughts were taking. "I need to go. Daddy's going to think I ran away."

"Okay. Well, I'll see you Sunday. Pick you up about six?"

"Maybe make it five-thirty?" Daddy would probably be back from Bowling Green by six and she didn't want to risk having to introduce Link to him. Or vice versa.

Link gave her a questioning look.

"Portia has school Monday. I don't want her out too late."

"Oh. Okay. Five-thirty then."

She shrugged and took another step back. "I really do need to go."

"Okay." He hesitated, then reached out to touch her arm. "I'll see you soon. Have a good day."

Shivering—and knowing it had nothing to do with the brisk wind—she nodded. Then, ignoring how desperately she wanted to stay out here talking to him, she turned and ran inside.

A swirl of dry leaves followed her in on a gust of cold wind, and she immediately went for the broom in the back room.

"Who was that?" Her father stood behind the cake case with hands on hips. "That the Whitman boy? Again?"

She pretended she hadn't heard him and took the broom and dustpan to the door and swept up the mess.

Daddy was still standing there, watching, when she started back with the full dustpan. "You hear me, girl?"

"I heard you. His name is Link."

"He the one almost ran over Portia?"

"He didn't almost run over her."

"That's not the story you told that day it happened." His gaze panned the humming dining room before it landed on Valerie, the college girl at the cash register. "I'll get the register, Val. You go make the rounds with coffee."

Shayla resisted the urge to roll her eyes. *Just say it, Daddy: Shayla here isn't pulling her weight.* But she grabbed a clean apron and looped it over her head. "You want me to start some potato soup?"

That seemed to derail his interrogation. "Yeah, but don't make as much as you did last Tuesday. We had too many leftovers."

"Portia and I can eat it while you're gone this weekend."

Daddy pulled the decaf carafe off the burner, dumped the old coffee in the sink, and started scouring the pot as if he thought the restaurant inspector was five minutes out or something. "I'm not going this weekend."

She froze. "You're not going? Why?"

"I'm just not. Leave it be."

"But Daddy—"

"I said leave it be."

"You weren't expecting me to go since you're not?" She hadn't been to visit her brother in prison for at least four months. Probably closer to five now. And the longer she could stretch that, the happier she'd be. She'd never gone by herself. And wouldn't. It was almost three hours each way and from what she remembered, it was rough. Daddy had already decided they wouldn't take Portia to see Jerry. A decision Shayla agreed with, even though it made her feel guilty. But then, what *didn't* make her feel guilty these days?

"I never said I expected you to go. I wouldn't want you going by yourself." He set the sparkling carafe on the counter and wadded up the dish towel he'd used to dry it. An impish grin flicked at the corner of his mouth. "Besides, I don't relish being stuck by myself all day with that little Energizer bunny."

Shayla giggled, grateful to see a side of her father she hadn't seen in a long time. But now what was she supposed to do about Sunday? She had to tell him. When Daddy headed to Bowling Green each Sunday to visit Jeremiah, she didn't feel obligated to tell him what she did with her time while he was gone, but she wouldn't lie to him. As Daddy liked to say, "A lie can travel halfway around the world while the truth is putting on its shoes." Probably one of his Mark Twain quotes. But it was true. Especially in a small town like Langhorne—speaking of Mr. Twain.

She took a breath. "Portia and I were going to go to a movie Sunday. In Cape. That okay with you?"

"What movie? Maybe I'll go with you. Unless it's a lame kids' movie."

"It kind of needs to be a lame kids' movie if Portia's going." This was not going the way she wanted.

She looked up to see her father looking at her with an expression that told her she was pretty much busted.

"You going with somebody else? That it?"

"I—"

"It's that Whitman kid, isn't it? What'd you say he's called—Luke?"

"Link. And yes. If you must know, he invited me and Portia."

"Like . . . a date?"

She affected a laugh. "You can't exactly call it a date if Portia's going."

"How'd this come about? Is that what you were talking to him about out there?" He waved a hand toward the front of the bakery. "You don't even know the man."

"I know him. He's a great guy. He's really good to Portia."

He narrowed his eyes. "When's he ever seen Portia outside of running her over with his pickup?"

"Daddy! He didn't run over her. It was an accident. In fact he did everything he could to *save* Portia. And he's apologized all over himself about—"

Two patrons came to pay their checks and Daddy slid behind the cash register to ring up their food. He made small talk with them like always, but when they walked out, he picked up right where they'd left off. "Are you *seeing* him? You done this before?"

She hadn't noticed how much gray there was in his eyebrows until they were knit together like this. "He took us to a movie . . . and the park."

Her father pressed his lips together and balled the dish towel up tighter, scrubbing at an invisible smudge on the case. "When were you planning on telling me?"

"It was nothing."

"One time is nothing. Two times might be close to nothing. But three times? You might think it's nothing, but I guarantee you that's not how Mr. Luke sees it."

"Link, Daddy. His name is *Link*."

Noise from the brick street wafted in through the front entrance. With a jangle of bells, the door closed behind an older couple.

Saved by the bell.

"Good morning, folks!" Daddy called. "Come on in. It's a chilly one out there, isn't it?" Her father turned so the couple couldn't see his face. He pointed a finger at her chest and lowered his voice. "Don't think I don't see those wheels of yours turning. And don't think you were saved by no bell. We'll discuss this later."

Her jaw dropped. "How did you—"

"I'm your father. I know everything." He tossed the towel at her, his eyes sparkling. "You go start some soup. I'll take care of our customers."

She huffed at him, even as she felt her lips form that same impish grin that he'd let her glimpse before.

It'd been a long time since she'd seen this side of him. It made her heart swell to know that playful side hadn't been buried with Mama after all.

Valerie appeared out of nowhere, as if she'd been hovering, waiting to talk to them. "I need to clock out if that's okay. I have a test to study for."

Daddy glanced at the clock. Almost eleven and the crowd had dwindled. "Sure, go on."

Shayla waved. "See you tomorrow, Val."

Her father went back to the register and Shayla trudged to the kitchen. At least he hadn't totally flipped out about Link. That was something. She tied a scarf around her hair, scrubbed her hands, and put a pot of water on to boil. Peeling potatoes, she rehearsed her speech.

She knew her father well enough to know there would be nothing playful about the man when it came time to discuss her dating Link Whitman.

A loud crash from the front of the store made her gasp. She quickly turned the stove down and ran out to see what had happened.

Her father and the elderly couple stood in front of a broken window, a pile of shattered glass littering the floor and tables near the window. The wind whistled eerily through the hole in the plate glass.

"Daddy? What happened?"

"Some kid threw something through the window." The elderly woman's voice quavered, and her face went pale as cream cheese frosting. "I saw him do it. This pickup drove by real slow and this kid leaned out the window and threw something. You need to report him. Call 9-1-1!"

"Get the broom, Shay," Daddy barked.

She started for the broom closet.

"That's him!" the woman yelled.

Shayla whirled around.

"They're coming back again!" The old man pointed through the jagged hole in the window.

Shayla rushed to the window in time to see a gray pickup coast by, a bulky white guy hanging out of the passenger-side window. His yellow hair waved like a flag in the wind. She froze. The guy from the movies. The one Link had gone after. She would have sworn to it.

"You really should call the police," the woman said.

Daddy kicked into proprietor mode. "We'll take care of it, ma'am." He ushered the couple away from the front of the bakery. "Neither of you are hurt, are you?"

"No, we're fine," the woman's husband said.

"Bert, did you get the license plate?"

"I couldn't see it," he said. "But I caught a glimpse of the driver. I'd know him if I saw him again. It was a kid. Had one of those crazy haircuts"—he ran his hands down the middle of his own scalp—"and he had those metal things through his eyebrow and his lip . . . staples or whatever they call them."

"I don't know why anybody would want to do that to their body," his wife said. "Plumb crazy, if you ask me."

"Folks, we're going to have to close the store until we can get that window repaired." He started herding them toward the front door. "Let me get you some pastries to go. On the house."

"Nonsense. Let us help," the man said.

"No, no. I appreciate the offer, but you don't need to do that. We'll take care of it. But we do need to lock up." He motioned toward Shayla. "Bag up some pastries, Shay."

Shayla walked backward toward the display cases, watching her father herd the couple toward the door. She quickly filled a bag with pastries, neatly folding the top down as she carried it to the couple. "Here you go."

"Well, thank you. You didn't need to do that." Reluctantly, the woman took the bag.

Her husband fished an old flip phone from his pocket. "I'll call the police department while you clean up."

"No, no. Thank you, but that won't be necessary." Daddy all but put the man's phone back in his pocket for him. "We can handle it. You folks don't need to get involved."

Her father would not call the police. Not now. Not later. He'd sweep up the glass, call the hardware store to order a new window, and sweep the whole incident under the rug.

Shayla didn't blame him. Not the way things were.

But if it really had been the bully from the theater the other night—the one Link referred to as Mohawk—would that make a difference?

Even worse, if she told her father what had happened—about Link confronting the jerk who'd taunted Portia—it would only give him ammunition against Link. And Lord knew he already had a full clip.

9

Hey, if you can't get a sitter, I understand."

"I'm sorry. I tried." It was true, but maybe she could have tried harder.

"Hey," Link's voice brightened. "Any chance you can get away next Tuesday evening instead?"

"Tuesday?" She switched her cell phone to her other ear and lowered her voice. Daddy was already in bed for the night. "I can't. Daddy has his prayer meeting, so there would be no one to watch Portia."

"Bring Portia too. My nieces will love having a new playmate."

An alarm went off in the back of her head. "Your . . . nieces?"

"I'm not on the schedule for late shift that night, so come have supper with us."

"Us?"

"My family. At the inn. We get together every other Tuesday night for supper. Remember?"

"Yes, but I thought you ended up going last week."

"Oh, I did. We're switching weeks because of Thanksgiving, so that makes two in a row."

"Link?" Her palms were sweating just thinking about the prospect. "I'm not sure I'm ready for that."

"Sure you are. They won't bite. I promise. I'd love for them to meet you. Well . . . get to know you I mean. I know you've already met some of them because of the bakery."

She blew out a calming breath that didn't do much to calm her. "I guess I could do that."

"Great. I'll pick you up at six and give you the lowdown on the way out there."

"Lowdown?" Why would dinner at his parents' involve a lowdown? What had she gotten herself into?

He laughed. "I'm just kidding. Well, sort of. Just come. It's totally casual. Nothing fancy. Oh, and hey, I told Mom I'd bring the bread, so maybe you can pick out a couple of nice loaves from the bakery and I'll pay you for it."

"Oh, I get it. You're just trying to get out of having to take care of the bread."

He laughed. "Well, there is that. But hey, I said I'd pay for it."

"Don't be silly. I'm happy to bring the bread."

They hung up a few minutes later and Shayla realized her hands were shaking.

Part of her was ecstatic at the invitation. Not only had she always wanted to see the inside of the Chicory Inn, but to think that Link wanted his family to meet her? She was beyond flattered. And a little bit surprised.

But another part of her was terrified. Link's family was close—and big. *Huge.* And she didn't know how they did things, what they would expect of her. Mama had taught her and Jerry good manners, but they didn't often have the opportunity to eat at nice restaurants. What if she didn't know which fork to use? Or what if they talked about things she knew nothing about?

A horrible thought struck her: What if they asked about *her* family? She wasn't even ready to explain everything to Link yet, let alone his family.

And what if Link's idea of "casual" was totally different than hers? His sister and sister-in-law had been pretty dressed up that day they'd come to the bakery to arrange the catering for Bree's reception. Maybe they were so dressed up because they had other errands that day, but she sure wouldn't have called their attire casual.

Remembering her conversation with Landyn, she smiled. She'd emptied two burlap coffee sacks since that day—never mind that she'd transferred a half-full bag into plastic bins in order to free up another sack. She could take them to Landyn Tuesday night. That would give them at least a little something to talk about. For the first five minutes anyway.

There were already three cars in the driveway at the inn when Link rounded the curve. It looked like everyone but Bree and Drew was here, and they might have ridden along with Danae and Dallas from Cape as they sometimes did.

"Here we are." He gave Shayla what he hoped was a reassuring smile as they wound up the long driveway.

She'd hardly spoken all the way here, although with Portia chattering, it wasn't surprising Shayla couldn't get a word in.

She twisted in her seat to speak to Portia in the booster seat. "Now you behave, young lady. Use your manners, you hear me?"

"I didn't do nothin' wrong!"

"You didn't do *anything* wrong," Shayla corrected.

"That's what I said."

Link and Shayla laughed. "I'm just reminding you, baby. Manners. And good grammar, please."

He patted Shay's arm. "She'll be fine. Things already get pretty wild with my eight nieces and nephews. One more isn't going to make it any rowdier."

She laughed, but Link thought it came off a little nervous sounding. He was nervous too. It had seemed like such a good idea to skip the movie and bring her and Portia to Tuesday night dinner instead, but suddenly he worried about how everyone would react. He hadn't told anyone he was bringing Shay and Portia. It had been a very long time since he'd had a girlfriend—not that Shayla would consider herself that. But still, that was where this was headed, and he hadn't wanted to make it too "official" by announcing that he was bringing guests. His family would make a big deal of it as it was. Especially his mom. And his sisters. And probably their kids.

He took in a short breath. He hadn't thought about his nieces and nephews until now. And it struck a tiny bit of terror in him. Some of them were old enough now that they might say something embarrassing. Tease Shayla or ask questions about why her skin—and Portia's—was different from theirs. He figured his sisters had taught them better than that, but they were just kids, after all, and he'd heard them say some pretty embarrassing things.

Then there was CeeCee. And who was he kidding? A small part of him worried what his family might think about him bringing home a biracial woman. It wasn't that they were racist. They weren't. But maybe they'd feel a bit differently when they realized it was more than a friendship—and especially given that Shayla had a child, to boot. Because regardless of how Portia was related to Shay, the girl *was* part of the package. And then there was the brother. In jail.

If Link tried to view things through his parents' eyes, there was a lot to object to.

With a hand on the door handle, he turned to Shayla now. "I did tell you about my grandmother, didn't I?"

"Yes, Link." She mimicked him. "Heaven only knows what CeeCee might say!"

He laughed. "Well, it's true. I'm just warning you. Some days she's fine, but if it doesn't seem like she's making sense, just smile and nod. She won't know the difference." He wasn't giving CeeCee quite enough credit. She was actually getting along wonderfully at the assisted living center, but the family didn't even pretend any more that his grandmother would ever move into the cottage Dad and Bree's fiancé, Drew, had built on the property for her.

Currently Mom and Dad planned to rent it out as a suite, but they hadn't put CeeCee's house on the market yet, so Dad was understandably a little antsy about the finances.

Though CeeCee had days when she was still her old self, Link saw the slow decline in her too. Made him sad. And he couldn't even begin to imagine a day when he might possibly see his own parents have to walk that same path.

He parked beside Chase and Landyn's minivan, turned off the ignition, and pocketed his keys.

"Is this your house, Mr. Link?"

Link looked at Portia over the back of his seat. "It's not my house now, but this is where I lived when I was a little boy about your age."

Portia giggled. "You ain't my age, silly."

"*Aren't* my age," Shayla corrected.

"No, I *aren't*"—he winked at Shayla—"but I used to be your age. A long time ago."

Portia wrinkled her nose as if she wasn't sure whether to believe him.

Shayla got out and helped Portia unbuckle. "We're going to meet Link's parents and a whole bunch of his family. So you be on your best behavior, okay?"

"You already told me."

"I know. I'm just reminding you."

"Is Link going to be on his best 'havior?"

Link laughed. "Probably not. You know how you sometimes act goofy when you're only with Shayla and Big Daddy?" Portia had corrected him enough times, he'd learned to refer to Mike Michaels by the "right" name when he was talking to her.

Portia nodded.

"Well, sometimes I act goofy when I'm with my family." He climbed out of the truck and shut the door behind him.

"Oh brother." Shayla rolled her eyes. "Am I going to be sorry I came?"

He winked at her over the hood of the truck. "Time will tell."

"Do you have the bread?"

He held up the three bags she'd brought from the bakery.

Huckleberry chose that moment to come flying around the house, the chocolate Lab's tail wagging wildly. Portia screamed and climbed Shayla like a tree.

"Hey, hey. It's okay." With his free hand, Link grabbed Huck by the collar and knelt down to hold him close. "It's just Huckleberry. Remember I told you about our dog? He's a friendly dog. In fact, Huck loves kids."

"I don't like him." She buried her face in the crook of Shayla's neck, peeking out at the dog.

"You don't even know him yet," Shayla chided.

Link wondered if there was a subliminal message there, but she set Portia on the ground without meeting his gaze. She took the little girl's hand. "He won't hurt you."

Link looped the bread sacks over one wrist and wiped his hands on his khakis. "Okay, let's do this."

Shayla studied him. "If I didn't know better, Mr. Link, I'd think you were nervous."

He had a feeling she was only saying that to make herself feel better. But he just grinned and put a hand at the small of her back, steering her toward the wide front porch of the inn.

Shayla looked up at the gabled roofline. "This has always been my dream house. Don't forget you promised me a tour."

"Don't worry. If I don't give you one, I guarantee my mom will. It's her pride and joy."

"I can see why."

The inn did look beautiful, dressed for fall. It struck him that he might invite Shayla and Portia for Thanksgiving.

The three of them climbed the steps, but before Link could reach for the front door, it flew open, and Corinne's three oldest girls plowed into him.

Portia squealed and jumped back three feet.

Link caught her and put his hands on her shoulders. "Hey, hey, careful there, ladies. I brought some friends with me tonight. Don't knock them over before they even get inside."

Sari and Sadie stopped short and stared up at Shayla, then Portia, and back again. Three-year-old Simone went straight to Portia and reached up to finger the beads dangling from her hair.

"Ouch!" Portia yelled.

Simone let loose and stumbled backward.

Shayla knelt between her niece and his. "Cut it out, Portia. You're okay." She turned to Simone. "Do you like her beads?"

Simone nodded solemnly, suddenly shy.

"I like 'em too," Sari said. "Mama did her hair like that once when they was in Jamaica. But we didn't get to go." She pouted like the slight had been yesterday.

"That was two years ago," Link told Shayla, laughing.

His mother appeared in the doorway just then. "Well, hi there." She gave Link a look that asked if he knew why the girl from the bakery was there.

"Mom, you know Shayla Michaels...from the bakery in Langhorne?"

"Of course." Her knit brow said she still hadn't caught on.

"This is Shay's niece, Portia. Oh, and"—he held up the bread—"tonight's bread is brought to you by Coffee's On, compliments of Shayla."

"Why thank you, Shayla." His mother beamed. "But you didn't drive all the way out here just to deliver that, did you?" His mother looked past them to the driveway, and Link could almost read her mind. She was looking for the delivery truck from the bakery. She didn't realize Shay and Portia had come with him—which was his own fault.

"Mom, Shayla is actually my—"

"Link!" His mom gave him a playful smack. "Didn't I tell you to write it down?" She turned to Shayla. "I'm so sorry if you made a special trip. This guy would seriously forget to eat if somebody didn't remind him. Hang on a minute and let me get you a little something for the delivery."

"*Mom*..."

She looked at him.

If his eyes had been lasers, she would have been toast. He put an arm around Shayla's waist. "Shayla is with me."

Slowly, painfully so, a light dawned in her eyes—a dim light, but better that than the blank stare she'd been wearing seconds earlier. Her hands fluttered in front of her face and she sputtered, "Oh! Of course. And supper is almost ready, so you all come on in." She hurried to open the front door, and as Shayla ushered Portia in, Mom asked, "Now what did you say your little girl's name is?"

Link pounced on the question. "Portia is Shay's niece, Mom. It's spelled P-O-R-T-I-A."

"Yes." Shayla shot him a look over her shoulder. "*Not* like the car."

Mom laughed as if she were in on the joke, and Link shot up a prayer of sheer desperation. If he survived this night, it would be a flat-out miracle.

10

Shayla's eyes adjusted to the dimmer indoor lights, and a strange sensation went through her. *This house!* She'd barely stepped past the foyer and already it was everything she'd imagined and more.

And it wasn't only the cream-colored woodwork and golden hardwood floors, or the colorful textiles and paintings on every wall, although all of that was stunning. There was a *warmth* about it that filled her up. And made her remember a time when their humble home above the bakery had felt the same way.

"I'm sorry," she told Link's mother, putting a hand to her throat. "I'm gawking. But your home is just so beautiful, Mrs. Whitman."

"Well, thank you, honey. That makes my day. And please, call me Audrey."

Shayla gave a nod, hoping she'd remember.

"We've certainly enjoyed the house." Link's mother led the way through the foyer. "Link may have told you it belonged to my parents. We raised our five kids here, and then when Landyn went off to college, we completely remodeled it and opened the inn."

"I've been telling Shayla you'd give her a tour of the whole place," Link said.

"Of course. I'd love to." Audrey beamed.

"I remember when it opened." Shayla made herself smile. She remembered because the open house had fallen on the one-year anniversary of Mama's death. But of course she didn't tell Audrey that. She'd wanted to come and see the house even back then, but it had seemed somehow an inappropriate and selfish way to spend such a somber anniversary. So she'd stayed home with

Daddy. In silence. Grieving in their separate ways, in separate rooms above the bakery.

"I'll give you the full tour after supper," Link's mom said. "Unless Link wants to do the honors." She turned to him.

He shrugged. "Either way."

"Well, let's eat first, while the food is still hot."

"It smells heavenly in here." Shayla took an appreciative whiff.

"Come on to the kitchen, Shayla." Audrey's heels clicked on the hardwood floor. "We'll introduce you to the rest of the family."

Seeing the house, she'd forgotten about being nervous, but the nerves kicked in big-time now. She wiped damp palms on her jeans. Then worried she shouldn't have worn jeans. Link had said casual, but if Link's sisters were all in dressy pants or skirts, she was going to feel stupid.

"Come on, Portia." She took her niece's hand and leaned down to whisper in her ear. "Remember your manners."

Portia wriggled her hand away, but gave a quick nod. Shayla prayed for the best. She looked around for Link, but he seemed to have disappeared.

Audrey led them through a dining room and into a large family room connected to a kitchen that was bigger than the bakery's. And a million times more elegant. The children were playing with Legos on the floor of the family room, and the rest of Link's family were scattered around the room in noisy clusters.

Shayla spotted Link's grandmother sitting in an overstuffed chair in a corner of the room, hands on the arms of the chair. She was more petite than Shayla had imagined, but her white hair and queenly demeanor fit the image the name "CeeCee" conjured for her. Shayla halfway hoped Audrey would introduce her to CeeCee first, but instead she went over to Link's father and sisters and another guy she didn't recognize, who were deep in discussion.

"Grant? Girls?" She finally patted her husband's arm to get his attention. They all turned and stared, looking as perplexed as Audrey had when she'd first seen Shayla. She was starting to get the impression that Link hadn't told his family she was coming. She looked furtively around the room. Where *was* Link anyway?

Audrey steered Shayla beside her. "Do you girls know Shayla Michaels from Langhorne? And this is her niece, Portia."

They all murmured hellos.

"Shayla, this is my daughter Corinne, and that's Landyn and her husband, Chase. And you know Grant, I think."

"Yes. Hi." She gave an awkward wave, then turned to Landyn. "Nice to see you again."

Landyn looked momentarily confused, and then recognition lit her eyes. "Oh! Of course. You're from the bakery. You're catering Bree and Drew's wedding."

"Oh, that's right," Audrey said. "I didn't realize you girls had already met with Shayla."

Landyn motioned toward Shayla's head. "I didn't recognize you with your hair down. Um, I think Bree's upstairs with the babies if you need to talk to her."

Shayla frowned. "Talk to her? About the catering, you mean?"

Landyn nodded, looking puzzled again.

Audrey cleared her throat. "Shayla and Portia are Link's guests tonight."

"Ohhh...I'm sorry. I didn't realize—" Landyn stammered, then quickly recovered. "Have you met everyone yet? Let me take you around and introduce you."

Audrey seemed grateful to hand Shayla off to her daughter.

And Shayla was *officially* going to strangle Link. Not only had he not told his family he was bringing her and Portia, he had apparently also failed to mention they were dating.

"Let's go meet the kids." Landyn held out her hand. "Come with me, Portia."

But Portia clung tighter to Shayla, suddenly shy.

"Come on. It's okay." Shayla gave her a little push. "I'll come with you."

Landyn bent at the waist and got eye-level with Portia. "How old are you?"

Portia held up five fingers, still clinging to Shayla with her other hand.

"Oh, Corinne's Sadie is five. I think." She smiled up at Shayla. "I can't keep track of all the nieces and nephews. Chase and I have twins. Oh, there they are." She pointed to the corner of the room near where Link's grandmother sat. Five little girls chattered and danced and giggled together.

Landyn cleared a path through the Legos and took Portia's other hand. "Girls? Hey, girls?"

They all turned and stared.

"Girls, this is Portia. Can you say hi? Portia and her mommy came with Uncle Link tonight."

"Portia, this is Sari and Sadie and Simone." She tapped each girl's head as she named them. "And these two are my girls, Grace and Emma."

"You look the same," Portia said, pointing between the twins.

Landyn laughed. "Even the family has trouble telling my twins apart sometimes. Tonight, Emma's wearing blue and Grace is in green."

"Grace and green," Portia repeated. "That makes the same *grrr* sound."

"That's right!" Landyn crowed, as if Portia was some kind of prodigy. "That's how you can remember them."

Sari, the oldest, held out a sparkly wand to Portia. "Do you wanna be the princess? It can be your turn."

"Okay." Portia took the wand, then quickly looked up at Shayla for permission.

She nodded. "Sure. Have fun, Princess Portia."

The Whitman kids giggled, repeated Portia's name, and launched into an explanation of how their little kingdom worked. Shayla let out a silent sigh of relief.

"Who's the little dark girl?" CeeCee's voice carried across the room, and Shayla looked over to see Link's grandmother leaning across to a young woman with a baby on her lap.

The woman caught Shayla's eye and gave her a smile that held an apology, before leaning in to speak softly to CeeCee. Shayla couldn't hear what she said.

Apparently CeeCee couldn't either. "What's that? You say they're with Link? The two dark ones?"

Landyn intervened. "Come and meet CeeCee." She leaned in and whispered to Shayla. "Our grandmother is a little confused sometimes, so just"—she shrugged—"forgive her if she's not exactly . . ." She couldn't seem to find a way to finish the sentence.

"Link warned—*told* me," Shayla quickly corrected herself.

Landyn didn't seem offended, and in fact, looked relieved. She led the way to the "throne." "CeeCee, this is Link's friend Shayla."

Shayla held out a hand. "Nice to meet you, ma'am."

CeeCee took Shayla's hand between her two frail, vein-lined hands. "Any friend of Link's is a friend of mine."

"Thank you, ma'am."

"Enough of this ma'am business. You can call me CeeCee just like the rest of the children do."

"Thank you."

CeeCee pointed to where the little girls were playing. "That little dark girl must be yours?"

"Well, she's my niece."

"Ah, yes, I thought I saw a resemblance."

Shayla looked over at Portia's fuzzy brown head amidst a sea of towheads and wanted to laugh, but Link's grandmother seemed completely serious. Shayla said, "Your little great-granddaughters made Portia the princess first thing when we got here. She'll never want to go home now."

"Well, they are good little children. They've been taught to accept everybody and treat everybody the same whether red or yellow, black or white." She smiled.

Shayla cleared her throat. If it had been anyone but Link's family, she might have been tempted to make a sarcastic, equally condescending remark, but she sensed that CeeCee meant well and didn't realize how her comment came off.

Landyn came to the rescue again. "Oh! I think Mom is trying to get everyone to the kitchen. She made lasagna tonight."

CeeCee clucked her tongue and hooked her finger for Shayla to come closer. "I swan, we've had enough lasagna in this house to feed all of Italy twice!"

Shayla laughed. "It's actually our favorite. But I hardly ever make it. My dad especially loves it." She'd have to get Audrey's recipe and make a pan for her dad. Maybe that would soften him up.

"Well, now why didn't you bring the rest of your family tonight? The more the merrier at this house."

"Oh, well, maybe another time." Shayla looked around for Link.

"CeeCee, you stay put," Landyn said. "I'll bring you a plate. We're not all going to fit at the table tonight, so you may as well stay where you're comfortable." She pulled a little tray over closer to CeeCee's chair.

"Well, now, I can be comfortable wherever you put me. Just tell me where to go. That's what everybody's been doing for the last year anyway. I don't see why you'd be any different."

Landyn laughed, but it sounded to Shayla like there was some pent-up resentment coming out.

"There you are." Link came up behind her and put an arm around her shoulders. "Hungry?"

"Uh-huh." She stiffened under his touch and refused to meet his gaze.

Either he didn't notice, or he pretended not to. "It's buffet style. Come on, let's get in line. It's every man for himself around here."

"Let me get Portia."

"Oh, Corinne already helped her fill a plate. She's at the kids' table with the other girls."

"Oh. Okay."

He handed her a plate and she took it without comment.

He studied her, frowning. "Are you all right?"

"I'm fine." She turned away, inspecting her plate as if she'd never seen one before.

"Uh-oh. That didn't sound so fine."

"Where have you been?" she said through clenched teeth, feeling inexplicably angrier than she'd been before he'd asked if she was all right.

"What do you mean where have I been? Right here." He was either winning an Oscar playing dumb, or he truly didn't know why she was upset.

They gravitated to the buffet set up at the kitchen bar counter. Link's parents were still setting the food out. She smiled, then looked away.

"What's wrong?" Link whispered plenty loud enough for them to hear.

She turned away from Grant and Audrey. "Not now," she hissed. "Please."

"Okay. So . . . you'll explain on the way home?"

Link's sisters and their spouses moved to the kitchen, jostling for places in line behind Link and her. Audrey tried unsuccessfully to direct traffic, and Landyn cut in line in front of them, announcing that she was filling CeeCee's plate. Shayla noticed it contained very little lasagna.

She and Link ended up at a smaller table in the kitchen with Bree and her fiancé, Drew Brooks, who Shayla learned was a brother to Danae's husband, Dallas. She'd never learn everybody's names, but it was probably a moot point. This family had a history together. They fit together like a jigsaw puzzle, and it was very obvious the puzzle was finished and she and Portia did not fit into it. And never would.

11

So, did you have fun?" Link waited until they were out of the driveway to ask the question. It had seemed like Shayla enjoyed the evening and fit right in, but that comment when they were dishing up their plates had him worried.

Shayla hesitated a few seconds too long.

"What? Did something happen? Did somebody say something?"

"No, Link. They were all very nice, very polite, very... politically correct."

He looked over at her, trying to read her expression in the dark—without success. "Somebody said something, didn't they?"

She glanced over her shoulder into the backseat where Portia was watching a video on Shayla's iPad with earbuds. "*Everybody* said something, Link. That's just it. I could tell I made them all uncomfortable. Everybody was tiptoeing around, doing their best not to say the wrong thing. Heaven forbid if somebody mentioned they didn't like black jellybeans, the rest of the room froze and watched me to see if I was offended." She gave a choked laugh. "One of your nieces told her mom it was too dark in the dining room and you'd have thought she used the N-word!"

Link couldn't help it. He laughed out loud.

"You think that's funny?"

He stopped. "You've got to admit, it is kind of funny, Shay."

A smile teased the corner of her mouth, but she didn't let it into full bloom. "Has your family never been around anybody of any color besides white before?"

"Hey, now, I'm offended by that remark." He was teasing, but by the way her posture stiffened, he didn't think she took it that way.

"And you didn't tell them you were bringing me, did you?"

"Why do you say that?" He was buying time because she was right. He *hadn't* told them. And he couldn't exactly tell her why. At least not all of it. He reached to touch her arm. "Shayla, my family loved you. I could tell. And it seemed like you liked them. If you didn't, you were sure putting on a good act."

She rolled her eyes. "Where did you go?"

"Where did I go?"

"You ushered me into your house and dumped me. I felt like an idiot."

"What? Why would you feel like an idiot?" He truly didn't understand what her deal was.

"I didn't know *anybody* there, and you just vanished and left me to fend for myself!"

"Shayla, I saw that Landyn was introducing you to everybody. I didn't know you needed somebody to hold your hand."

"Well, it would have been nice."

"Are you serious?"

She gave a little growl. "You can be so clueless sometimes, you know that?"

He rolled his eyes. "So I've been told. Listen, I'm sorry if you feel like I abandoned you. I was just down saying hi to the guys—okay, and maybe checking the score of the game. But seriously, with every girl I've ever brought home, things were tense at first. That's just the way it is getting to know someone new, coming into a situation where you're the new person. And yeah, maybe the color of your skin made them afraid they might say something that would offend you. No different than if you'd worn a Chicago Cubs T-shirt to dinner with my Cardinals family. But that doesn't mean you didn't fit in. I promise you they'll get over any differences—even something as horrible as if you were a Cubs fan—"

He stopped short and stared at her, waiting until she met his gaze. "You're not a Cubs fan are you?"

She laughed. "No, bud. You can rest easy. Cardinals all the way."

"Whew! You scared me for a minute there. But seriously, Shay, nobody will even think about the color of your skin a month from now except maybe my sisters who will be jealous of your tan. Unless, of course, *you* make an issue of it."

When she angled toward him in the seat, he quickly realized he should have stopped while he was ahead.

"I am not making an issue of it," she said. "Did you see *me* cringing in fear when I asked for a slice of white bread? That jelly bean thing really happened, Link. I wasn't just imagining it."

"I'm not doubting you. I'm just saying..." He grappled for an example. "Let's say you had a friend who was handicapped. How would you handle that? You're probably not going to change some people's discomfort with being around handicapped people any more than you can change people's discomfort about being around anyone they perceive as different from them. So what do you do?"

"Am I hearing you right? Are you comparing black people to handicapped people?"

He looked askance at her. "Are you saying being handicapped is an insult?" He chalked up a point for him on an imaginary blackboard. "Ha! See my point? So my question again is, how do you handle people's discomfort with your imaginary handicapped friend?"

She shrugged. "Ignore them?"

"I have a better idea. How about educate them? Just by example. Being a good friend yourself. I remember Corinne had a friend in high school who was in a wheelchair. Belinda couldn't walk, but she was funny, talented, super brainy. And smokin' hot. I had a little crush on her if you want to know the truth."

"Man, did you have a crush on every woman you ever met?"

"No. And I was twelve so that wasn't happening. But my point is, some people treated Belinda like she couldn't see or hear or think. Yes, they were idiots for thinking that way. But Corinne just redirected stupid questions and went on."

"What do you mean?"

"Well, like if they were in a restaurant together and the server said to Corinne, 'What would your friend like?' Corinne would just say, 'Why don't you ask her?' Not in a sarcastic way, but—"

"But it still got the point across." Shayla laughed.

"Right. I admit I would have been tempted to say, 'my friend? I've never seen this weirdo before in my life.'"

"Link!" She slugged his arm. "That is so not politically correct."

"But do you see my point? Shay, you apparently felt as awkward with my family as they felt with you. Neither of you are right or wrong. In fact, everybody was just trying not to hurt anyone else's feelings."

She nodded as if she agreed.

Which he took as permission to continue. "There's been so much pain and misunderstanding and division in our history. Clear back to slavery, yes. But way too recently too. Things like Trayvon and Charleston don't help. And Ferguson was way too close to home. But those are just the things that make the news. That's not us. Our families are the kind that want to be *solutions* to the problem. And it can start with us. You and me."

"You really think your family would welcome me with open arms if they knew we were . . . more than friends?"

His eyes went wide and he couldn't hide the hope her question gave him. "Are we? You know how *I* feel. Are you trying to tell me something?"

"Would you quit wiggling your eyebrows—and changing the subject! I'm asking you an important question."

"Of course they would, Shay. You don't know this, but my parents—my mom especially—were really leery about Bree getting married again. Not because they had anything against Drew, or any of the other guys she dated, but because they were afraid of losing her. But when it came down to it, they just wanted Bree to be happy. And now they love Drew like their own."

"I don't get it. Why are you telling me this?"

"I'm just saying that my family wants me to be happy. The only thing that would bother them is if you were an atheist or something. They *are* probably prejudiced when it comes to faith."

"Or the Cardinals."

He laughed. "Yes, and not necessarily in that order. Oh, and"—he made his eyes bug out—"you don't have any tattoos, do you? My dad is *not* a fan. My brother-in-law—Landyn's husband—has a big ol' Celtic cross on his left pec and I'm not so sure Dad doesn't still hold that against him."

"No tattoos." One corner of her shapely mouth tipped up. "Yet."

"Don't do it! That's a deal breaker." He let his smile fade, knowing they were skirting the real issues. "Seriously though, Shay, I guarantee you my parents will ask me if you love Jesus long before they ask about anything racial."

Shay looked at her hands in her lap. "Well, I wish I could say the same about Daddy. Not the faith part. That's first for him too. Jesus. But Daddy's just . . . He's changed. Everything changed after Mama died. And then after Jerry went off the deep end . . . My dad expects the worst from people. And too often that's exactly what he gets."

"I'm sorry, Shay. I really am." He risked taking her hand, feeling a little like he was taking advantage of her emotions. But he liked the feel of her small hand in his too much to let go. She didn't pull away either.

He held her hand across the console until they crossed over the Langhorne city limits. He drove slowly, but the bakery was only a few minutes away. He pulled into a parking space in front of the store and put the truck in Park, but didn't turn off the ignition.

"Can I finish my movie, Shay?" Portia hollered over the seat, talking louder than necessary with her earbuds still in place.

Shayla motioned for her to take them out and waited until she did. "Maybe in the morning if you get your chores done before school."

"No! Tonight! It's a good movie."

"I guess if you're going to argue about it we'll just send it back to the library and—"

"Okay, okay. I'll watch it in the morning."

"*If* you get your chores done in time," Shay reminded.

There were lights on upstairs, and although Link wanted more than anything for Shay to invite him in, carry Portia up to bed, and then come back to sit in the dining room with coffee and him for another hour, he knew better. Those lights probably meant her father was still up waiting for her, and he would surely find a reason Link needed to leave and Shayla needed to get to bed.

And to be fair, she did need to get to bed. Running the bakery meant she was sometimes up with her father before four a.m. He needed to get home too. He was back to working two shifts tomorrow. But he wouldn't drive away until he had a sure date on the calendar.

Shayla opened her door, then closed it partway and turned back to him. "I did have a good time tonight, Link. I don't want to sound ungrateful."

"I did too. And I promise it'll be easier next time and the time after that."

She laughed as if she wasn't sure there would be a next time.

"We only have family dinners every other week. I can't wait that long to see you again. How about a movie Sunday?"

"I'll see."

"You're not going to back out on me are you?"

She pursed her lips and looked straight ahead through the windshield. "I don't know, Link. Let me think on it for a while, okay? I'll call you before Saturday."

"That's kind of mean to make me wait that long."

"You're a big boy. I bet you'll survive." She opened her door and a blast of cold air whooshed in.

He reached for his door handle. "I'll help you get Portia."

But she waved him off. "I've got her."

She climbed out, shut her door, and opened the back door. "Unbuckle, baby."

"I already did."

Link put his arm over the seat, watching, feeling a little useless.

Shayla set Portia on the sidewalk and started to close the door, then gave a little gasp. "Oh! I forgot to give your sister the bags."

"What bags?"

"The coffee bags she wanted."

"Which sister? I can give them to her."

She looked distraught. "I can't believe I did that! I totally forgot they were behind my seat."

"No worries. I can take them to her."

Shayla snatched up the shopping bag. "It doesn't matter. She probably didn't want them anyway. Goodnight, Link."

He didn't like the note of sadness in her voice when she said it.

12

Link says there's no such thing as fairies." Portia bobbed her head as if that made it so. Since the minute she'd popped out of bed, the girl had been chattering about Link and their night at the Chicory Inn.

Shayla cringed inwardly and glanced across the table in the kitchen alcove where her father sat. Thankfully he was engrossed in the newspaper, having been up since four a.m. baking. She hadn't told her Dad about going to the Whitmans'. Link had dropped her and Portia off before Daddy got home from his prayer meeting and she'd made a point to be in bed when he came home, so she didn't have to answer any questions about where they'd been. If Portia didn't hush, there would be plenty of questions to answer.

Shayla scooted the lime green cereal bowl closer. "Eat your oatmeal, baby. You've got school today."

"Does Link go to school?" Portia giggled.

"No, silly, he's a grown-up. He goes to work. Now eat."

She stole a sidewise glance at her father. Their eyes met.

Daddy put the paper down. "Speaking of school, we'd better get moving, baby girl. And just who is this Link you keep talking about?" His question was aimed at Portia, but he didn't take his eyes off Shayla.

To her surprise, he hadn't brought the subject of Link up again since that day the bakery window had been shattered. Except to tell her on his way to bed that night, "I trust you, girlie. I know you'll do what's right."

She knew he expected her to take that as a decree *not* to see Link. But he hadn't forbidden her, and she truly didn't think seeing Link was wrong. That didn't keep her from shaking in her shoes right now though.

"Link has a whole bunch of kids at his house. The *big* house." Portia spread her arms wide and launched into a description of her evening with Link's nieces and nephews. Though Shayla had tried to shush her and change the subject, Portia had talked of little else since.

Daddy set his coffee mug on the table. "You went to his house? After all we talked about."

You mean after all you *talked about, Daddy.* "His parents' house. Well, the inn they run." She worked to sound nonchalant, but the quaver in her voice gave her away.

Her father let the newspaper fall over his half-eaten scrambled eggs. "So you decided to take up with the guy who nearly ran Portia down? Are we talking about *that* Link Whitman?"

"You know we are, Daddy. And for the hundredth time, it was an accident."

"Link says I'm a character," Portia spouted with a grin. She was totally smitten with the man.

"Hush and eat your breakfast, Portia." Shayla hadn't meant for it to come out so harshly. And she knew the fact that it had only made her father more suspicious.

He took a sip of his coffee. She recognized the demeanor that said he had plenty more to say. "So what's the deal with this Link? What are his intentions?"

"What do you mean?"

"You know good and well what I mean. Are you dating him?"

"We're friends, Daddy. I don't know beyond that."

"And when are you seeing him next?"

Warmth rushed to her cheeks. "Maybe Sunday. If I can find a sitter."

"You're not taking Portia with you this time? I don't like the sound of that."

"Why?" She wasn't sure she wanted to hear his reasons, so she quickly told him hers. "I don't want Portia to get attached to him . . . in case it turns out not to be anything."

He glanced over at Portia. "Too late for that, I'd say."

"We're just friends, Daddy."

"And what if he wants more?"

"I'll deal with that when—if—I have to."

"You'll have to. You know you will. Best deal with it before things get ugly."

"What are you talking about?"

He scraped his chair back from the table. "You know very well what I'm talking about."

"Daddy, I'm thirty-three years old. I think I can handle this." She was a little shocked to hear the defiance in her own voice. Even grown men didn't talk back to Mike Michaels. Unless they were looking for a fight. But it seemed like she'd been doing her share of it recently. And she was not looking for a fight.

She *did* know what he was talking about. But Link wasn't like the handful of other men she'd dated. He was different. She just knew he was.

Her father folded the newspaper into thirds and placed it on the table, giving her a look that said this conversation wasn't over yet.

Link pulled up in front of the bakery and jumped out of his truck, leaving it running. He was a little later than he'd told Shayla. He should have called to let her know he was on the way. As it was, they'd be late for the movie if they didn't hustle. He was almost tempted to toot the horn, but if his sisters had taught him one thing in life it was that you did not, ever—unless you were looking for trouble with the girl *and* her father—sit in a car in front of said girl's house and toot the horn.

The bakery door was unlocked, which was unusual for a Sunday. He started to step inside, then hesitated, feeling like he was trespassing. He knocked on the door, and when no one had responded after a minute, he stepped inside. "Shay?"

He called her name again and heard movement above him. A door creaked open upstairs, and Shayla's father appeared and started down the steps.

Link took a step backward and removed the baseball cap he'd been wearing. "Sorry to just walk in, sir."—he pointed over his shoulder to the front of the store—"The door was open. I wasn't sure Shayla could hear me knock."

"She heard."

"Is she ready? She and Portia? We're going to a movie."

Shayla's father reached the bottom of the stairs and stood there, feet spread wide. "We need to have words, you and me." He motioned between them.

"Yes, sir?" He extended a hand, which Michaels ignored. "I don't think we've been officially introduced. I'm Link Whitman."

"So I've heard. Have a seat." The man indicated a four-top in the middle of the room. Link pulled out a chair and sat, not sure what was coming and more than a little nervous about it.

"Is everything okay, sir?"

Mr. Michaels sat across from him, elbows on the table. "That depends on you."

"I . . . I don't understand."

"I'm not sure you understand my daughter's situation."

Link waited, wordless. What situation was he talking about? And where was Shayla?

Mr. Michaels cleared his throat. "I don't know what Shay's told you, but she has responsibilities here"—he waved a hand that encompassed the bakery—"and that generally doesn't leave time for anything else."

"Has Shayla said she doesn't want to see me?"

The man shifted in his chair, making it scrape along the tiled floor. "Whether she wants to see you or not isn't the topic at hand."

"If by responsibilities you mean Portia, I understand that." He was pleased his voice came out sounding steadier than he felt.

"Yes, Portia is part of it, but—"

"Portia has been invited to go along on our dates. She's a sweet girl."

Mr. Michaels cocked his head. "Shay told you about Portia? Why we have her?"

He nodded. "That she's her brother's daughter? Your son's. And that Portia's mother died."

"Do you understand what that means?"

Link wasn't sure enough about what he was getting at to want to answer that question. "I'm not really—"

"Link?"

Footfalls sounded on the stairway, and Link looked up to see Shayla descending. Her eyes were red and swollen. What was going on?

"Daddy, what are you doing?"

Her father scraped his chair back and looked up at her.

"Link." Shayla's voice wobbled and she looked at her father even though she was addressing Link. "Could we please go for a drive? We need to talk."

He pushed away from the table and rose slowly.

"Daddy, I'll be back in a few hours. I need some time away. Portia fell asleep upstairs. She'll be hungry when she wakes up."

Mr. Michaels stood, mouth gaping, as if he wasn't accustomed to taking orders from his daughter.

Shayla disappeared around the corner near the back door. Feeling her father's eyes on him, Link became extremely interested in the pattern of the tile floor. But Shayla returned a few seconds later with her coat and purse slung over her shoulder.

"Come on, Link. Please."

He followed, feeling oddly torn between going and staying.

The fire in Mr. Michaels' eyes made his decision for him. He gave the man a brief nod and headed for the front entrance, holding the door open for Shayla. He half expected to feel her father's grip on the scruff of his neck.

Outside, Link opened the passenger door for Shayla, tucking her coat out of the way before he closed the door. He jogged around and climbed into the idling truck.

"Can we not go to the movie?"

"Sure. Of course. But what's going on?"

"Just drive, would you? Please. If we sit here for ten seconds, he'll think of a reason to make me stay."

"You have a fight or something?"

She huffed. "Fight implies there were two people arguing."

"Oh." He didn't have a lot of experience with women, but he did know that sometimes it was best just to listen. He backed out of the parking space and headed toward Cape Girardeau. "I know a coffee shop in Cape. That sound okay?"

She nodded, then flipped the visor down and inspected her makeup in the mirror. "I'm a mess."

"You look great."

She gave him a *what are you smoking?* look.

"Okay. You've maybe had better days, but I like your hair like that."

That made her laugh. But her expression quickly sobered again. "Can we just go park somewhere and talk?"

"Okay. Your dad's not going to report me for kidnapping or anything, is he?"

She rolled her eyes. "I'm thirty-three years old, Link. I don't have to do what my daddy says."

Link glanced at her again. Four years older than him. He hadn't realized that. But did realize—too late—that his expression revealed his thoughts.

She studied him and sighed. "You didn't know I was thirty-three, did you? Well, let's just start getting secrets out of the way."

He shifted in the seat. "No. I didn't."

"Yeah, well, deal with it. How old are you? Twelve?"

He managed a laugh. "Twenty-nine." It was only four years, but wow, thirty-three did kind of throw him. He would've guessed twenty-five at most. But then, his sister Corinne was the same age as Shayla, and she didn't seem old to him. Age was just a number, right?

But in the back of his mind he heard his sisters talking about biological clocks ticking, and he remembered how hard Danae had tried to become pregnant—before she and Dallas had adopted their precious sons.

Women had babies in their thirties, didn't they? And everything was fine? He wanted a family. He would never have confessed it to Shayla, but he'd imagined what *their* babies together might look like—and in his mind they were adorable. But he was in no rush. And at thirty-three, Shayla might be.

But he was getting way, way ahead of himself. And they weren't together to talk about how old Shayla was. Why were they here? She still hadn't said.

"I know this lake out in the country. Would you be comfortable if we drove out there to talk? It's real pretty. And it's quiet. Nobody'll be out there this time of year."

"Yeah, sure." Her shoulders hunched and she pulled her knees up to meet them, looking like a wounded child.

They drove in silence most of the way along mostly deserted county roads, and when they turned onto the lane that led to the lake, Shayla straightened and put her feet on the floor, looking out the window. "This is nice. I've never been out here."

A misty fog hung over the small lake and seeped over the banks to the edges of the pasture. The wind whipped up little white caps on the surface of the water and at intervals, the fast-sinking sun caught them and turned them to diamonds. The grass and brush were brown, but the canted sunlight burnished them gold against a baby-blue sky.

"It's been a while since I've been out here." He pointed toward the lake, which looked more like a pond all these years later. "It's not as big as I remember. One of my high school buddy's grandparents own the land. They used to live in a trailer right over there"—he pointed—"but they moved into town a while back. To the same place CeeCee lives. They used to let us come fishing out here. I always wished for enough money to buy this property."

"I can see why. It's gorgeous."

He'd never even told his family about that dream. It was nothing more than a stupid daydream really. But with Shayla he didn't feel foolish admitting to it.

He drove off the lane and through the bumpy pasture, parking on the slope of a ridge that afforded a view of the water and the vista beyond. Leaving the view of the road behind them, they couldn't get much more secluded than this.

He shut off the engine, and in the stillness of the truck's cab, he could hear Shayla's quiet breaths. He unbuckled his seatbelt and faced her, stretching his arm over the back of the seat. "So tell me what's going on."

"I don't even know where to start. And I know how it's going to end, so really—even though I don't want you to—you'd be justified in taking me back home."

"Huh-uh. You're not getting away with that." He touched her shoulder gently. "Just talk to me. Trust me, okay?" Even as he said the words, he wasn't certain what he was about to get into. Or whether he wanted to get into it at all.

She looked thoughtful for a moment, then breathed out a sigh. "Here's the thing, Link. Portia doesn't call me 'Mama,' but truth is, I *am* her mama."

"You mean—" He stopped. Looked at her. "What are you saying?"

She held up a hand. "No, no. I just mean that I may as well be her mama. The responsibility for her falls on me. Pretty much always. And it always will. Do you understand what I'm saying? Unless I cut out like I did today and give Daddy no choice, I'm all Portia has. Jerry's not getting out any time soon, and even if he did, he'd be worse than Daddy when it came to taking care of a little girl. It doesn't matter how much I wish things were different, they're not. And I have to consider how everything I do will affect her."

"I understand." He could *imagine*, but how could he really understand. And he had to admit, it was a part of Shayla's life that gave him pause. Serious pause. Although, the fact that she had a brother in jail—for drugs—actually bothered him more than the fact that she essentially had a child.

He admired Shayla for taking the responsibility of her niece so seriously. And it irked him that her father left it all to her.

Shayla shook her head. "I'm not sure you do understand. And that's what Daddy and I were arguing about. I love Portia. And if she was my own daughter, I'd be really careful before I let someone into my life. Until I knew it was serious. She's been let down...had her heart broken too many times already in her short life. I can't let it be broken again if I can help it."

What was he supposed to say to that? He looked at the steering wheel, scrambling to come up with words.

"I'm sorry," she said. "I know it sounds like I'm putting a lot of pressure on you. But—"

"No. It's okay. I understand." He kept telling her that, but did he? He wasn't sure he understood. Or wanted to.

"No. What I'm saying is, I'm giving you an out. I know we're a lot to take on. And I don't blame you for not wanting the package deal. But that's what I am. A package deal."

Wow. He swallowed hard. "I...Let me—"

She held up a hand. "There's more. And I'd just as soon get it over with in one pass, okay?"

13

Can we get out and stretch a little?" Shayla squirmed in the truck seat, dreading the conversation to come. Part of her wishing she could stay out here in this beautiful place with Link forever, while another part wanted to crawl under the truck and pretend she'd never started this conversation.

"Sure." Link took the keys out of the ignition and stuffed them in his coat pocket. "Will you be warm enough? I think there's a blanket in the back." Without waiting for her answer, he jumped out and rummaged in the backseat. "Here you go."

She caught the blue plaid throw blanket he tossed her and wrapped it around her shoulders. They met in front of the truck and Link led the way down toward the pond. The evening fog had dissipated, and now the sun slipped below the horizon, a huge neon orange ball. A small herd of black cows appeared on the other side of the pond, dotting the grassy expanse.

Watching his lean form navigate the uneven pastureland, a wave of sadness rolled over her. Why had she ever thought it would be a good idea to embroil Link in her crazy life? She'd known for a long time what her future held—and what it didn't. Was she only being selfish to drag Link into it?

She didn't like the silent answer to that question.

It wasn't as if she had a miserable life. She liked her work at the bakery. She truly did love Portia. The girl made her laugh every day, sometimes hourly. And she loved Daddy too. Harsh as he could be, he was a good man who'd been through difficult things these last few years. Things that might have broken a lesser man.

"So talk to me." Link's soft voice interrupted. He stopped walking and turned her gently toward him. "What's going on with you?" He brushed back a strand of her hair that had fallen over her eyes. But he didn't let go and instead coiled it around his finger. She hated to guess what she looked like. Thanks to the blowup with her father, she'd cried off every trace of makeup, and even if she'd had time to straighten her hair it would have been a mass of frizz by now.

She sniffed and bowed her head. "I must look like a hot mess."

He lifted her chin, his gaze suddenly so tender it made her ache. Then that tiny lopsided smile of his. "You look hot."

She laughed, but took a tiny step back, away from his touch, embarrassed by his compliment.

He took her arm and steered her to one side. "Careful where you step. It's kind of a minefield, thanks to the cattle."

She looked down to see a giant cow pie. "Thanks! Nice save. But you must be going blind, Whitman. I didn't even have time to do my hair today."

"I like it this way"—he touched her head again—"all curly and a little wild."

"Then you're crazier than I thought."

"No, seriously." He shrugged. "Maybe it's because that's how it looked the first time I saw you. It just seems more *you*."

She frowned and shook her head. "You're weird."

He frowned. "What is the deal with you *women* and hair? And speaking of cows, I'm probably stepping in it big-time here, but you're just like my sisters—always moaning and groaning about their hair. Corinne wishes she had Landyn's curly hair and Danae wants Corinne's darker hair. Mom wishes she still had as much hair as the girls, and they all hope they look like Mom when they're her age. Why can't you ladies just be happy with the way God made you?" He ducked as if she might slap him.

Which made her laugh. It felt good to laugh after all the tears today.

They were quiet for a minute before he spoke again. "I suppose that was a super sexist thing to say. But seriously? Guys don't spend half their lives worrying about their hair."

"Oh, I know a few guys that just wish they *had* hair."

He laughed. "Well, there is that. But seriously, we don't spend half our lives wishing we looked like some other dude! Besides being a huge waste of time, it's just stupid."

"Oh, and now you're calling me stupid? Wow, you're on a roll." She wondered if he knew how close to home he was hitting.

But he looked smug. "Yep, and to think you agreed to go out with me." He started walking again, one hand lightly at the small of her back.

It was dusk now and his face was cast in shadow. His expression grew serious, reminding her why they were out here in the first place.

She cleared her throat. "About that, Link. I'm grateful I agreed to go out with you. More than you realize, but I want you to know my whole story. I need for you to know."

"So tell me. I'm listening."

She shivered. Not so much from the cold, but Link must have thought so because he stopped and pulled the blanket tighter around her shoulders.

The sun had all but disappeared, and the landscape was cloaked in dusky shadows. She felt a little braver for it and plunged in. "My mom died—cancer—five years ago. Right before Portia was born. Portia's named after her, but Mama never got to meet her first—her *only*—grandchild." Before tonight, she hadn't been able to utter those words without crying, but now they came easily. Almost clinically, detached from emotion. "I came home from college to take care of Mama after her first cancer surgery while Daddy kept the bakery going."

Link reached for her hand. "She must have been sick a long time."

She nodded, relishing the warmth of his touch even while she knew she was playing with fire to allow it. "Nine years. She had a short remission, but then it came back with a vengeance. It's a horrible, horrible way to die. But I wouldn't trade one day I got to spend with my mother while she was dying. Not now. But when it was happening"—she lowered her head, fighting tears of shame—"I resented having to drop out of school. Having to come home and work in the bakery. I was the first one in Daddy's family to go to college. I won a little scholarship and Daddy was so proud of that. He and Mama already had a little savings set aside and once I got the scholarship money, they started saving for Jerry to go next."

"That must have been so disappointing. For all of you."

She shrugged off his sympathetic words. "I'd only been in the dorm a couple of weeks when Daddy called to tell me Mama was sick. I left school of course, and came home. I didn't mind. I truly didn't. I wanted to be with my mom. Daddy couldn't run the bakery by himself, and I knew Mama's radiation treatments would take up all the money they'd saved. But as time went on, and the writing was on the wall that I wasn't going back to school—and I had no life outside of the bakery and taking care of Mama... Resentment set in. Of course, that was right in the middle of all that stuff with Jerry. And Daddy was so harsh with *me*. I understand now that he was struggling with his grief and guilt." She swiped at her cheeks with her free hand. "I think we've gotten through it. I'm not mad at my parents anymore. But long story short, I never got back to school."

Link rubbed his thumb in slow circles on the top of her hand, but he didn't interrupt or ask questions.

She was grateful. She wasn't sure she could finish if he did. "I'm not mad at Mama or Daddy. But I am mad at my brother."

"Why him?"

"As if losing Mama wasn't bad enough, after she died, Jerry went off the deep end. He pretty much went down the list of bad stereotypes people have of black people. He started running with a gang. He stole from the few people who would hire him. Then, he started doing drugs, then dealing them. Finally, right on schedule, he landed in jail."

"I'm so sorry, Shayla. That had to be tough, especially when you were still grieving your mom. But that stuff your brother did isn't confined only to black people." He gave a short laugh. "Shoot, the only person I know who's in prison is white."

She threw him a look. "For what?"

"Murder, actually."

"What? Who do you know in prison?"

"She's the birthmother to my sister's little boys. It's a long story, but Danae and Dallas were kind of foster parents to Austin after his mother killed her husband."

"Why did she kill him?"

"He was abusive to her, but it wasn't self-defense. And she went to jail. Turned out she was pregnant, so Danae and Dallas got the baby too. Two kids almost overnight."

"Wow. That's unbelievable."

He grinned. "They are awesome kids. But my point is that no race has a corner on the sin market. Well, except maybe the human race. So don't be too hard on your brother."

She rolled her eyes. "You haven't heard the whole story."

"There's more?" He looked almost scared.

Shayla swallowed hard. "The rest is Tara's story, I guess. But it's Jerry's too." She took a heavy breath. "Tara was pretty messed up in the head. It got worse after Jerry went to prison. We tried to help her as much as we could, but she'd sometimes disappear for days at a time. Usually leaving Portia with us. We were terrified they'd take her away."

Link shook his head, his features pained. "Looking at Portia now, I'd never guess that was her history. Amazing how resilient kids are."

"You don't know the half of it. One night Daddy took some food over to Tara. That girl was always out of money, no matter how much Daddy gave her. Anyway, he heard Portia crying. Screaming at the top of her lungs. The door was locked, but he knew where Tara hid her keys. He let himself in and knew something was wrong the minute he stepped inside."

14

They were close enough to the water now to hear it lapping against the shore. Shayla sucked in a hard breath. She'd forgotten how suffocating it was to relive the memories. And her poor dad. If it was this bad for her, even three years later, what must it have been like for him?

Link watched her, the concern in his eyes deepening, and she pushed on, wanting to be done with the telling of it all. "The bathroom was locked, but Daddy found Tara in the tub. She'd sliced her wrists. Both of them."

Link stopped walking and stared at her in disbelief.

Shayla closed her eyes tight. "She'd cut them the long way too—the way somebody does when they're serious about dying."

A gust of wind brought a swirl of dead leaves to dance around their feet, and she shivered again.

He put an arm around her. "I'm so sorry," he whispered, his voice gentle. "For her. For you and your father. And Portia."

The ache in her chest fanned out, and it was all she could do to continue. "Tara was already gone when Daddy found her. For probably ten or twelve hours by then, EMS said. Portia was in that crib alone in the house all that time."

He made a guttural sound and squeezed her hand tightly. "But why? How could someone do that? She had a child!" Disbelief and anger sharpened his tone. "How old was Portia when that happened?"

"Barely two." She could see his mind working, trying to imagine the cheerful little girl he knew today in that horrific situation back then. It touched her to hear the genuine concern in his voice. To see it in the handsome profile of his face. "And why? We'll probably never know. She didn't leave a note or anything. But like I said, she was always a little... *off*."

"I'm so sorry, Shay," he said again. "And Portia... I can't even imagine."

He stooped to pick up a small pinecone lying on the ground, and as he rose, he threw it hard into the water.

"I'm just thankful she was protected from seeing anything. Anyway, even before that happened, Daddy had no use for Tara. Not because she was white," she explained quickly. "But because she and Jerry had a baby—and they weren't married."

"That must be where Portia gets her blue eyes. I've wondered about that."

Shayla shook her head. "Mama had blue eyes too. I don't understand how all the biology works, but somebody told me once that it took Mama *and* Tara—two sides of the family—for her to get those blue eyes. I didn't have a chance at them." And oh, how she wished she'd inherited Mama's eyes.

Link smiled and ran his finger down the bridge of her nose. "I like your eyes just the way they are."

She waved a hand. "You sound like a broken record, you know that? Anyway, of course Daddy blamed Tara—not Jeremiah—for the whole baby-out-of-wedlock thing. So maybe you can see why he doesn't want me getting involved with somebody who's... not black."

Link made a face. "Not exactly fair."

She shrugged. "Maybe not, but it is what it is. Tara's pregnancy was a big embarrassment for my parents. Daddy was a deacon in our church—in Cape—and he stepped down after that. Never mind there were three other out-of-wedlock babies being brought up in that little church at the same time. I think he'd always prided himself in thinking our family was above that."

Link seemed to think about that for a minute, started to say something, then chewed his bottom lip.

She ignored that and pressed on. "All of that with Tara happened almost three years ago. I don't think Portia really has any memories of her. Or Jerry for that matter. We don't talk about him. Sometimes I think—because she calls my dad Big Daddy—she doesn't understand that she doesn't have a father in her life. She knows I'm her aunt, but does a five-year-old really have a concept of what that means? And we tell her that her mama is in heaven, but I don't know if she is, Link. I don't know. How could she be . . . with what she did?" Her voice climbed an octave.

Link gave her hand a quick squeeze. "That's God's business. We don't know what happened in those final minutes, Shay. So we can't know for sure."

"I guess." She sighed. "Here's the thing. And I know this sounds awful. Selfish. But I went from taking care of Mama to taking care of Daddy after my mom died. And now I'm taking care of Portia. And if Jerry gets out when he's supposed to, I know it'll be me that takes care of him too. Because I know Daddy won't. By the time Portia's grown—and God knows I love her to death—but by then, I'll be forty-six, maybe forty-seven. So"—her voice broke—"you don't want to be waiting around for me to be free, Link. Because I don't think I'm ever going to be free. At least not while I'm young enough to enjoy it." She affected a laugh that came out more like a sob.

Link peeled her hand from his and put his hands on her shoulders, turning her back toward the truck. For a minute, she thought he was just going to take her home. Instead, he took her hand again. "It's getting dark. We should get back to the truck while we can still see." He brought her hand to his mouth and kissed each finger. "I know you feel caged, Shay. And I don't blame you. I would too. But caring for Portia, for your mom, even the way you take care of your dad now—that's what makes you who you are, what makes you so special, so amazing in my eyes."

She wanted so desperately to believe him. But she knew the truth. "I don't think you get to count sacrifice when it's so full of resentment." Tears clogged her throat, and she regretted ever confessing any of this to him.

But he only held her hand tighter. "That's like saying being brave doesn't count if you're scared. Of course it counts. You're doing the right thing. Anyone in your shoes would have moments of resentment. But I've seen you with Portia, Shay. I know how much you love her. What a great life you're creating for her. And I hear the love in your voice when you talk about your mother."

"I do love them both. Daddy too. Even Jerry. But I hate what happened to our family. I used to have a family like yours, Link. We laughed together. We prayed together. I didn't realize Mama was the one keeping us from falling apart. And why"—her voice faltered—"if it was God who took her from us, as some say, why would He do that when He knew it was her holding us all together?"

Link shook his head, frowning. "I don't know the answer to that one. But I do know that some things just aren't meant for us to understand. Not on this side of heaven anyway. Sometimes—well, maybe *always*—we just have to take it on faith that God knows what He's doing."

She tensed and pulled her hands from his grasp. "So you're saying you *do* think God took Mama?" She huffed softly. "Well, if God took her, then I don't have much respect for Him. I can't believe a good God would do that. I just can't. Especially not after everything that's happened since she died."

"I understand why you'd feel that way," Link said quietly.

But a slight change in his tone gave her the impression he didn't agree.

They trudged toward the truck in silence, Link staring off toward the road in the distance, his thoughts seeming far away.

"I shouldn't have put you in this position," she said. "I'm sorry. Please forgive me. You . . . you've been a good friend, and I was wrong to drag you into all this."

He stopped walking and turned to look at her. "First, you didn't drag me into anything I didn't want to be dragged into."

She gave a humorless laugh. "Then you're weirder than I thought."

But even in the near dark, she could see that he didn't crack a smile. "And second," he said, "you mean way more to me than merely a *good friend*, Shay. And if I've done a poor job of communicating that up until now, then that's my fault."

A shiver stole down her spine, but not an altogether unpleasant one.

"I'm not saying the complications of your life don't scare me a little. And I'll go ahead and admit I'm a little terrified of your dad." He shot her a smile that said he was kidding. Mostly anyway. "But I'm drawn to you, Shay. Ever since the first time I saw you at the shelter—you probably don't even remember it—I haven't been able to get you out of my mind. And as much as you're trying to scare me off—at least that's what it feels like—my feelings for you aren't going away, which—you may not want to hear this—I sort of take as God's leading."

She shook her head, even though her heart was nodding—and smiling. "Be careful. You may find yourself regretting those words one day." She meant it to be teasing.

"Stop it!" His jaw tensed, and his eyes narrowed. "Please." He touched her arm as if to soften the harsh words. "Quit putting yourself down like that. It's not becoming. And it's not showing much gratitude to the one who made you."

At first she thought he meant Mama. But she quickly realized he was referring to God. And she felt chastised. And realized Link was right. She hated the way her whining made her sound. And yet, she'd felt obligated to warn him.

They reached the truck, and he dug the keys from his pocket and went around to open her door.

But instead of climbing into the truck, she grasped his arm. "Link—one last thing."

He turned, a question in his expression.

She inhaled a shallow breath. "When my mother married Daddy, her parents kicked her to the curb. Mama and Daddy hadn't done one thing wrong—not like Jerry and Tara. But Mama's parents cut all ties with their own daughter because of one thing—the color of my dad's skin. They never even took the time to get to know him. And if that wasn't bad enough, the day I was born, my grandfather officially disinherited my mother. Because of *me*."

"Oh, Shay..." His voice was a whisper.

"You can guess the label he had for me. Of course, Mama never told me that herself, but I overheard her and Daddy talking one night. I could tell it about killed her. And I think my dad felt guilty that it was because of him that Mama lost her inheritance. Her parents had quite a bit of money."

"Shayla, that's on them." Link shook his head and leaned back against the side of the truck. "Surely you don't think their bigotry, their hate, has anything to do with you? *Or* with your parents. Anybody with a heart can see how wrong they were."

She tried to think how to answer. Honestly. "I know in my mind they were wrong. That they missed out on so much when they rejected Mama. And me. And later Jerry. So"—she looked away—"why is it that I sometimes wish that my skin... That I looked like Mama?"

"What's wrong with a woman wanting to look like her mother? That's probably every little girl in the world." He paused as if her meaning had just penetrated. "If you mean you wish you weren't *black*? Don't let them do that to you, Shay. They're not worth it." He reached up and cupped her cheek in the palm of his hand. "You are so beautiful. How can you not see that when you look in the mirror? I... I wish you could see what I see."

It took everything in her not to melt into him. Let him comfort her. But she turned away. "But I'm no better than them. I know I judge as bad as they did. On something people can't even help."

"None of us are sinless, Shayla. We have to just learn to control those thoughts. My dad used to say"—he paused—"he'd tell us to take every thought captive."

Shayla nodded. "It's in the Bible. 'Take captive every thought to make it obedient to Christ.'" A wry smile came. "Sunday school memory verse. But I guess I haven't been very good at that."

"It's hard. Thoughts are tricky things. But it must be possible, or God wouldn't have told us to do it."

"Oh, Link. I've hated people I didn't even know. Mama's parents... I never even met them. Didn't want to. But I've *hated* them."

"Are they still around?"

She shrugged. "Last we knew, they were in St. Louis. But like I said, they wrote Mama off. As far as I know they didn't even attend their own daughter's funeral."

"How sad."

"Of course, I doubt Daddy wasted any time trying to contact them when she died. They never forgave her for marrying a black man and then embarrassing them with black grandbabies. Apparently they pretended Jerry and I didn't exist."

"At least they got out of your life. They could have made it pretty miserable."

"Well, don't think they didn't. If my parents ever fought about anything it was what had happened with Mama's parents. It broke her heart. Mama told me once—after she got sick—that my dad's family wasn't all that thrilled about their marriage either. But they came around. Grandma and Grandpa Michaels ended up being like parents to her. And it eased some of the pain of her own parents' rejection."

"Are they still living? Your dad's side?"

She shook her head. "They died within a few months of each other when I was in middle school. We still lived in Cape back then, but I have a lot of happy memories of holidays spent at their house for Christmas and Easter. Sometimes Fourth of July. Maybe that's why I've always felt more black than white." She lifted her arm and inspected the back of her hand. "Well, that and the fact that my skin sort of didn't give me any other options."

"You are so beautiful," Link said again. "Just the way you are." He didn't try to touch her this time, but he spoke more emphatically, as if he knew it would take some convincing.

"It's not like I hate myself or anything, Link. I don't. And until I was seven or eight—when I found out what Mama's parents had done—I didn't even think about race. But if I could click my heels and have Mama's creamy white skin and her straight blonde hair, I'd do it in a heartbeat."

She wasn't about to tell him the truth—that loving him had only made that desire stronger. To look like his sisters. Fit into his family.

Loving Link.

Did she love him? Did she even know what love was?

It didn't matter. Even if she did truly love him—even if Daddy would give his blessing on them being together—she couldn't ask Link to take on the burdens of her life.

And she needed to tell him that before she lost her courage.

15

Link held the passenger door and waited for Shay to climb in. "I need to get you home. Your dad will be worried. Don't want him thinking I've kidnapped you." Even though he'd like to do just that.

He climbed in behind the wheel and slipped the key into the ignition. Nearly nine o'clock. He switched on the truck's headlamps and the beams illuminated the darkness before them, casting pale white light across the now-still pond.

The last thing he wanted to do was face Shayla's father. But he would. After everything Shayla had told him, he was hopeful the man did, indeed, have a good side, and he intended to get on it.

"I went with you of my own free will, Link. Don't let my father accuse you otherwise." Her voice still bore the breathy quiver of tears, and it tugged at his heart. He wasn't usually one to let a woman's tears get to him. After all, he'd grown up with sisters.

But Shay's emotion seemed genuine, and she had every reason to feel trapped and disappointed with life. Even though it felt like a dangerous prospect, he had a strange feeling he could change things for her.

But at what cost? Would he really help her if he ended up feeling just as trapped and alone as she was? Not to mention, he wasn't exactly in a position to support a ready-made family.

He turned the key and the engine sputtered—and died. "Oh, no."

"What's wrong?" Shay leaned forward, sitting up straighter. Link thought he saw something stronger than mild concern in her expression.

He tried again. Same results. *Lord, please! I need this truck to start.* He turned the key and held it engaged a few seconds longer this time, but that only created an awful, high-pitched grinding. He turned the ignition off and gave Shay what he hoped was a reassuring smile. "Don't worry. It's done this before. I think I know what's wrong." Where was Ruiz when he needed him? Now if only he could remember what Izz had done to fix this junker of a truck the last time it conked out in the parking lot at work.

He popped the hood release and opened the door. "Be right back."

He found the lever and opened the hood. The headlamps were nice and bright, but they didn't shed any light under the hood. He aimed his phone's flashlight on the engine and wiggled a few of the same wires he remembered his coworker fiddling with. He wasn't a total whiz with cars, but his friend had taught him a few tricks. He checked the battery cables and didn't see a problem with the connections, but he jiggled them anyway.

Leaving the hood up, he climbed back in the cab and turned the key again. Same grinding noise.

"Do you know what's wrong?" Shayla watched him closely.

"I'm not sure. But you'd probably better call your dad and tell him we'll be a little late."

She gave him a look of disdain. "I don't have a curfew, Link. Besides, I walked out on him, remember?"

"Yes, and why do I feel like *I'm* the one who's going to be in trouble for it?"

She gave a one-shouldered shrug that almost felt like she agreed.

"Let me try something else. Hang on." He got out again, racking his brain to think what it could be.

"Try praying," Shayla called through the open driver's side door. "That's what my dad does whenever the stupid delivery van breaks down. It usually works too."

"Believe me, I've been praying." *Mostly that her father wouldn't ask for his head on a platter.* He tinkered with some hoses and belts, and after a few minutes, he lowered the hood partway and looked through the windshield. "Could you try starting it for me?"

Shayla leaned across to the steering column. Almost instantly the truck sputtered to life.

Thank you, God! He slammed the hood, hopped back in the truck, and put the gearshift in reverse. "You must be a good pray-er."

She gave a wry grin. "Where two or more are gathered..."

He fastened his seatbelt and checked the clock on the dashboard. After ten. "Buckle up. We need to get you home."

Wordless, she did as he asked.

It was hard to make out the unmarked edges of the lane, but he managed to get back to the highway and head toward Langhorne. "So your dad is going to be a hard nut to crack. Is that what you're telling me?"

"He's a good man, Link. He really is. That whole mess with Mama's family was bad enough, but when she died... He changed. And after Jerry and Tara, I think something just snapped in him. He hasn't been the same since."

"I can't blame him. That's a lot to bear. For you too."

She didn't reply, and he drove for a while in silence, his thoughts a swirl of conflict and horror at all Shayla had revealed about her family. His family had grown stronger and closer after his brother's death. But it was different losing Tim as a hero. The Whitmans had been surrounded by comforting words and accolades, as if they'd done something honorable simply by being Tim's family.

But if they'd buried him in shame or sent him away to prison. If they'd had sorrow after sorrow on top of what happened to Tim, would Link have been able to say the same thing about how his family had weathered their grief? He doubted it. It gave him a new perspective on Shayla's father, and he knew he would've spoken differently to him if they'd had this conversation before.

"Hey?" He patted Shayla's knee.

She looked up at him with doleful eyes. "What?"

"I'd like to talk to your father in private, okay?"

"Without me, you mean?" She looked nervous. "What are you going to say to him?"

"I just want a chance to plead my case."

Her eyes narrowed and she tipped her head. "Your case?"

"If your dad has a problem with you going out with me, I want to talk to him about why. I want his blessing before I see you again."

"Then you might as well drop me off in the street because you're not going to get it."

"Just let me try, okay? You don't know my persuasive powers." He gave her his best puppy dog eyes. And wished he believed his own bravado.

But Shayla wouldn't be teased out of her mood, so they rode in silence until they reached the bakery. Still, she didn't argue when he got out of the truck and walked in with her, his nerves growing tauter with every step.

A dim lamp in the back of the bakery did little to dispel the shadows.

"Daddy?" Shayla called.

Link followed her through the dining room. Rustling came from the seating area at the far end of the store. An overhead light came on and Mr. Michaels appeared.

He barely acknowledged Link's presence before turning to Shayla and hooking a thumb toward the stairway that led to the living quarters. "I told Portia you'd tuck her in."

Shayla touched Link's arm. "Don't leave before I talk to you." She swept past him and hurried up the stairs.

Link shuffled his feet on the tile floor. "I apologize we're so late, sir. My pickup wouldn't start. I'm sure that probably sounds like a version of 'the dog ate my homework,' but I swear, it's true."

Michaels leveled his gaze. "You ever hear of a phone?"

"I did ask her—Shayla—to call, but..." He hadn't meant to throw her under the bus, but her father had a way of making a guy quake in his boots.

Now Michaels waved a hand, dismissing Link.

It was now or never. "Sir... I'd like to speak with you for a few minutes. Please, sir."

Shayla's father cocked his head. "I'm listening."

"Um, could we go sit down somewhere? Please?" It came out sounding far braver than Link felt.

Michaels motioned for Link to follow him to a round table in the corner. He pulled out a chair and sat. Link followed suit.

"Mr. Michaels, Shayla tells me you don't want her dating me. And I'd like to plead my case. If you'll let me."

No response.

"Sir, I'm not sure exactly what your objections against me are. But I assure you I have the utmost respect for your daughter. I think the world of her, and I think the feeling is mutual, and I'd like to have your blessing to court her." He wasn't sure where that word had even come from. *Court* her? But it did seem like maybe Shayla's father was the kind of man who would appreciate that old-fashioned term.

"You think the feeling is mutual, huh?"

"Yes, sir, I do."

"And I assume Shay's told you about her situation?"

"Portia, you mean?" He wished he hadn't spoken so quickly. Maybe that wasn't what her father was referring to at all.

"Oh, yes, there's Portia. But that's only the half of it. What I mean is, do you know what it means to tie yourself to a black family."

"Sir?"

"I bet Shayla hasn't told you about all the birthday parties she didn't get an invite for when she was in middle school. You ready to explain that to your children someday? For your little girls to come home cryin' to you with their hearts broke because the boy they like doesn't date black girls? If the feeling is so mutual as you say." His voice dripped sarcasm.

Link cleared his throat. "I realize that—" That was all he could get out—not that Mike Michaels would have let him speak anyway.

"I don't suppose Shay mentioned how her brother got cut out of his group of friends at school? So he fell in with the only bunch left to him. And of course they're just what you'd expect. Gang bangers and"—he gave a sharp laugh—"what you'd probably call thugs. That what you want for your kids someday? 'Cause that's what you got ahead of you if this turns into anything. If this is so *mutual* as you say."

"I'm sorry, Mr. Michaels. I'm truly sorry those things happened to you. And to Shayla. To Jerry. To your family. I know the world isn't perfect. And I don't deny there are still prejudices here. But I truly think things are better now. That it would be a little easier for our kids—I mean, if we ever *had* any kids. After we got married, I mean. *If* we ever got married . . ." He was digging a hole so deep he'd never get out.

Mike Michaels gave a humorless laugh. "You think so, huh? You think *all that*"—he stretched out the words—"everything I just told you, happened way back in the olden days? Then I don't guess Shay told you about the bottle that come sailing through our front window here just the other day. Your parents ever had a bottle come smashing through a window out there at their fancy bed and breakfast?"

At first Link thought he surely must be attempting a joke. But despite his condescending tone, nothing in his demeanor hinted at a joke. So Link sat there with his jaw slack wondering what he'd done to deserve the vitriol Michaels was dishing out.

"Yeah," the man said shortly. "I didn't think so."

"A bottle? You mean somebody threw a bottle through your window *here*? At the bakery?" Shayla hadn't said a word about it. He wondered if she even knew.

"Cost me over a thousand dollars to get it fixed, and of course I have a fifteen-hundred dollar deductible on my insurance. That's a lot of doughnuts and coffee I gotta sell." He leveled a hard gaze at Link. "So you never had something like that happen to you, huh?"

Link looked away briefly. "No sir. I haven't."

"This ain't the olden days, son. This happened last week."

"Are you saying it happened because of your race? Because you're black."

"Well, now, the character that threw that bottle didn't leave a message rolled up inside explainin' himself, but judging from the looks of him, I think you and me would draw the same conclusions."

Link wasn't sure what, exactly, he was implying. But he could guess. Although, given some of the conversations he and Shayla had had, he was tempted to call Michaels on judging a person by his looks. "I'm sorry it happened, sir. And no, I didn't know about it. Did they catch the guy that did it?"

"Like I said, it was a drive-by. He didn't leave his name and address, and he probably looked like a hundred other pierced and Mohawked white kids around here."

"Mohawked?" His heart lurched. "Did he . . . Was his hair dyed yellow?"

Michaels eyed him. "You know the guy?"

"No, but Shayla and I had a run-in with a guy with a yellow Mohawk at the movies a few weeks ago. A big guy? Pasty white complexion?" Why hadn't Shayla said anything? "Was Shayla here when it happened? The broken window?"

"She was here, but she never told me anything about a run-in. What do you mean by that? Does *Shay* know this guy?"

"No. He was just some jerk in line at the movies. He made some smart remark about Portia. He must have thought she was ours . . . together. Shayla just ignored it, but he wouldn't let it go, so

I finally told him—more or less—to shove it." Maybe that would gain him some points with Shayla's dad.

But Michaels shook his head and clenched his jaw. "That there? What you just told me is exactly why I have reservations."

"About me?" Link pointed to himself. "I don't understand."

"That's right. You don't. And Shayla and Portia are the ones who'll suffer for it. It didn't cross your mind that that yellow-haired genius might follow you out here? Might find out where Shayla lived so he could even the score?"

"Is...is that what happened?" Link felt sick to his stomach. Shayla's father was right. It never crossed his mind there might be retaliation for what he'd done. He thought he'd sent a clear message that the guy had better not mess with Shayla. Or Portia. But if he was honest, he'd also been trying to be their hero. Trying to win Shayla over.

He swallowed hard. "No sir. I admit I never thought of that. But if he was going to come after anybody, it should have been me. I'm the one who egged him on. Besides, we didn't see anyone following us." He hadn't been looking either. He'd been too busy patting himself on the back for defending the little ladies.

"And what if you had seen him? Would you have jumped out and given him what-for? You think that would have ended it? If you do, then you don't have a clue what it takes to keep my babies safe in this wonderful modern world where apparently 'things are better now.'" His imitation of Link's voice made Link cringe.

He dipped his head. "I'm sorry. I should have let things be. Shayla tried to tell me, and I ignored her. She didn't do anything wrong and—"

"Never said she did. I raised her to know how to handle herself in this world."

"Sir, I was just trying to defend them. Protect them. My dad taught me to speak up if somebody was bothering my sisters and...any woman."

"Well, I'm sorry to tell you, your paradigm done got shifted, son. I only wish it'd shifted before I lost my front window."

"Are you saying the window is my fault?" That sent his blood into a slow simmer.

"I never said that. As Shay likes to say, it is what it is. But I'll thank you to keep your heroics confined to your sisters in the future."

Link clenched his fists and prayed he wouldn't say anything he'd regret. He was surprised at the words that came to him next. "Sir, I am truly sorry if my actions caused that trouble"—he pointed toward the sparkling clean new window—"and I'll be glad to help pay for it." How he'd find the money, he didn't have a clue. Unless he tapped into his savings and stayed in his dumpy apartment for another year.

Mike Michaels shoved his chair away from the table. "I don't need your charity, but thank you all the same."

Link rose with him. He saw clearly where Shayla got the chip on her shoulder. "I wasn't offering charity, Mr. Michaels. I was offering restitution." He raked a hand through his hair. "I think it might be best if I leave. Would you please tell Shayla good-bye for me. I'll call and talk to her."

"She has a busy week ahead."

"I understand, but I told her I wouldn't leave without saying good-bye, and I'd like to explain why I did." *Because her father is a hard-headed—*

"Suit yourself. The door is unlocked." Michaels pushed his chair in and went to fiddle with the lock on the back door, effectively dismissing Link.

Link shoved his own chair under the table and strode to the front door. He didn't realize until he reached for the door handle that his fingers were still balled into fists. He hadn't felt this frustrated since his boss had unfairly accused him of exaggerating his hours a couple years ago. But Shayla's father may as well have had his own fists up. He'd been begging for a fight the whole time.

Hand on the door, he paused, hesitant to leave without speaking to Shayla. After all, he'd given her his word. But if he stayed, he feared he'd say something he'd regret. If not to her father, then to her.

What a tangled mess this entire night had turned into.

And why hadn't Shay told him about the broken window, about that kid retaliating? He'd looked like an idiot to her father. And maybe he'd *been* one. He'd only meant to defend Shayla and Portia, like he'd said.

But if it was true that Mohawk had followed them to Langhorne, to the bakery, then his attempted heroics had put Shayla—and her whole family—in danger. It had cost them a small fortune. And it was starting to look like it might cost him the woman he was growing to love.

16

Hey, Dad, Mom said she thought you were tinkering in your shop. Um, can I talk to you?"

Grant looked up from under the hood of the car to see Link standing there. The expression on his son's face caused him to straighten and lay aside the wrench. "Sure, bud. Shouldn't you be at work? It's Monday morning. Everything okay?"

"I might have . . . gotten myself into some trouble."

Grant attempted to read the seriousness of his son's tone, while also willing his pulse to return to normal. Did young men of a certain age have any clue what came to a father's mind when a son said he might have gotten himself into trouble?

"How so?" Grant aimed for a casual tone, wiping his hands on a clean corner of a grease rag. *Whatever it is, Lord, give me a cool head and wise words.*

"What do you have going on under here?" Link peered beneath the hood and tinkered with the oil dipstick.

Grant took the hint and leaned back beneath the hood. "Just giving 'er a tune-up. Already changed the oil, but it seemed like maybe the spark plugs could use changing too." He was no mechanic, but they were on a squeaky tight budget for a few months, and he figured he could save a small fortune if he figured out how to do some of the car maintenance himself.

"Have you changed them yet?"

Grant tried not to look too sheepish. "I can't even *find* the stupid things. Why do they have to hide everything in these new vehicles?"

Link laughed. "I wouldn't exactly call a 2005 Saturn Ion a new vehicle, Pops. But hey, hand me that screwdriver. Spark plugs happen to be one of the few things I do know." He undid a few screws and popped a cover off to reveal a row of individual compartments.

"Well, I'll be! I'll call you *first* next time I overhaul an engine." He smiled. "Where did you learn this stuff anyway? It sure wasn't from your old man."

"Necessity is the mother of invention."

For a split second, he felt miffed that his son had apparently had car trouble and hadn't called his good ol' dad to help him out.

"And," Link piped up. "It probably doesn't hurt that I have a mechanical buddy at work. You remember Izz? Isaiah?"

"Sure. Nice guy." Eager to get to what was bothering his son, he knew better than to press.

Link pushed his way under the hood and started working the plugs out of their housings with a ratchet.

Grant let him take over, grateful for the assistance. "So how are things with you? What's up? That girl still in the picture? Shayla?"

"Yeah, she is. At least I hope so. That's why I need some advice."

"Okay. Shoot." He kept his head down, careful not to meet Link's gaze. He and Audrey had both noticed how reticent their son had been recently and were, frankly, starting to get a little worried about him. Especially since they saw so much less of him these days, now that he was working extra shifts. They'd been thankful to hear he was dating but wished they could get to know Shayla better.

With the old spark plugs removed, Link worked to install one of the replacements. Grant was relegated to "mechanic's assistant," handing him various tools as he requested.

Link gave the ratchet a final twist and held a hand out for the next plug. "So how important do you think it is for a girl's parents—her dad specifically—to approve of her boyfriend?"

Grant watched his son's profile, trying to read him. "I take it this isn't hypothetical?"

Link screwed up his mouth. "Not exactly."

Grant didn't have a clue how any girl's father wouldn't be thrilled beyond belief to have Link Whitman interested in his daughter. But then again, he was more than a little prejudiced when it came to this handsome son of his. "So what's not to like? She's not seventeen or anything?" He spoke the thought as it flitted to mind, then wished he hadn't.

"No." Link laughed. "More like seventeen times two."

Grant furrowed his brow, doing the math. "Shayla's thirty-four? I wouldn't have guessed that."

"Well, thirty-three. Same difference."

"If anything, I would have guessed she was much younger." That information shocked him until he realized she was only older than Link by four or five years. When had their kids gotten to be not just adults, but *old* ones? "Is that a problem for you? Her age?"

He shrugged. "Not really."

"But she still lives at home?"

Link nodded. "Otherwise I wouldn't worry so much what her dad thought."

"So what's his objection? He think you're too young?"

"More like too white."

He straightened. "What? He doesn't want her dating you because you're *white*? He said that?"

"Not those words exactly. Shayla's mom was white. I don't know if you knew that."

Grant nodded. "I don't think I ever met her, but I remember when they bought the bakery." It had caused a bit of a stir as Grant recalled, especially when the business began to draw people from the Michaelses' church in Cape—black people. He shook his head. He would never understand the way some people thought. Busybodies and troublemakers. Always trying to stir up trouble where there was no reason for it. Thankfully things had settled down and stayed that way as far as he knew. "And I remember hearing when Mike's wife died. That's been a while now, I think."

Link nodded. "Five years. And Shay said her dad was really broken up when her mom died. So I don't know what his deal is. It just seems a little odd to me that her dad has a problem with a white guy dating his daughter." Link sighed. "But there are a lot of other complications."

"Like?" Grant studied his son's expression, hoping for a clue.

"Like, Shayla's mom's parents disowned her when she married a black guy. And her brother got in some trouble with the law."

A fluorescent light in the rafters overhead buzzed and flickered. "What kind of trouble?"

"Drugs. I don't know the whole story."

"Well, is he still... messed up?"

"I don't know. Shayla doesn't talk about him much. She doesn't see him."

A knot formed in Grant's gut. He sensed Link was hedging, and wondered what he wasn't saying. He and Audrey had always prayed their kids would marry into good families. Mike Michaels had seemed like a nice guy the few times Grant had talked to him at the bakery. But he hadn't known about the son with drug problems.

Link cleared his throat. "I might as well tell you, Dad. Shayla's brother is in jail. Prison."

The knot in his gut tightened. Not exactly the kind of family he'd hoped for. Still... Best wait and hear the entire story. "So the brother—the one in prison—he's the father of the little girl?"

"He is."

"And where's the mother?"

"She passed away. It's too long a story... I'll just leave it that they've had their problems."

"Wow. I guess so." He stepped back and stared at the concrete floor, processing everything he'd just heard. Praying for wisdom. "That's a lot to bear. For the whole family, I mean. After all that, Shayla's dad, Mike, is probably reluctant to lose his daughter too."

Link frowned. "Lose her?"

"Whether it's accurate or not, son, I think every father feels like he's losing his daughter when another man steals her heart."

"Oh." He grimaced. "Hadn't thought of that, I guess."

"Yes, and he's already lost a lot. That might be what's going on here. You know how much I think of your brothers-in-law, and Mom and I feel blessed they haven't dragged your sisters off to the far ends of the earth. But I'm here to tell you if any one of those guys ever dared to hurt my little girls—Bree included—I'd make them sorry they ever laid eyes on me."

Link gave a droll laugh. "I don't think you have anything to worry about, Dad."

"I don't either. The girls chose well. I'm just saying." He echoed Link's laughter. "So Shayla's thirty-three? An older woman, huh?" Things weren't stacking up to his liking. "She's not divorced, is she?" He knew it sounded judgmental, but thirty-three was getting up there to still be single. And Lord knew marriage was hard enough without throwing exes into the mix.

"Nope, never married," Link said. "Shayla took care of her mom full-time while she was dying of cancer. Otherwise somebody would have snapped her up. You saw her. She's gorgeous. And very sweet," he added a little too quickly.

His son sounded smitten. "How did you two meet anyway?"

"At the homeless shelter last summer. She was delivering day-old stuff while I worked on their computers. And since then I've talked to her at the bakery." He shrugged. "We just hit it off. So I finally got the nerve up to ask her out. We've been taking Portia on dates with us. But when I tried to get Shayla to go out, just the two of us, her dad got all bent out of shape. Shay's brother apparently got his girlfriend—Portia's mom—pregnant, and I guess Shay's dad was pretty upset about that. He was a deacon in their church and it was pretty humiliating. So that might be part of it."

"Understandable," Grant said, working to hide his growing discomfort about this girl's family.

"The thing is, Portia lives with them full-time, and Shay's pretty much taking care of her. Her dad doesn't seem willing to give her any time off. And she already works long hours at the bakery six days a week as it is."

Link settled the last spark plug into its socket. "All set. You want to hand me that well cover?"

"I can take it from here, bud. Thanks. You likely saved me a trip into town. And more than a few dollars."

Link straightened and stretched, giving Grant a lopsided grin. "No problem. You've done a favor or two for me over the years."

Grant took the opportunity to give his son a frank look. "Are you sure you want to get caught up in all this, Link? It sounds like Shayla has a lot on her plate. A lot of responsibilities. And if her father isn't on board with you, might not be something you'd want to get tangled up in."

"I'm already tangled, Dad. I really like her. Believe me, I've thought about what I'm getting into. And that's what kind of convinces me she might be the one. Because there was a time I would have run fast and far away from complications like that. But with Shay, it doesn't scare me. Not really. This is what her life is like, and if I really love—or care about her, then I don't have any choice but to accept her the way she is. Baggage and all."

Baggage was a polite way of putting it. "*Are* you in love with her, bud?" He was almost afraid to ask the question.

Link nodded without speaking.

Grant couldn't tell if his response was uncertain, or if he was too choked up to risk voicing his feelings. But judging by his glassy eyes, it was the latter.

"Then I think you'd better get things straightened out with her father. That needs to be your first priority. Sounds like there are enough complications without starting out with him against you. You'll have to win him over somehow."

He and Audrey had been praying so long for their son to find the right woman. Link'd had a few girlfriends throughout high school, and had dated a little since then, but it seemed the older he got, the fewer and farther between those dates were. His sisters had tried to set him up with young women they knew, and

Audrey had a famously failed matchmaking attempt with the daughter of one of her friends. After that fiasco, they'd decided to let Link—and God—handle things.

Audrey had commented just the other night, when they were speculating about why Link had made himself so scarce lately, that at his age, they might need to be prepared for him to meet a divorcée or a single mom. Grant had thought she was being a little dramatic. Twenty-nine wasn't that old . . . not for a man.

But now he wondered.

"There's something else, Dad."

Grant lowered the hood support rod and snapped it in place, then slammed the car hood shut with both hands. "What's that?" He braced himself for what, he wasn't sure.

"Shayla's dad is blaming me for something that happened at the bakery. And"—he glanced away, his expression pensive—"it probably *is* my fault. But I'm not sure what to do to fix it."

17

The bakery was quiet on a Monday morning. *Too quiet.* Shayla went to offer refills to three college students studying in the corner nook, then came back to start another pot. Even though she'd barely poured five cups from the last one. But people would complain if their morning java wasn't fresh.

Already Thanksgiving week, yet they had barely half the orders they usually did for Daddy's fluffy crescent rolls and his famous pumpkin pies. She hadn't thought much of it at first, but now she was beginning to suspect word had gotten around about the broken window, and people were staying away because of it.

She felt sick to her stomach when she thought about the things her father had said to Link last night. She'd listened at the top of the stairs to their strident voices, unable to make out the words, but knowing her father'd had the upper hand. But she'd been too much of a coward to defend Link—to come down and make her father understand that Link's intentions were only good where she and Portia were concerned.

Except Link could be clueless. Like egging on that jerk at the movies. Link might have thought he was being a hero, but he was showing off too, trying to get in her good graces by playing the tough guy. Except he didn't understand how guys like that operated.

She couldn't blame him. It wasn't his fault he'd never had to deal with challenges she'd grown up taking for granted. She loved Link's innocence. Loved that he was blind to the prejudice that was still all around them—at least in this part of the country—

even if it was usually subtle. But if Link was going to be part of their lives, he had to learn.

Who was she kidding? If things weren't already over between them after they talked last night, they surely were over after her father dragged Link through the fire. Over, with a capital O.

The bells on the front door jangled, and she looked up, ready with her usual welcome greeting. "Good morning. What can I—" Her heart stopped. "Link?"

He gave a little wave.

"I thought you had to work."

"I'm going in a little late today. Can we talk?"

"Daddy's out back working on the delivery truck. I have to work the counter."

He looked around the nearly empty space. "Doesn't seem like you're too busy."

"Okay." She nodded, excited to see him, yet apprehensive at the same time. She didn't dare let him guess her real feelings, for both their sakes. "But if anyone comes in, you need to leave."

"I understand."

"And if my father comes in, you may get thrown out on your ear."

He looked at her as if trying to figure out whether she was teasing.

"Just hurry. What is it?" She hated the coldness in her voice, but it was for his own good. It didn't matter how much she loved being with him, touching him, feeling his strong arm around her shoulders, watching every nuance of those expressive blue eyes. Things would never work for them, and the sooner she accepted that, the sooner she could get on with her life. And Link with his.

The oven timer sounded and she headed for the kitchen.

Link followed her around the counter.

"You can't be back here."

"Sorry." He raised his arms and retreated to the other side of the display cases.

She hurriedly pulled a batch of pecan-and-date cookies from the oven and took the pan back out to the bakery counter.

Link didn't miss a beat. "First, I wanted to say I'm sorry I didn't tell you good-bye before I left yesterday." He rolled his eyes. "Your dad didn't seem too keen on me hanging around."

"I'm sorry if he was rude." She grabbed a spatula and lifted the cookies from the pan one by one, placing them on a cooling rack.

"He was just worried about you. I'd probably feel the same if you were my daughter." His soft smile tore her up. But the smile faded and a hard edge came to his expression. "Why didn't you tell me about the window?"

"Window?" She stilled.

"Your dad told me about the broken window. And about who did it. The guy with the Mohawk?"

She froze. "Did you tell Daddy about what happened at the movie?"

"Of course I told him. I can't believe you didn't. Why would you keep that from him?"

"What did he say?" Daddy had to be furious that she'd kept that from him, and yet, he hadn't confronted her. Of course, she'd avoided him all morning. Thankfully, the broken down delivery truck made that easy.

"What did he say?" he scoffed. "He lectured me for an hour, that's what. Pretty much the gist of it was, there is no way in heaven, on earth, or any other planet, for that matter, that I'm going to touch his daughter."

Shay steeled herself. "And he's right."

Link studied her. "Is that you talking? Or your father?"

"It doesn't matter, Link. The results are the same."

"No. I'm not ready to accept that. But we'll talk about that topic after we talk about the window. Why didn't you tell your dad? Is it because you couldn't tell him we were at the movie together? Have you lied to him about us spending time together?"

She huffed. "As if I could keep anything secret with Portia around."

A hint of a smile played on his features but quickly faded. "Why didn't you tell me about the window? Why would you keep that from me—*or* your dad? The police need to know what that guy did."

She closed her eyes. "You don't get it, Link. My dad didn't report it, and he's not going to do anything about it. That would only make the situation worse."

"How can you say that? And how can *he* be so irresponsible? Especially when he told me he thinks that thug followed us to the bakery that night after the movies. That makes sense. How else would he know where you lived? He targeted you and you could have been—"

"Link! Listen to me." She tossed the metal spatula into the sink and it landed with a clatter. "You don't understand."

"Then help me understand."

"If you'd lived your whole life getting routinely pulled over—multiple times in a year—just because you were a man who happened to have black skin—"

"Pulled over? Well, then I must have some black blood in me, because I'm paying sky-high insurance premiums right now, thanks to two speeding tickets."

The smug look on his face made her clench her teeth.

She tilted her head. "And *were* you speeding?"

"Well, yes," he admitted.

"And therein lies the difference. My dad was not."

He had the decency to look shocked. "Not even a little?"

She stared at him. "If anything, he drives five miles an hour below the speed limit. You know *that* stereotype don't you? Well, there's a reason for it."

"Whoa, are you serious, Shay? I guess I—" He regarded her. And apparently her expression made him change gears. "I guess I'll shut up before I dig myself in any deeper. I didn't realize it really was that way, Shay. I mean, you hear things, but . . ."

"But you don't believe them. I know you don't get it. Most of *you* don't." She released a sigh. "And sorry if that sounds racist. But until you've experienced it again and again, you can't understand."

"Well, I guess I can imagine how I'd feel if I'd been stopped if I *wasn't* speeding. Unfortunately, I earned my tickets fair and square."

"Like I said, therein lies the difference. You have a choice, Link. You can stop the pull-overs if you just quit speeding. Not everybody has that privilege. And I'm telling you, my dad is not going to report what happened. We've had enough run-ins with the police to last a lifetime. Some of them deserved, with Jerry. But many of them not. For sure not with my dad. So you can see why Daddy's sure not going to call the authorities about some bigot vandalizing the bakery."

"I still—"

She held up a hand. "It's over and the window is fixed. The last thing we need is rumors about the bakery being targeted." She waved a hand over the dining room, empty except for the students studying in the nook. "Although I'm guessing news already got out that it's not safe to come in here anymore."

"What? You can't be serious, Shay. Of course it's still safe."

Apparently her expression revealed just how serious she was. His face fell, and his shoulders slumped, his expression revealing so much. Regret. Anger. Comprehension. "Shay, I'm sorry."

"I realize you didn't grasp the possible consequences of what you did at the movies that night. But now you do."

"Your dad accused me of not understanding some of the things you guys face, that I *don't* face. He was right. I feel terrible. And that's the other reason I came. I'd like to offer to pay for the window." He nodded toward the front of the store. "Or at least part of it. Your dad said it didn't meet the insurance deductible. I feel really bad about everything."

"No." She shook her head. "No, Link, I'm telling you right now, don't even offer. Don't even suggest that to my dad—"

"Too late."

She stared at him.

"I apologized. And I did offer to pay. It didn't go over so hot."

"I don't think you understand what a proud man my dad is. To him, it looks like you're offering charity, and he is nobody's charity case."

"That's not how I meant it. I told him I feel responsible. So, what can I do?"

"Do?"

"To get his blessing, to get permission to be friends with his daughter again—his thirty-three-year-old daughter."

She stared at him trying to decipher his sarcasm, trying to decide whether to ask him to leave or try to make him understand. Again. "How can you even want that—to be friends—after everything I told you last night? After my dad's lecture?"

"Because I know what I want, Shay." The piercing look he gave her said he wasn't taking no for an answer.

"Link..." She didn't have the first clue how to respond to that. "Hang on. I... I need to make sure I turned off the oven." She hurried back to the kitchen, thankful he couldn't see her face, read the longing in her eyes. *I know what I want.* Why did he have to go and say things like that? Why did he have to make it so much harder than it already was? Bracing her arms on the counter, she took in deep breaths.

Finally, composing herself, she went back out to the dining room where Link stood. "Sit down." She pointed to a table where he'd be hidden from view if Daddy came in the back door. The weight in her chest was almost more than she could bear. But she knew what she had to do. "We need to talk."

Link perched on the edge of the chair. Across from him, Shayla watched his face with an expression he couldn't read. "What's going on?" He glanced toward the bakery's entrance, then the back door, praying no one came through either. Especially not her father.

"Link, I laid awake half the night wrestling with God, struggling to plot out some scenario that would make this work. But I can't get past the truth—there *isn't* a scenario. We can't do this. It just won't work."

"Are you saying... because of your father?"

She sighed. "It's so much more than that. I don't even know where to start. And I feel like I've given you all the ammunition you need. I don't know why you can't take a hint."

"I'll tell you why. Because I don't believe you." He exhaled. Was he really ready to put it all out there? He'd chided her for keeping things from him. If they were going to be honest with each other, let it start now. "Tell me you don't feel something, Shay? Tell me you don't think we're good together. Good with Portia even. You're not giving us a chance, and I don't understand why. It's not fair. It doesn't even make any sense."

"If you weren't so blind, it would make perfect sense." She scrubbed her face with her hands and gave a growl of frustration. "Link, if it was just you and me and we could move to a desert island, everything would be just peachy. But we can't. We have to consider the real world we live in. And the different worlds we live in. That's where we'd have to make *us* work. In the midst of both of our families. With me working right here at the bakery. And with Portia in the picture. All the time. Every day. And people like that stupid Mohawk character everywhere we go. Not every day. No. Most people are kind and understanding and accepting. But not everybody. And those are the ones we have to think about."

"No." He straightened and leaned closer. "Why should we let those kind of people dictate our lives? Why would we do that? Why not expect the best of everybody and ignore the idiots of the world?"

"Oh, you mean the way you ignored Mohawk? No, Link, because the idiots won't ignore us."

"So we deal with it, Shay." He held up a hand. "And I don't mean the way I did. I might be a slow learner, but I *can* learn. And maybe we can set an example and change the world just a little bit along the way. At least our part of the world."

"I wish it was that easy, Link. I truly do. If we both came from families that supported us in this. If Portia wasn't in the picture, we might have a prayer. But there's so much going against us. And it's not going to get better. Someday Jerry will get out, and then things could get a whole lot worse."

"You don't know that. Why are you borrowing trouble? Why are you building an impossible case against us?"

"I'm not building anything, Link. I'm showing you the blueprint. I'm trying to save you from building something that's doomed to collapse."

He shook his head and looked at the table. He didn't want to keep arguing with her. But he hated hearing the hopelessness in her voice.

And for some strange reason, he was still determined to find a way to keep seeing her. In some ways he was surprised she hadn't scared him off with all the drama that seemed to dog her family. He'd gotten the feeling his dad thought he should bail while the bailing was good. But something drew Link to her. Something more than just the physical attraction he felt for her.

He scooted his chair closer to the table, closer to her. "Would you give me some time? Give me the rest of the year to convince you that we—"

The front door opened, jangling the bells, and two guys strode in wearing coveralls with the local auto parts shop logo on their breast pockets.

Shayla jumped up, pasting on a smile Link knew she didn't feel. "Hey, Rick, Gary. Is it coffee break already? What can I get you guys?"

She waited on the men, pouring coffee and bagging pastries, making friendly small talk. That was the Shayla he'd fallen in love with. The one he'd flirted with whenever he came in. He hadn't known all the undercurrents that were there.

Link willed the men to order their food to go, but they took their coffee in mugs and settled in at a corner table. Thankfully, they were soon engaged in a good-natured—but loud—political discussion.

When Shayla came back to the table, he lowered his voice. "You guys have been through a lot," he said. "But I think maybe I understand your dad's feelings a little better now." His talk with Dad had helped.

"Then you know why I can't see you any more, Link."

He leaned back. "No, I don't know that at all. Why would you say that?"

She looked at him with a pained expression. "Did you hear *anything* I just told you? I'm sorry I ever let you think this could go anywhere. I wanted it to. I really did, Link"—her voice broke—"but it won't. And it can't. It just . . . it wouldn't work."

"I think you're wrong."

At that moment, the back door opened and someone came in, whistling.

Mike Michaels strode around the corner and stopped short when he saw Link. His gaze panned the room, and seeing the guys from the auto parts store, he motioned to Shayla. "You've got customers."

"They've been taken care of, Daddy."

Link prayed the men's coffee cups weren't empty. Even though the sign by the coffee pots clearly offered free self-serve refills.

"Then you can take the day-old stuff in to the shelter in Cape. I'll man the counter. I can't do any more on the van until I get a couple of parts in."

"Daddy." She said it respectfully, but through gritted teeth. "I have company."

"It's okay," Link said, patting her hand. "I need to go anyway. I'll call you." He turned to her father. "Good morning, sir. I was just leaving."

He didn't wait to see what kind of reaction that got from Michaels but strode to the front door, returning the brief greeting from the auto parts guys with a nod before giving the door a decent slam.

18

That was rude, Daddy." She followed him to the kitchen, not looking back to see whether the auto parts guys were watching. "What did Link ever do to deserve that kind of treatment from you?"

The line of her father's jaw tightened and he grabbed a bar rag and twisted it. Shayla got the impression he wanted to do the same thing to her neck.

"I thought I made it clear he is not welcome here."

"He's my friend. Are you truly telling me my friends aren't welcome here now?" The truth was, Daddy hadn't exactly been welcoming to the few friends she had left. Kind of like now.

"Sit down, Shay."

"What?" She reached for a stool at the baking counter, even as she wondered why she let him boss her around like that. Speak to her that way.

"Listen, baby, I just don't want you to get hurt, that's all. Whether we like it or not, Portia is our responsibility. It's just a fact that no guy is going to be happy about that. I just don't want you—"

"Daddy, Link already said he doesn't mind about Portia. He told you that. And he knows she's part of the package. That she comes with me. I explained it all, and he's fine with it."

"He says that now, baby. But you mark my words. It'll start to wear thin. That's a lot to ask a man to take on."

"But that's my decision to make! Not yours. If I get hurt, I get hurt."

"And what about Portia? She's already crazy about the man. You let him get any closer and it'll break her heart."

Hadn't she told Link that same thing? And meant it. She'd always been careful that Portia didn't get attached to any guy—well, the few guys—she'd dated. But that didn't make it fair that she had to consider her niece, as if it was her fault Jerry had saddled them with his daughter.

She looked at her father and though she knew she shouldn't let the words fly, a rebellious spirit rose up in her. "What about my heart, Daddy? When will it be my turn? You say Portia is *our* responsibility, but why is it always me who ends up with her?" She couldn't believe the words were coming out of her mouth. Her father had never laid a hand on her in anger, but given the rigid set of his jaw, she half expected him to strike her now.

But he didn't, and it made her brave. Too brave. She'd never dared to speak to him this way. Still, she was a grown woman. And she had put in her time with Mama. With Jerry. Even with her dad. "I love Portia, and you know I'm in it for the long haul with her. I'm resigned to that. No, I *accept* it. I love her. You know I do." Her voice broke.

But he only stared, as if waiting for her to finish.

She took a deep breath, fighting back tears. "Daddy, I can't do this if I have to be in it alone."

"Alone? And what am I? Chopped liver?"

She knew he was merely trying to tease her out of a fight, to stave off her tears. But she had things she needed to say while he was still listening. And while she still had the courage. "I know you do what you can, but I'm burning out. Link... he brought some fun and laughter back to my life. And Portia's too. He's good for us. Why can't you see that?"

"What I see," he said slowly, "is what I saw with your mama's family. And it only gets worse. And it ends badly. You know that, baby. Why would you want to willingly walk into it?"

"Are you saying because he's white? Because Link's white? Are you seriously saying that? Because the dad I remember, the father

I trust, raised me to believe that the color of our skin didn't matter. That it was who we were inside that counted." She gripped a fist to her chest.

He looked at the floor. "That was your mama's influence, God rest her. And it sounded good in theory. But your mama, she had a Pollyanna streak a mile wide. That had its advantages. I'm not saying it didn't. But your mama didn't always see the truth. Even when it was staring her ugly-like in the face."

"Well, I wish some of the Pollyanna had rubbed off on you! Mama would be so ashamed of you. That you're—"

"Shayla." He clenched his fists at his sides as if he wanted to throttle her.

She actually flinched. What had they come to, standing off against each other? She hated this. *Hated* it.

Looking stricken, her father unclenched his hands, rubbing them as though they ached.

She'd already pushed him too far. But she was desperate to make him understand. "Daddy, please." She worked to keep her voice low and steady. "I'm begging you. I need a friend, and I've never met anyone like Link. Who understands about Portia. Who—"

A scraping of chairs came from the dining room and he held up a hand. "I need to check the front. I'll be right back."

He left, and she heard him asking the men if they needed refills. She felt completely dismissed.

But he was back in a few seconds and picked up where they'd left off. No. Where *he'd* left off. "You say you need a friend. If you think Link Whitman is just a friend, you're blind. I see how he looks at you. That's not friendship, baby. It's just not."

How could she argue with that? There was definitely more than mere friendship between Link and her. But they *were* friends. Were becoming *dear* friends. Wasn't that what her parents had modeled for her and Jerry growing up? She tried that tack now. "When I was little I used to watch you and Mama together. And even back then, I saw how you were friends. That's what I always wanted, and I've found it in Link. Why can't you see that?"

She took a deep breath but rushed right back in, needing to get it all said before he could argue. "All I'm asking is for you to let me make my own decisions. And my own mistakes. I promise you, I'll go in with my eyes wide open. And if Link proves you right, you can say 'I told you so,' and I won't make you listen to me whine or cry. But give him a chance. *Please.*" Her father had never been persuaded by tears, but she couldn't help that they came now.

He clamped his lips into a tight line and stared at her for an uncomfortable minute. Finally, he shook his head slowly.

Hope welled up inside of her. Why hadn't she spoken her mind to him long ago?

"You're a grown woman, Shayla. You're right about that." He gave a little moan, as if he were in pain. "But I can't give this my blessing. I can't—and I won't."

Her heart sank. "Daddy. Please. I'm begging you."

"I love you, Shay. You got to know that. But there's been too much hurt. Too much pain. I just want it to stop. I don't think either of us can take any more."

She opened her mouth to tell him that Link had never hurt anybody. But she knew before a word left her mouth that her father would point to the newly replaced window and say otherwise. Prove otherwise.

The bells on the front door jingled.

"I've got it." Daddy grabbed a fresh apron and swept past her, obviously relieved to end their conversation. "You go on and take the day-olds in to Cape. Keep your phone on too. I may need you to pick up a part for the car on your way home. If you don't mind," he added quickly. His concession to their discussion about her being a grown woman, no doubt.

Before she could think of another argument or better words to persuade him, he left the kitchen, letting the door swing behind him.

With a growl of frustration, she washed up the dishes in the deep sink, then went to load the boxes of day-old pastries in the car to deliver to the homeless shelter.

Sitting behind the wheel of his truck in the parking lot at Carson Tech, Link tried Shayla's cell again. Straight to voice mail like it had been doing all afternoon. He'd tried calling her on his lunch break too. And left three text messages. She was hiding. He knew she'd been headed to the homeless shelter in Cape when he left the bakery, but she should have been home by now.

He Googled the bakery's phone number and called there.

"Coffee's On. This is Mike. How may I help you?"

Link froze, then quickly pressed End. He'd said all he had to say to Mike Michaels. He started his truck. Only an hour before he had to be back on second shift, and he needed a burger—and a quick nap—before he faced another shift. Besides, he wasn't going to fix things between him and Shayla with a twenty-minute phone call. He tossed his cell phone on the passenger seat. He'd try her again tomorrow. Her dad was usually gone to his prayer group on Tuesday nights so maybe she'd be able to talk.

He felt bad about walking out of the bakery on a sour note this morning. But Shayla's dad hadn't given him much choice. He wanted to invite her and Portia to Thanksgiving dinner at the inn Thursday, but if he couldn't get her to take his calls, that'd be a challenge.

Maybe he could have his mom call with the invitation. Might make up for him not telling his family she was coming last time. He drove to Culver's and ordered a burger and fries, then called his mom while he waited at the drive-through window.

"Hey, bud. How's it going?"

"Good. I'm between shifts so I need to make this quick, but I wondered if you'd do me a big favor?"

"Depends. How much is this favor going to cost me?" There was a smile in her voice.

"It's going to cost you about three minutes of your time."

"Okay, then shoot."

"Would you mind calling the bakery and inviting Shayla and Portia to Thanksgiving dinner—that is if you don't mind having extra guests."

"Of course we don't mind. But what about Shayla's dad?"

"What about him?"

"Well, it wouldn't be very nice to invite Shayla and Portia and leave him home alone for the holiday."

"Oh." Sometimes he really wished life had a rewind button. "I hadn't thought about that." He shook his head. He was being selfish, but having Mike Michaels at his Thanksgiving dinner did not sound like something to be thankful for. *It's not always about you, Whitman.* He blew out a breath. "Yeah, sure. Go ahead and invite him too, I guess. But I kind of doubt he'll come."

"Why do you say that?"

He hesitated. "Let's just say I don't think he's a fan."

"A fan? Of the inn? Or of you?"

The drive-through window slid open and a pretty teenage girl handed out a Coke and straw. He tucked his phone between his ear and his shoulder, speaking into it as he took the drink. "You know what? I—"

"What?" the girl said, her smile revealing that she thought he was flirting with her.

"Oh. No, sorry. Not you. I was talking to someone." He held up his phone as if he owed her proof.

She blushed crimson, and he gave her the courtesy of looking away as he put his phone back to his ear. "Never mind, Mom. I need to go."

"Well, let me know if you change your mind, honey. I don't mind calling."

"No. I'll figure it out. Thanks anyway." He hung up before she could argue.

He drove back to Carson Tech and sat in the parking lot wolfing down the burger with one eye on the clock. Thank goodness it was a short workweek because of Thanksgiving, but three straight days of back-to-back double shifts just might do him in. He had to get out of this place.

But for what? Some other dead-end job? He had a business degree. What did he want to do with it? What did he want to do with his whole stinking life?

And that was just the problem. As for the job, he didn't have a clue. As for his life, it was starting to look like the one thing he did want—Shayla Michaels—he couldn't have.

19

Hey, baby, you have everything you need for the Whitman wedding?" Her father took one last sweep with the broom and leaned it in the corner near the storage closet.

Shayla scrubbed an imaginary spot on the glass of the pastry case and came to a slow boil. Daddy had been pretending everything was back to normal ever since Link walked out of the bakery in a huff on Monday.

No, worse than normal. Her father had been extra sweet and attentive. Trying, she knew, to get back in her good graces. "I have the wedding under control. And all the other December events. I've got three kids from the college lined up to help. That okay?"

"Now, you know I leave that up to you, baby."

If he called her baby one more time, she just might come unglued.

"You've never wasted my money," he continued. "And you know better than I do what it takes to run an event that size."

"Well, I could probably get by with two helpers, but this close to Christmas I don't want to take any chances that somebody might decide to go home early for Christmas and cancel on me. We should still come out ahead, even paying three." She found herself measuring her words carefully. And it took everything she had to speak back to him as kindly as he was treating her. Was that what they meant by killing someone with kindness?

"Like I said"—he sidestepped and patted her on the back—"I trust you."

She knew what that meant: he trusted her not to get involved with that evil, evil Link Whitman.

"Listen, baby, there's something I wanted to talk to you about."

Yep, here it came.

"I'd like you to come with me to see Jerry tomorrow."

She stilled. This wasn't what she'd been expecting. "No, Daddy. Who would we get to babysit Portia on Thanksgiving Day?"

"I thought we'd take her with us. To Bowling Green."

"What? I thought we agreed it wasn't good for her to have to see him."

"I know, but I've been rethinking that. She's going to want to know about her father one of these days sooner than we know."

"You really want her to see him in that jumpsuit with a guard eyeing him like he might make a run for it or something?" She'd tried to block those images from her last visit out of her mind, but they came back in living color now.

"I think she's old enough to handle it. And I think it might do Jerry a world of good to see her, to take some responsibility for her. Have somebody counting on him."

"It's a little late for that, don't you think. What, you think he's going to help feed and clothe her?" She couldn't keep the sarcasm from her voice. "You think he'll pay for her college?" She turned away, knowing Daddy wouldn't tolerate that kind of sass.

But his reply came quiet and steady. "You know he can't do any of that, Shay. But that doesn't mean he can't still be a father to her in some ways."

She shook her head. "I don't want to go, Daddy. Maybe at Christmas." But she knew she'd come up with another excuse before then.

"I'm asking you, please, Shay. If you won't do it for Jerry, for me, then do it for your mama. You know she'd be heartbroken about everything that's gone down."

"Maybe Jerry should have thought about Mama before he decided to get mixed up in that gang. Maybe he should have thought about her before he got Tara knocked up and brought a baby into the world that he couldn't take care of. Maybe he—"

Her father held up a hand, and she knew he'd reached the end of his tolerance.

She worked to keep her voice steady. "Daddy, I've done what you wanted and let go of the best friend I ever had next to Mama." She thought, too late, how that might make him feel. But she had to say her piece before she lost her nerve. She could apologize later.

She took a breath. "I'm resigned to raising Portia, to working here with you to keep the bakery running. I don't have any other options because of Portia. And I'm resigned to never having a family of my own. But even though I live under your roof, I earn my keep here, Daddy. I'm a grown woman, and it's my decision whether I go visit Jerry or not. And I've made my decision. Now I'll ask you to honor it the same way I'm honoring yours."

He took three long strides and grabbed the broom he'd been sweeping with earlier. "Suit yourself." He yanked the dustpan and a whisk broom from inside the storage closet and attacked the pile of debris he'd collected earlier as if it were a vicious animal.

She stormed back to the kitchen, more furious than hurt. She'd made up her mind to break things off with Link. She would have to tell him eventually. Face to face. Or at least on the phone. Unless she took the chicken way out and sent him an e-mail. But for now, she was simply ignoring his phone calls and texts.

And worrying about why he'd quit calling. He'd bombarded her with messages on Monday and Tuesday morning, but she hadn't heard a peep out of him since. Had he given up on her that easily? He'd said he wanted to talk to her about Thanksgiving. She hoped he didn't plan to invite her to his family's Thanksgiving dinner. Although that might beat going to Bowling Green.

Except she wasn't going. And neither was Portia. She didn't care what her dad said.

Locking the door to the bakery, Shayla watched her dad's car disappear down the street. Some Thanksgiving. Daddy wasn't happy she'd refused to go with him to see Jerry, but he hadn't pushed it.

She went to check the back door locks, then slipped her phone out of her pocket and checked it again—for the third time in as many minutes.

Link's last message had been sent Tuesday afternoon. If he hadn't called again by now, he wasn't going to. And she had nobody but herself to blame. But what did it say if he gave up trying to reach her after less than forty-eight hours?

"Portia!" She hollered up the stairs. "Portia Beth? Get down here." She heard her niece clomping around on the wooden floors and a minute later, she appeared on the landing.

"I picked up my toys like you told me."

"Okay, then, let's load up. Get your heavy coat on. It's cold outside."

"I wanna wear my *Frozen* jacket."

"No, if you wear your *Frozen* jacket, you'll *be* frozen. Now get your big coat on. And hustle."

Portia huffed and stomped, but she went for the coat.

She and Portia would do what they'd always done on Thanksgiving Day since Mama died. They would take boxes of bread and pastries and pies—fresh made for this occasion, not day-old—to the homeless shelter in Cape, where a big turkey dinner was always served.

It had been Daddy's idea to do that the first Thanksgiving after Mama passed. And they'd kept it up. It made the holiday easier than setting the table in the kitchen alcove and staring at Mama's empty chair.

Shayla wasn't sure what had made Daddy decide to go spend Thanksgiving with Jerry. And what had made him suddenly think it would be a good idea for Portia to go along. But she was glad to have the day away from her father.

She loved the man. She had to keep reminding herself of that. But it seemed lately he'd made it his goal in life to keep her from anything that made her happy—like Link—and steer her toward the very things he *knew* upset her. Like Jerry.

Well, her father would be happy to know she'd already decided to honor his wishes and not see Link again. Daddy would make life miserable for her if she didn't. He'd proven that.

The irony did not escape her that she felt miserable anyway. And maybe Daddy was right about Link. If he could give up so easily, maybe she'd made the right decision anyway. But even if Link was still calling her every hour, she'd made up her mind. She simply couldn't ask him to make all the adjustments he'd have to make to fit into her life. It was too much. To take on Portia, to deal with Daddy. To be tied to the bakery forever because Daddy couldn't run the place alone, and he couldn't afford to hire full-time help. They were doing good to make payroll for her and the few college kids they employed.

No, she was stuck here. This was the hand God had dealt her, and she was determined to make the best of it. If for no one else, for Portia. But her niece was all the more reason she couldn't drag Link into the cage that was her life.

She sighed and looked at the clock, then toward the stairway. Where was that child? If they were going to have the bread there in time for Thanksgiving dinner they needed to get on the road. "Portia? Hurry up, girl. We need to go."

"I'm comin'!"

Shayla heard clomping in the hallway above her. The door at the top of the stairs opened, and Portia came out, closing the door behind her as she'd been taught. She descended hanging on to the rail, and before she was halfway down Shayla could see that Portia had her heavy coat on—over her *Frozen* jacket.

She smiled to herself and said nothing. There were plenty of hills to die on. This wasn't one of them. Portia was a sweet child—and creative—but she could be a handful.

Shayla sighed. Link Whitman had the right to a normal life, a normal family. His own babies. *Keep talking, Shayla Jean. Talk enough and you might even convince yourself.*

When Portia got to the bottom of the stairs, she folded her arms across her middle in a stubborn stance Shayla recognized all too well. "I don't wanna go. Can't we just stay home?"

"No, baby. We need to take this food to the homeless shelter. You want those people to have some good bread and pies for their Thanksgiving dinner, don't you?"

"Can't they just eat turkey?"

She laughed and tweaked Portia's little pug nose. "*You're* a turkey."

That brought a glimmer to the blue eyes.

"I'll tell you what." She waited until she had Portia's full attention.

"What?"

"After we make our delivery, we'll come home and eat our chicken dinner, and then after your nap we'll have a girls-only day. We'll paint our toes and watch movies and eat Cheetos 'til we pop."

Portia's eyes grew big. "I want purple this time! Purple polish on my fingers too?"

"We'll see if we have time before Big Daddy gets home." She felt a little better just seeing the joy on her niece's face. Portia had lost so much. And it took so little to make her happy.

Why couldn't *she* be more that way?

20

Link popped a second snickerdoodle, whole, into his mouth and surveyed the inn. Today it looked the way the old house had that time Mom had let him and Tim have a team party there after they won the state championship. Huge platters of half-eaten food covered every surface, with empty plates stacked high beside the sink, and the living room littered with bodies. Mostly his nieces and nephews, since the guys were downstairs watching football, and the women were gathered around the table making some crafty thing—party favors, he thought—for Bree's wedding.

The wedding was two weeks from Saturday, and for some reason that fact depressed him like nothing had in a long time. He knew Mom and his sisters had struggled with Bree remarrying. Although that seemed to have turned out okay, given that Drew and Bree spent almost as much time at the inn as the natural-born Whitman kids did.

He was pretty sure his depression had more to do with Shayla Michaels than it did with "losing" Bree to Drew Brooks—who was a great guy and likely to keep close ties with the family, since his brother was married to Link's sister.

Maybe it was the whole thing about being the last man standing. No doubt he was going to have to listen to a bevy of little old ladies ask when they could expect to see *him* heading to the altar. And no doubt he'd be the focus of every would-be matchmaker's attention. Shoot, Bree was already teasing him about catching her bouquet.

But he'd already met the only woman he wanted to be matched with. He just couldn't get her to take his calls. Or texts. Or answer his e-mails, apparently. He'd finally taken a hint after she'd ignored him for two days. He couldn't force her to communicate with him. But it hurt to think she was ignoring him.

"Hey Link, come here." Landyn beckoned him across the room. "We need an opinion."

He shook off the heavy thoughts and put on his happy face. "If it's about food, I'm your man."

"Bro! You are a bottomless pit," Corinne said laughing. "I don't know how you could even think about eating another bite."

"Besides, it's not about food." Bree held up something shiny and round. "It's about these favors."

He lifted his hands in truce. "Now you're pushing it. You know I'm not crafty."

"No, you don't have to be crafty. You just have to tell us if a guy is going to 'get' this as a favor."

He gave a little growl, knowing they wouldn't stop until they had his opinion.

Bree handed him one of the tiny tins they'd been affixing stickers to. The sticker had a silhouette of what looked like the climbing tree out in the meadow, and it said "Drew and Bree sittin' in a tree." He flipped it over. Nothing on the bottom. He shook it. Something rattled inside. Something dense. "Can I open it?"

"Not yet!" Landyn grabbed it from his hand. "First, do you get it?"

"What do you mean, get it? Is it a joke?"

"More like a riddle," Bree said. The women were all cackling like a brood of hens now.

He took the box back from Landyn and inspected it. "Drew and Bree sittin' in a tree? Hmm. Is it supposed to be like that song?"

"What song?" They all spoke at once.

"You know. K-I-S-S-I-N-G," he sing-songed.

"That's it!" They cheered in unison.

"That's it? I still don't get it."

"No," Bree said. "That's a clue."

"A clue to what?"

"To what's inside," Danae said, bouncing Tyler on her lap.

"Now I have to guess what's inside?"

"Yes, but now you have a clue."

"Well, it's kind of stupid, but it beats the last wedding favor I got."

"What was that?" Bree was still smiling, so hopefully he hadn't hurt her feelings.

He shook his head. "You don't want to know."

"Come on, Link." Corinne tugged on his shirtsleeve. "You have to tell us now."

"Mom's not going to like it."

His mother rolled her eyes. "I think I can handle it." She looked around the room, checking, he knew, to be sure none of her grandkids were listening in. "Danae, cover Tyler's ears."

Link cracked up. "It's not *dirty*, Mom."

"Well, just in case. Now come on . . . Give."

"It was a hangover kit."

"What?" the hens chorused.

"How romantic," Corinne said, rolling her eyes and looking a lot like Mom.

"I'm almost afraid to ask," his mother said. "What in the world is a hangover kit?"

"It was just a little baggie with aspirin and mints and"—he shrugged—"I can't remember what else was in it." He waited a beat. "I was too drunk."

Their reaction didn't disappoint. They all squealed like a bunch of banshees.

"Link! You were *not*," his mother huffed. But her expression begged him to reassure her.

He laughed. "You're right, Mom. I was not."

If she could have reached him from the other side of the table, Link was pretty sure she would have smacked him upside the head.

"Like I said. Stupid." He brushed a hand through his hair. "Okay, I played your silly little game, now can I open it?"

They dissolved into giggles again.

"No, you have to guess what's inside." Landyn spoke to him as if he were a two-year-old. "You have your clue now."

He scratched his head.

"You were on the right track with the song," Corinne hinted, sing-songing the rhyme like he'd done.

He humored them, repeating the clues and sing-songing again, but drew a blank. "I give up. You guys are too clever for me."

Landyn grabbed the tin from him and popped open the lid. Candy kisses wrapped in pink and green went flying. The nieces and nephews came scrambling on all fours, as if a piñata had just broken. Then Huckleberry skidded into the scuffle, nosing the floor.

Link grabbed his collar. The crazy dog had already had one unpleasant run-in with chocolate in his life. They didn't need a Thanksgiving run to the vet.

When things quieted down, Link eyed the table of women. "Okay, ladies, can I go now?"

"Go!" They all shooed him off.

But he returned, stepping over nieces and nephews. "Bree?"

She looked up from pasting on another sticker.

He gave her a thumbs up. "Edibles are always good. Let the women figure out the riddle, the men can eat the candy, and everybody will be happy."

"'Preciate it, bro." She gave him the smile he knew had made Tim fall in love with her.

And he couldn't help but think about the smile that had made *him* fall in love. Despite being in this house full of people he loved, there was an empty spot in his heart. He wondered what Shayla was doing today. And whether she was thinking about him the way he couldn't help thinking about her.

There were twice as many cars as usual in the parking lot at the homeless shelter. Shayla parked as close as she could to the entrance and went around to help Portia out of her booster.

"Stay right beside me, baby. I don't want you getting hit by a car."

"I'm a big girl, Shay."

"Yes, you are. But you're not bigger than a car. If one of those cars backed out and hit you, it would squash you flatter than a bug."

"You're funny. Mr. Link's truck didn't squish me flatter 'n a bug."

"I'm not trying to be funny. And his truck sure could have squished you. You just stay beside me." Ever since what had happened that icy day with Link's truck, she lived in fear of Portia running out in front of a car again. The child was fearless. "Stick to me like glue, Portia, because I can't hold your hand. I have to carry the bread in."

She went around to the trunk and stacked up the boxes that had slid en route. Balancing them on one arm, she managed to get the trunk closed.

"I'll need you to push the doorbell button for me, baby. You remember how to do that?" The shelter was usually locked for security purposes when she came, though sometimes on holidays, with so many people coming and going, they relaxed the rules a little.

"I can do it." Portia skipped ahead. "Let me do it."

"Get back here right now! You can push the doorbell, but I need you to stay right beside me. I promise, I'll let you push it."

When they reached the entry portico, Portia stretched to press the button, then looked up at Shayla. "How's come they're not letting us in?"

She laughed. "Give them a chance, honey. It takes more than two seconds to get down the hallway. You remember that long hall don't you?"

"I remember." She suddenly went quiet and Shayla wished she had time to ask what her niece was thinking about. There were usually some interesting characters here, and Shay supposed it could be a little scary for a five-year-old.

Within a minute, the door opened and one of the volunteers, a woman Shayla had seen here before, let them in. Her nametag said *Nadine*, but Shayla knew volunteers sometimes didn't use their real names here.

"I hope I'm not too late with the bread," Shayla said around the stack of white bakery boxes.

"Not at all. Thanks so much for bringing it. Here, let me take a couple of those."

Shayla bent her knees so the volunteer could reach the top boxes. "We brought some pies and other goodies today too."

"I can smell them!" the volunteer said brightly. "Who's your helper here?"

Shayla smiled down at Portia. "This is my niece, Portia." She spelled her name as she always did—and as she remembered her mom always having to do. She'd been a little miffed at Tara for taking Mama's name for her baby. But of course Jerry had just as much right to the name as she did. And though she'd always wanted to name her first daughter after Mama, with all the trouble Portia's name gave them, she had second thoughts about saddling a baby with a name she'd have to spell and pronounce and explain all her life.

She pushed the thoughts aside. It was silly to be ruminating about a choice she wasn't ever going to have to make in her lifetime anyway. Looking down at Portia, standing up so straight and polite beside her, it suddenly struck her that she *had* a little girl named Portia.

"Will you stay and eat with us?" Nadine asked. "You know there's always plenty."

"Not unless you need someone to help serve."

"We have plenty, so it's up to you." Nadine led the way to the kitchen and she put the boxes on the counter where the volunteer indicated. "If you don't mind helping me cut up these cakes and pies before we put them on the buffet, I'd appreciate it."

"Sure, glad to." Shayla shed her coat and laid it, along with her purse, on a chair by the door, then got out her iPad to entertain Portia while she waited.

Another volunteer named Betty came in to help, and the three of them made short work of cutting the desserts and plating them on paper plates. Shayla wished she'd thought to stop and pick up some holiday paper napkins for the shelter. It didn't quite seem like a proper Thanksgiving with flimsy white paper plates and napkins. Never mind that she and Portia were going home to eat grocery store rotisserie chicken—and Cheetos. She smiled, actually relishing the thought. If she simply kept busy, kept her mind off of what she *couldn't* have and dwelled on what she did have, she could forget the ache in her heart that had awakened her this morning—and reminded her in idle moments what she'd chosen to give up. She'd made the right decision. She had to rest in that. And find fulfillment in the life she already had.

The two older women arranged the dessert plates on trays while Shayla sliced the bread and placed it in baskets. She helped the volunteers carry trays into the dining room where the residents milled about, waiting for the meal to be served.

She slid a tray of sliced pie onto the end of the buffet and looked for Portia. She was standing beside Betty, staring at a middle-aged woman who looked like there wasn't a square inch of her exposed body that hadn't been tattooed—and plenty of her body was exposed. *Lord, please don't let Portia say anything rude.*

"Portia? Come here, baby. Stick close. They're trying to get dinner on, so you need to stay out of the way."

"I'm hungry." It was a broad hint, no doubt motivated by the cherry pie that was at eye-level to Portia.

"We'll eat as soon as we get home. Remember we have plans?"

Portia's expression took on a new perkiness. She looked up at Nadine. "I get purple polish."

Nadine gave Shay a questioning look.

"We're having a spa day." She winked. "At home. Just us girls."

"Well now, doesn't that just sound like a treat? You two enjoy yourselves."

"We sure will. If I can—" She felt a tug on her sweater and looked down to see Portia pointing behind Shayla. She stooped to her niece's level, praying she would keep her voice to a whisper.

"It's him, Shay. Look." She pointed.

"Who, baby?"

"That guy."

Portia was pointing toward a cluster of half a dozen men holding paper plates and looking impatient that it was taking so long to get the buffet ready.

"What guy?" She pushed Portia's hair away from her ear and whispered, "Don't point, honey. That's not polite. And I don't see who you're talking about."

"You know"—Portia's voice climbed an octave—"that guy... that dumb teenager from the movies."

"What movie?" She couldn't remember any shows they'd watched recently that had teenagers in them.

"Nooo!" Her volume went up with her frustration. "That one movie Link went to with us. And that one boy with that yellow hair." She pointed again. "That dumb teenager. You know."

"Shush, Portia!" She put a gentle hand over the girl's mouth, but she doubted there was anyone in the room who *hadn't* heard her. Trying not to be too obvious, she scanned the group Portia was pointing to for someone with hair that might make her think of Mohawk.

She'd hoped her niece had forgotten that incident. But she apparently remembered details. Shayla's adrenaline flowed faster just thinking about it. *Picking on a five-year-old?* It didn't get much more cowardly than that.

She held Portia's hand down to keep her from pointing. "I don't see him, honey. Listen, are you ready to go have our girls' day?" She made her voice bright.

But Portia wouldn't be dissuaded. "He's right there, Shay!" She freed her arm from Shayla's hold and pointed again. "See? But he took off his funny hair."

She followed the line of Portia's finger and recognition hit. The guy sported a freshly shaved head now, but she recognized the spiked piercings in his lip and eyebrow.

To her horror, he chose that moment to look her way—and leer. If she hadn't been certain it was him before, she knew now. She would have known that smarmy grin anywhere.

"Told ya, Shay. Told ya it's that same dumb teenager."

"Portia, hush!" Shayla knelt to whisper a stronger warning. And to scan the room for an escape route.

21

The beefy young man turned his stare on Portia and sneered. "Who you calling a dumb teenager?" He took a menacing step toward her.

Portia shrank back, but the boy laughed and quickly retreated, his goal apparently met.

The guys clustered around him laughed.

"Whatsa matter, Billy, you scared of a little kid?" One of his cohorts challenged him like a schoolyard bully.

Billy. So he had a name after all. Shayla drew Portia closer and started edging her way backward.

"I'm not scared of anybody," Billy growled. He lunged at them again, arms out in a juvenile bogeyman pose, never taking his eyes off Portia, who screamed and wrapped her arms around Shayla.

"Leave her alone!" The tremor in Shayla's voice gave her away.

Mohawk—*Billy*—guffawed.

Fury made Shayla forget her fear. She lifted Portia into her arms and took a step toward him. "Can't you see you're scaring her?"

He slapped his cheeks and made a comical face. His minions roared.

She scanned the room frantically for Betty or Nadine. But they'd apparently gone back to the kitchen. Cradling Portia close, she turned and wove her way through the gauntlet of people queued up, waiting for the signal to eat.

"Oh, sure," Billy taunted from across the room. "Leave just when we're starting to have fun."

Shayla kept walking, forcing herself to move at a natural pace—when what she really wanted to do was sprint full out to the parking lot.

Behind her, a low, male voice took command. "What's going on here?"

Shayla was grateful one of the volunteers had come to their aid. But she didn't dare turn around to see.

"Just having a little fun. Some games for the kiddies," Mohawk said behind her, all innocence.

She couldn't dignify the man by even thinking of him by his given name. What a despicable piece of humanity.

"Well, knock it off," the low, cultured voice said. "Is that how you thank the people who feed you and give you a place to come inside and get out of the cold?"

"I don't need your freakin' charity. My truck is nicer than this craphole."

"Fine then." The male volunteer spoke in a barely controlled tone. "If you feel that way, why don't you just go get in your truck and get on out of here?"

She risked turning to look over her shoulder. Mohawk glared at the man, but didn't make a move toward the door.

Shayla sucked in air and hiked Portia higher on her hip. Her purse and coat were still in the kitchen. She needed to get them and get out of here.

Hurrying down the hall, she struggled to catch a breath she hadn't realized she'd been holding.

"Miss?"

The voice came from behind her, but Shayla kept walking.

"Miss? Ma'am?" It was the volunteer who'd confronted Mohawk—a tall, white guy, probably about her dad's age.

She turned, eager to dismiss him. She just wanted to get out of here.

He hurried toward her and, when he was close enough, he put one hand lightly on her arm, the other on Portia's back. Portia buried her face in Shayla's hair.

"I sincerely apologize for that...back there." He hooked a thumb toward the dining room. "That was inexcusable. You shouldn't have to listen to that. Not with everything you guys do for us."

Shayla waved him off. "It's okay. We...we've had run-ins with him before."

"With Billy? Billy Waverton?"

"I don't know his last name. But yeah, him."

"I'm so sorry. I assure you he'll be on his best behavior next time—or there won't be a next time. He can sleep in his truck if he can't show some common decency."

The man reminded her a little of Link. For all the good their well-meaning threats did.

"I need to get my niece home." She nodded toward the kitchen. "We'll just get our coats."

"Of course. And again, I'm sorry you had to listen to that."

She forced a smile. "Have a happy Thanksgiving."

He looked relieved. "You too." He got in close and tickled Portia's chin. "You too, little cutie. What's her name?"

"Portia. I really have to go."

"Of course. I won't keep you." He took a step back. "I'll walk to the kitchen with you and make sure it's unlocked."

"Thank you." She wanted to ask him to walk to the parking lot with her too, but for all she knew he wasn't any more trustworthy than Billy Waverton.

Shayla hurried down the corridor and out to the parking lot toward her car, groping inside her purse for her keys.

"I don't like him." Portia clung tight as ever to her neck.

"I don't like him either, baby. We're just going to forget about him. Let's go home and paint some toes and eat some Cheetos. What do you say?" She forced a smile she didn't feel.

"Purple?"

"Purple Cheetos?"

"No! You're bein' silly."

"You can have whatever color you want, Princess Portia. If you want rainbows and puppy dogs painted on those little tootsies, then that's what we'll paint."

That got a giggle. *Lord, please erase the memories of that monster from this sweet girl's mind.*

She watched over her shoulder while she helped Portia buckle into the backseat. She jogged around and got in, locking her car doors as quickly as possible. She breathed a little sigh of relief. And wondered how she was going to get out of delivering the day-old bread from now on. Because if she never saw that Billy whatever-his-name-was again, it would be too soon.

She drove around the building to the parking lot's entrance, searching the lot for a gray truck that might be his. She'd barely gotten a glimpse of it that day he'd thrown the bottle through the bakery's window. And she wasn't good at makes and models. There were only two pickups in the lot, neither of them gray. She didn't know whether to be glad or worried.

She pulled onto the street in the direction of home. She'd planned to stop at the grocery store for a few treats for their girls' day, but now she just wanted to get home. As quickly as possible.

A light mist had started to fall, hazing the windshield. She switched on the windshield wipers, which only created a murky mess. She turned the wipers on high and pressed the button to squirt washer fluid. Better.

Even though it was only one p.m., most of the cars on the highway had their lights on, so she flipped hers on too. She stretched to check on Portia in the rearview mirror. The little girl's eyelids were at half-mast. Poor thing. It had been a very strange, but hopefully not too memorable Thanksgiving. They could end on a happier note with their girls' day.

The light ahead was yellow, and she tapped the brakes, slowing down well ahead of the intersection. The roads could be slicker in this kind of rain than if it was icy. She came to a full stop, but the pickup coming up behind her looked like it was going too fast to get stopped. She checked traffic around her, prepared to run the light if it looked like that truck was going to hit her.

But it stopped in the nick of time. When the light turned green, she started forward, checking her mirror again. It was hard to tell in the glare of headlights through the misty rain, but it looked like the truck was silver. Or gray. With a faded Confederate flag sticker on the front bumper.

She shivered. She was probably letting her imagination run away with her, but she couldn't seem to shake the foreboding that skittered up her spine.

She went straight through the intersection, praying the truck would turn. But it stayed behind her. She pressed the accelerator, speeding up. The truck did the same. And was gaining.

22

Sitting stiff behind the steering wheel, eyes trained on the image in her rearview mirror, Shayla held her breath. The gray pickup truck was still behind her. Kingshighway was a main road, so maybe it meant nothing that the truck had followed her through the intersection. So had several other vehicles.

But when she turned onto Highway K, the pickup stayed with her, dropping back a ways, only to gain again and tailgate her, then drop back again. With her rear wipers going and the truck's smeared windshield, she couldn't see the driver well enough to tell if it was him. The truck finally settled in about a dozen car lengths behind her. Maybe he wasn't following her at all. Maybe he was just looking for a place to turn around. Or ask directions.

Checking to be sure Portia was still asleep in her booster in the backseat, she slowed the car. Let the jerk pass her and go his merry way.

But he didn't pass. Instead, the truck rode her tail for the next three miles. Not too close. But close enough that she could still make out the Confederate flag on the bumper. *His* bumper.

It was simply too much of a coincidence for it *not* to be Mohawk. But she still couldn't see through the windshield—almost as if the glass was tinted darker than the law allowed.

With one eye on the road and the other on her rearview mirror, she blindly fished her cell phone from her purse. It wouldn't do any good to call her dad. He was more than three hours away.

She considered calling Link. But what could he do? And the Whitman family was in the middle of Thanksgiving dinner.

Besides, she was a little afraid of what Link might do if she told him what was happening. He'd take matters into his own hands or call the police, which could be worse—at least as far as her father was concerned.

She glanced at the clock on her dashboard. With Daddy gone, she wasn't about to drive home and be a sitting duck. Especially not with Portia in the car.

She tried to remember if there was a good place to turn off this road and circle back to Cape. If he followed her then, back into town, she would drive to Walmart or some public place. She'd drive straight to the police station if she had no other options. And sit there and honk her horn.

There weren't any polite words for a man like that. A *kid* like that. He was big—physically—but seeing him today, without the Mohawk—she doubted he was twenty yet.

She checked her rearview mirror again. He'd backed off a little. Maybe he'd grown tired of his little game. Maybe it wasn't even him. She hadn't seen that truck in the parking lot, but he might've had time to beat her out there while she was getting her coat and talking to the volunteer in the hallway.

She glanced back to see Portia still sleeping soundly—thank the Lord. She started watching for a place to turn around. A minivan waited with its blinker on to turn onto K from the north and she thought about stopping and telling whoever it was that she was being followed. But even though the mist had lifted a little, she couldn't tell who was in the car. What if it was a young mom with little kids? Or an elderly couple? She knew she'd be terrified if someone involved her that way.

And if they refused to help her, she'd be a sitting duck—headed off the highway on an unpaved, unfamiliar road—when the pickup caught up with her.

She passed the van and watched in her mirror as it turned east, toward Cape. It took a while for her to spot the pickup once the van passed it. And when she was sure it was the same truck, it seemed like it had dropped back again. She sped up gradually, hoping to put enough distance between them that he'd eventually lose sight of her. Then she could turn off somewhere. Ditch him.

The truck lagged a little more, and she sped up. Gradually. Terrified that if she went too fast, he'd pursue her.

But he didn't. Her speedometer passed sixty, then sixty-five. The speed limit was fifty-five along this stretch. Daddy had taught her never to exceed the speed limit by even a little, but right now, she was more scared of that gray pickup than she was of being stopped for speeding. Which was a lot.

She realized she could no longer make out the bumper sticker or the color of the truck. Was she gaining that much ground? She saw a flash of red on the pavement behind the truck. Brake lights? Then the headlights flashed off, then on. Then off again. Like some kind of Morse code she couldn't decipher. She slowed the slightest bit, not wanting to surrender the distance she'd put between them, but curious what the truck was doing.

It turned into a field entrance. The brake lights flashed bright, then dim, then bright again as the truck did a jerky one-eighty and pointed back toward Cape.

Foot still on the accelerator, Shay let out a shaky breath and checked the mirror one more time. The tail lamps in her rearview mirror grew smaller and dimmer until finally the mist and fog obliterated them.

Her hands stiff from gripping the wheel so tightly, she let go long enough to stretch her fingers out in front of her. They trembled like cottonwood leaves.

Portia still dozed in the back, her neck bent at an uncomfortable angle, her little mouth hanging open, completely oblivious to what had just happened.

Shayla scrambled to decide. She was almost to Langhorne Road. There were no vehicles behind her and she'd only passed two cars on K since she'd lost site of the gray pickup. Did she dare go home? Mohawk obviously knew where the bakery was. But did he know she lived there? Not likely.

It crossed her mind—briefly—to keep driving until she came to the Chicory Inn. Link would be there today. At least she would be safe there. But she simply couldn't barge in on their Thanksgiving like that. Or embarrass Link. It wasn't like she was in immediate danger. At least, not anymore.

Mohawk had merely been toying with her. Getting his jollies by scaring her silly. Well, it'd worked. She hoped he thought it was worth it. She would look up Billy Waverton—probably William?—on Google when she got home. Maybe there'd be something there that would help her decide how dangerous he really was. Her turn was up ahead. She had to decide. *Lord, give me wisdom.*

Almost instinctively, she turned toward Langhorne. Toward home. She and the curly-headed cutie in the backseat had a girls' day date. And she refused to let an idiot skinhead ruin it.

Shayla parked the car behind the bakery, leaving room so her dad could get his car in the garage beside the delivery van when he got home.

Portia woke up as soon as Shayla cut the engine. Portia sat straight up in her booster seat, a huge grin on her face. "Is it time? For girls' day?"

Shayla laughed. "It is! But we have to get in the house first. And remember we're eating our chicken before we polish toes. Got it?"

Shayla heated up the chicken and started potatoes frying, then set the table in the kitchen alcove where there were no windows to the outside.

"Is this breakfast?" Portia wrinkled her nose.

"Chicken for breakfast? I don't think so. What makes you say that?"

" 'Cause this is where we eat breakfast."

"I just thought it would be fun to eat Thanksgiving dinner in here too. Do you have a problem with that?"

"Is it fancy?"

"How about we make it a little fancy?" Anything to not have to explain why she was afraid to sit in the open dining room. She grabbed some colorful cocktail napkins from a cupboard that held leftover catering supplies. "Here—let's fold these fancy." The napkins were more fitting for an Easter brunch, but they'd do. She demonstrated, then left the task to Portia. "Fold enough for our snacks later too."

She cast about the kitchen looking for something else Portia would deem "fancy" and landed on a trio of cornucopia baskets they sometimes used to decorate the tops of the dessert cases. She couldn't remember the last time they'd put them out though. Maybe not since Mama died.

She washed off the dust and filled the baskets with fruit from the refrigerator. Anything special or "stylin'" had always been her mother's department. Shayla had forgotten how Mama had always had flowers on the tables—even if they were just wildflowers she'd gathered from the ditches alongside the road. And tablecloths. Mama had been a stickler for a well-appointed table.

These days it was paper plates more often than not. Watching Portia carefully fold the colorful napkins, Shayla longed for her to have the magic of those special touches. Mama wasn't here to do that for the precious girl. But *she* was. She needed to be more intentional about creating special moments for her niece.

On a whim, she rummaged some plastic daisies out of a basket near the cash register and plopped them into the cornucopias with the fruit. Glancing around the bakery looking for decorations, she realized the whole place could use some sprucing up. If they weren't going to be busy, maybe she would make that her project for the coming weeks.

Surely things would pick up again for Christmas. Thankfully they had the Whitman wedding coming up. But she might need to cancel that third student helper after all. On one hand, she looked forward to the wedding at the Chicory Inn. On the other, it would be awkward, seeing Link after the way things had ended between them.

Had they ended? She was determined they had. And yet things felt so *unfinished* between them. But whose fault was that? He'd tried to call and text her, even sent an e-mail, and she'd ignored them all. But then he'd quit trying. Too soon. That said something, didn't it?

Sighing, she dished up their plates with hunks of the rotisserie chicken, green beans, and fried potatoes, putting sprigs of slightly wilted parsley from the restaurant fridge on each of their plates. Shayla said a simple blessing over their dinner and Portia chattered the entire rest of the meal.

Shayla had planned bubble baths for part of the evening's entertainment, but something about undressing and stepping into the tub after what had happened today . . . She couldn't bring herself to let down her guard, be that vulnerable. She opted to do hair instead of bubble baths.

Three hours later, with beautifully coiffed hair and brightly colored toes and fingers, Shayla snapped selfies to mark the occasion—and to show Daddy later—then settled Portia in the playroom.

"I'm going to clean up the kitchen, and then I'll be down in the nook if you need me. I love you, sweetie."

Portia gave her a funny look.

"What's wrong?" But she knew what was wrong. And it broke her heart. "I don't say that often enough, do I?"

"Say what?" Shayla could have sworn the girl was testing her.

"That I love you."

"It's okay."

"No, baby, it really isn't. I should say that more." She knelt in front of her niece. "You know Big Daddy and I love you like crazy. You know that, right?"

Portia nodded, looking solemn.

Shayla opened her arms wide, and Portia fell into them, giggling.

"I love you too." The words seemed to come so easily for the five-year-old. "You're *my* Shayla."

"Yes, I sure am."

"And I love Big Daddy. And I love my mama in heaven. And I love my other daddy."

Tears welled in Shayla's eyes. She couldn't talk about that right now. Not without breaking down. But if Portia listed her "other daddy" in the list of people she loved, they needed to start addressing that. She'd have to do some research to discover how much a five-year-old could really understand about a daddy in prison. And a mama who'd taken her own life.

She shook off the memories and hopped to her feet. "Okay, kiddo. You have fun playing. I'll be downstairs if you need anything." She grabbed a couple of magazines and the novel she was reading from her bedside table and took them down with her.

As she was finishing up the last of the dishes, Daddy called to say he'd gotten a late start and wouldn't be home until after nine. She wondered how his visit with Jerry had gone. If it was like the last time she'd gone with him to see her brother, they weren't even allowed to eat together. There was a break during the seven-hour visiting period when prisoners went back to eat in the secure dining room like usual. That meant her dad might have eaten alone in a McDonald's somewhere. She hoped Jerry realized that. And apologized.

He could have eaten with you and Portia if you hadn't been so stubborn.

The realization jarred her. She'd only been trying to protect Portia. But no, if she was honest, it wasn't only about Portia. Shayla had her own reasons, her own resentments that had made her refuse to go with Daddy today. So maybe she owed him an apology too.

Seemed she had a lot to learn. And a lot of growing up still to do. Sighing, she took her magazines and curled up on the couch in the corner nook. Settling in, she looked up and at the reflection in the darkened window glass. It had never bothered her before that the windows of the bakery were open to the world on three sides. Besides the street-facing front, the windows looked out over a parking lot and the detached garage in back, and across the alley to a brick wall on the north. They had blinds on the front windows, but had never needed them on the back or north side, thanks to the two-and-a-half story insurance office next door. No one could see in during the day, and at night, the streets of tiny Langhorne were all but empty. But tonight, she looked at her reflection in the black glass and she could only see *his* face.

Shivering, she looked up to the top of the windows wondering if there was a way she could tack up a bedsheet or blanket.

Coffee bags. You could put them on rods with curtain clips.

She remembered the excitement in Bree Whitman's voice that day she and Landyn had come in to talk about the catering for Bree's wedding.

She still had the two coffee sacks she'd planned to give Landyn, and there was another one half empty in the storage room. Mama's sewing machine was in the back of the broom closet. If only she could remember how to thread it. Her mother had usually done that for her.

She ran upstairs for the coffee bags and laid them out on her bed. They still carried a strong coffee smell—which was actually a plus. She ran back downstairs and got a tape measure from the drawer by the cash register. She measured the windows, then ran back upstairs and measured the bags. If she only covered the bottom half of the windows—enough that no one could look in without a tall ladder—three bags would give her enough fabric to cover all the windows in the corner seating nook.

She checked on Portia, then went to empty the third bag of coffee beans into another container. She'd learned from the bags she saved for Landyn that they needed to be shaken out to get rid of stray beans, dust, and burlap fibers.

She had one hand on the back doorknob when a chill rolled up her spine. Given what had just happened at the shelter, maybe it wasn't such a good idea to go outside alone. *Oh, grow up, Shay.*

She'd seen the truck turn around and head back toward Cape. As far as she knew, Mohawk didn't know they lived at the bakery. But it wasn't exactly a secret. Anybody in town could have told him that. But no one knew Daddy wasn't home. And it was Thanksgiving. Surely, even people like that jerk had better things to do on Thanksgiving Day.

She was not going to let fear win. She would not let somebody like Mohawk relegate her to her bedroom for the rest of the winter. But the realization that she also would not feel safe sitting in the nook until those windows were covered—and her excitement about the curtain project—won out. She ran halfway up the stairs and called for Portia.

The patter of little bare feet came, then Portia poked her head around the door. "I'm not Portia. I'm a princess."

"Well, Princess Portia, please come out to the balcony so I can talk to you for a minute."

Her niece stepped onto the landing and struck a pose in her raggedy *Frozen* nightgown, which was heavily accessorized with costume jewelry. "You summoned me, Wicked Stepmother?"

"Hey!" Shayla laughed and struck her most regal pose. "I am not a wicked stepmother! I am Queen Shayla"—she affected a pathetic British accent—"and I have summoned you to tell you that I am stepping outside the castle for a few moments. So should you request my services, that is where I shall be."

Portia broke character long enough to ask, "Where you goin'?"

"Just out back to shake out some coffee sacks. I'm not leaving. I'll be right back. I just didn't want you to worry."

"Okay." She twirled, fully back in character, and pranced back to her room.

Still smiling, Shayla flipped on the outside light and peered through the window in the back door. The parking lot was empty, and the sliding door to the garage where the delivery van was parked was padlocked as Daddy'd left it. He was still waiting on parts. She could get by with her car for smaller deliveries, but she needed that van running before the Whitman wedding. In a little more than two weeks. She made a mental note to remind him. *Nagging*, Daddy would call it. Whatever.

She grabbed the dusty coffee sack and went outside, pulling the door closed behind her. She gave the bag three or four hard shakes, sneezing at the dust that blew back in her face. She peered inside the burlap bag, but it was too dark to tell if she'd gotten all the debris.

As she folded the bag, something rustled out near the garage. She whirled, panic rising in her like steam in a boiling kettle. She stumbled backward toward the house, her gaze constantly scanning the edges of the darkness. Mohawk may have thought he was only playing a game, giving her a scare on the highway, but she wondered if she'd ever feel completely safe again. To go anywhere. Or worse, to be home alone.

She hurried inside and locked the door, checking the locks twice. After checking on Portia again, she hauled out the sewing machine and set it up on one of the tables in the dining room, grateful to see there was already a spool of gold-colored thread ready to go. It wasn't an exact match to the burlap, but close enough. *Thank you, Mama.*

For the next two hours she measured and cut and sewed and measured some more. As she worked, she could almost feel her mother's arms around her. See Mama's white hands upon her dark ones, helping her guide the fabric through the machine, keeping her stitches straight and even.

She'd never missed her mother so deeply, and yet there was profound comfort in performing this task that Mama had taught her so many years ago. Together, they'd hemmed all the dish towels for the bakery, singing and sometimes being silly as they went. Now, Daddy just ordered towels from the restaurant supply where they got their other baking supplies.

She looked down at her hot pink nails and smiled, remembering Portia's delight this afternoon when Shayla had chosen that color for herself. Sometimes it was too easy to forget that Portia would have been Mama's first granddaughter. Mama surely would have taught her to sew too. In fact, Shayla had probably been about Portia's age when Mama first taught her to use the sewing machine. She made a mental note to find some of that fabric her mother had liked so well for dish towels—if they even made it any more.

It had been a day filled with fear, with longing for what she'd lost, but also with sweet discoveries. And even though there was a huge hole in her heart that Link had filled for so brief and sweet a time, it struck her that maybe Link Whitman had come into her life to remind her of what she already had. Of what yet remained. And that was something to be thankful for.

23

The dining room was littered with a few "Black Friday" customers. Mostly, Shayla suspected, college students who hadn't gone home for Thanksgiving break. Right now half a dozen kids had congregated in the seating nook, laughing and talking—several of them international students, judging by the cacophony of unfamiliar languages swirling through the space. Their camaraderie made her a little jealous of the whole college experience she'd missed.

But she had to smile as she made the rounds with coffee refills, then stood behind the counter admiring her handiwork. The new coffee themed curtains gave the place just the right funky vibe. She'd strung the half-curtains on twine, and tied up the edges to give them a little style. The effect was exactly what she'd been going for in the seating nook. She had to think it was one reason the students had gravitated to the cozy, private cave this morning.

There were enough scraps left over that she sewed a couple of throw pillows for the nook as well. They probably wouldn't last a year with all the handling they'd get here, but she could save coffee bags forever and make new pillow covers when they were needed.

While she made the soups for lunch in the kitchen early this morning, Daddy had handled the morning doughnut rush before turning the cash register over to her at eight.

He'd walked right by the seating nook on his way out to work on the delivery van and hadn't said a word about the transformation. She didn't know if it was because he hadn't noticed or if he was still upset with her for not going with him to Bowling Green yesterday.

She'd made a point of being in bed when he got home last night and hadn't said more than to holler goodnight when she heard his footsteps in the hall when he came up.

She checked the trays in the cases, rearranging some of the baked goods to make the cases look tidier. They didn't expect a very big crowd on this holiday weekend, but you never knew. Daddy always baked like it was a normal day. And the shelter was always glad to have the leftovers.

A knot still twisted in her gut whenever she thought about what had happened at the shelter yesterday. And how could she avoid going there again—at least as long as *he* was there? Now that she knew his name, she'd considered calling the shelter before she went, to make sure he wasn't on the premises. Or maybe she'd ask if someone would come out to the car and pick up the boxes of pastries. She'd think of something. Because the thought of seeing *him* again sent a shiver through her.

She'd Googled his name last night but the only thing the search turned up was a 2011 obituary for a woman named Phyllis Waverton with a surviving son named William. The woman had been sixty-two, which made her a little old to have a son the age of Mohawk. But then, maybe people would be saying that about the survivors in her own obit someday.

She knew she should tell Daddy about the incident. But there were so many reasons not to, foremost being it would only remind him that this whole thing had started because Link couldn't leave a taunt unanswered. Link was a subject she wanted—no, *needed*—to put behind her. It was over. She'd made her decision, and as much as it hurt, she was determined to make the best of it.

Sprucing up the bakery had been a start. Her *revelation* about Portia—and about what that child needed from her—had helped her wake up this morning with a renewed determination to make the best of things. To discover little joys in life, even though she'd been denied the things she wanted most. With God's help she would focus on what she did have. On what God had called her to do, by virtue of the fact that those tasks were part of the life she *had*. Not the one she'd dreamed of.

Scuffling on the floor overhead made Shayla pause and listen. Portia must finally be waking up. She was glad there was no school today so her niece could catch up from the late bedtime last night.

The back door opened and she turned to see her dad poke his head through. "Good morning. You doing okay in here?"

"I am, except I hear Portia stirring. Can you watch the counter for a few minutes while I go check on her?"

"I can." He came on inside, shedding his coat. He started to grab a clean apron from the hook, then called back to her. "Would you rather I help the girlie get ready or run the register?"

She studied him. That was a new one. "I'll get her. But . . . thanks."

"Suit yourself." He looped a clean apron over his neck, then tied it behind him. He seemed awfully chipper this morning.

She ran up and nudged Portia, who'd apparently gone back to sleep. "Hey kiddo. Up and at 'em."

Portia rolled over and stretched. The girl was about to outgrow the child-size bed. When had she gotten so big?

Portia stretched again, catching sight of her purple fingernails as she did. A huge smile bloomed on her face. "They're still on!"

Shayla laughed. "Yes, baby. They stay on for days and days—if you don't pick at them and chip them up."

"I won't. Promise."

"Well, if they chip off, we'll put some new polish on."

"Can I have green next time?"

"We'll see. Right now, you need to get your skinny butt out of bed and come down and eat some breakfast before we sell all the doughnuts."

"Huh-uh." Portia looked smug. "Big Daddy always saves me some."

Shayla laughed. "Yes, and I'd like to know how you stay so skinny eating doughnuts every morning." She made sure Portia got her fruits and vegetables, but there *was* always a little paper plate set aside from the morning's first batch. She'd been known to snatch an old-fashioned or a blueberry crumb off of it herself, on occasion, though she was more of a yogurt-and-granola-for-breakfast kind of gal.

She helped Portia get washed up and dressed, and together they went down to the dining room. The college kids had left, and the only customers were two middle-aged women at a table in the front. The usual coffee break crowd likely wouldn't be in today since few were working today, so it might be a quiet one.

"Hey, baby girl." Her dad came from around the counter and held his arms out. "I missed you."

"Big Daddy!" Portia ran for a hug, then launched in to an enthusiastic account of their girls' day. Shayla arrowed up a prayer that the girl wouldn't say anything about seeing Mohawk at the shelter.

Her dad grinned and winked at her over Portia's head. It was more than just a response to Portia's chattering. Something was up. There was . . . a twinkle? . . . in his eye.

Curious, but a little disconcerted too, she grabbed the watering can from the kitchen and filled it, then went to water the plants in the nook.

She sensed someone behind her and turned to find her father watching her. "Do you need something?"

He looked past her, and his surprised expression told her he'd noticed her curtains for the first time. "What's going on here?"

She felt suddenly shy. And also wondered how she could explain why she'd been so eager to cover those windows when they'd never talked about the possibility. She couldn't even tell him where she'd gotten the idea, since it'd come from Link's sister-in-law. "What do you think?"

He studied it for a minute too long, his expression serious. She braced herself.

"Those are coffee bags?"

She nodded, more riding on his response than she realized. "I heard they did that at an upscale coffee shop in St. Louis so"—she shrugged—"I thought I'd try it."

"Well, this is no upscale coffee shop, but it does class the place up a little." He pointed to the sofa. "You make them pillows too?"

"Uh-huh, with leftover scraps."

He looked at her like maybe he was seeing her for the first time in a while. "You get that from your mama, you know. That creative streak. You have a lot of your mama in you."

Nothing her father had ever said to her meant as much as that handful of words.

Her father looked around the bakery. The two women at the front table were still deep in conversation, but otherwise the dining room was empty. Daddy lowered his voice. "I have something I want to tell you." He steered Portia toward the kitchen. "Portia, baby, you go get you a doughnut from the box on the table in the alcove. Sit in there to eat it. And don't make a mess. I mopped in there already."

Now Shayla was dying of curiosity.

When Portia disappeared behind the counter, her dad looked down at her. "I know you don't have much use for your brother right now, but I want you to keep an open mind."

She sighed. Was this about her and Portia going with him to see Jerry next time? "What is it?"

"I come away yesterday feeling a new hope in my heart. You know my prayer group has been praying up a storm. And I wasn't seeing anything happen for it. But yesterday. Yesterday there was just something different. I sensed it the minute your brother walked into that room. Something in his eyes."

Shayla tilted her head. "Something in his eyes?" Was that sparkle she'd seen in Daddy's eyes this morning a reflection of what he'd seen in Jerry's?

Daddy's grin turned to a full-on beam. "My boy's been going to a Bible study. There at the prison. He's still struggling. He needs our prayers, Shay. But this is the first time I've felt a bit of hope—a good bit—walking out of that place."

She didn't know what to think. It was almost a joke that prisoners found Jesus. Sure they did. Maybe it was a way to sway a parole board—though given the severity of his drug charges, Jerry wasn't up for parole any time soon. Maybe "religion" was just something to pass the time. She didn't know. But if the sparkle, or whatever it was, was like Daddy's, it was the real deal. She couldn't let herself hope too much. But maybe it was a start.

"I'm not going to bug you about it, Shay, I promise. But I'd like you to pray...just pray that God will show you if maybe it would be good—for our Jerry's sake—if you came with me next time." He held up a hand. "I'm not talking about Portia. We made a decision, you and me. And it was the right one. At least for now. But Jerry...he asks about you. He misses his sissy. It'd be real nice if you could go. Sometime."

She closed her eyes briefly. "I'll pray about it. I really will."

He put a hand on her forearm and squeezed gently. "I know you will."

Shayla almost hated the grain of hope her father's news had planted inside her. But even more, she hated the very first thought that came to her: She wished she could talk it over with Link. Hear his insight and wisdom on the topic.

But maybe God wanted her to figure this one out on her own.

24

All set?" Grant paced nervously in the fellowship hall of Langhorne Community Christian.

"Set as I'll ever be in a tie." Link tugged at the noose around his neck and plotted how soon he might be able to escape the thing.

He guessed it could be worse. Bree could have asked them to wear tuxes. He pointed at his father's chest. "Come here, Pops. You're crooked." He slid the knot of his dad's tie up and straightened it, then took a step back to check. "Better."

Link glanced through the wide doorway to the floor-to-ceiling windows out in the foyer. Bree hadn't gotten the "dusting of snow" she'd hoped for on her wedding day, but recent rains had left the landscape washed clean, and now the sun shone in a deep blue sky—as nice a day as mid-December days came in Missouri. But the church was decked out in Christmas greenery and white lights. Rented English-style lampposts and a full dozen Christmas trees aglow in twinkling lights flanked the entrance to the sanctuary. Link and the brothers-in-law had set up the trees and strung the lights last night after the rehearsal dinner. A miserable job, but he had to admit it was worth it. The effect was a little like walking through the wardrobe into Narnia—well, minus the snow.

Link spotted his mom through the branches of a pine tree and went to see if she knew what they were supposed to be doing next—and why on earth they'd had to get here an hour before the wedding was supposed to start. "You clean up nice," he said, leaning in for a quick one-armed hug. Mom did look especially nice today. She'd done something to her hair. Highlights or whatever it was called. "So, how soon can we get out of these monkey suits?"

"Not anytime soon." She looked askance at him. "You're worse than the grandkids. Austin's having a meltdown about his bow-tie"—she pointed down the hall toward the Sunday school class-rooms—"and Dallas wasn't having much luck getting him calmed down last I checked."

"Can't say I blame the boy. But isn't he the ring bearer?"

Mom nodded her head. "That was the plan."

"Speaking of plans, what's next?"

"We're supposed to do family pictures in about ten minutes. Bree and Drew are having their big reveal moment right now."

"Big reveal?" He frowned. "Are we supposed to be there?"

"No, silly. It's just the two of them. So he can see her in her gown before we take pictures."

He shrugged. "Hey, I don't know this stuff."

That made her laugh. But it also made him ask, "How are *you* holding up, Mom?" He put his arm around her again, knowing this wasn't an easy day for her, with Tim's memory coloring everything.

"I'm okay. I really am." She didn't quite meet his eyes. "I'm happy for Bree. And Drew is—" Her voice broke.

"I know. He's a good guy." He pulled his mom closer. "They're going to be really good together."

"Yes, they are." Mom took a deep breath and gave a faint laugh as she fanned a hand in front of her face. "Now quit being so sweet. You're messing up my mascara."

He grinned and gave a little salute. "Yes, ma'am."

She looked over his shoulder to the front entrance. "You haven't seen any of Corinne's crew, have you?"

"No. You want me to give her a call?"

"Not yet. I'm sure they'll be here soon." Mom glanced at the clock in the foyer. "You sure you're okay with slipping out early?"

"I'm sure." He'd volunteered to leave the ceremony a little early and go unlock the inn so the caterers—aka Shayla—could set up for the reception there. He told himself he wasn't making an excuse to see her or force her to see him. Though that *had* crossed his mind. But seeing her again would be a lot less awkward if they weren't surrounded by a houseful of wedding guests—not to mention his entire family.

It'd been almost three weeks since they'd last talked. It felt more like forever to him.

"The house is locked," his mother reminded him. "You have your key?"

He patted his pocket. "I've got it. And if I don't, I'll just crawl in through a window like any self-respecting burglar."

"I'm going to see if I can help with Austin." She started down the hall, ignoring his joke.

It seemed to be all the rage—ignoring him.

He went back to the fellowship hall to see if anyone else was here. Weddings were crazy. Why anyone wanted to get all dressed up in the world's most uncomfortable clothes for twenty minutes of pomp and circumstance, he'd never understand.

If he wasn't so apprehensive about seeing Shayla again, he'd have been glad for the privilege of being designated official gofer. And he'd already decided a perk of the job was getting out of this tie a half hour earlier than everyone else.

Mom beckoned from halfway down the hall and he gathered his dad and the others who'd drifted in. He felt for the poor photographer, trying to wrangle the entire Whitman crew—twenty of them, including Bree in her wedding gown, and Drew, who wasn't even officially one of them yet. But they managed to get a couple of shots the photographer assured them could be edited so that all eyes were open, all tongues inside mouths, and all princess pink petticoats under wraps. He made the mistake of picturing himself in the groom's spot and made a quick note-to-self: *elope*.

Drew tried to kiss his pretty bride-to-be before they headed off to their separate dressing rooms, but she pressed a manicured hand over his mouth. "Uh-uh! Not until we're married."

The nieces and nephews tittered and whispered about kissing, and Mom, along with Bree's mother—serving as co-wedding planners—herded the little ones to their appropriate places.

An hour later, Drew collected on that promised kiss, following a ceremony that Link had to admit was very touching—not a dry eye in the house, including his. He wondered if Tim was witnessing it all—from heaven's balcony, as CeeCee liked to say. And if so, how he felt about it.

As the pastor presented Mr. and Mrs. Drew Brooks to the guests, Link slipped from his pew and out a side door, loosening his tie the minute he hit the foyer.

He drove to the inn, his nerves growing more on edge by the mile. The Coffee's On catering van and another car were already parked in the driveway when he pulled in. He waved and got out of his truck, holding up his keys.

Shayla waited in the driver's seat of the van and rolled down her window as he approached. She looked as beautiful as he remembered, her hair wild and curly the way he liked it. She looked good even in her simple uniform of crisp white shirt and black pants.

"Hi." He hoped his eyes conveyed how much he'd missed her, how good it was to see her again. But she wasn't alone in the van. He looked past her and gave a quick wave to the college-age kid riding shotgun.

"You guys are going to want to park around back and come in through the garage doors. Why don't you go ahead and drive on around"—he pointed—"and I'll go through the house and let you in. Everything should be set up and ready to go inside. I can help you carry everything."

Shayla shook her head. "You don't need to do that. I brought help."

"That's what she pays us the big bucks for," the good-looking black kid in the passenger seat said.

Link gave the guy a thumbs-up and winked at Shayla.

"Oh. Sorry," she said. "This is Derrick. Derrick, Link. And that's Valerie in the back."

"Glad you're here, man. Thanks for coming." Link gave a short wave and jogged to the front door of the inn. He unlocked it, leaving the door open behind him. He walked through the house to go unlock the back door.

The inn had been transformed, thanks to Mom and his sisters, along with Bree's mother. Bree's parents, who lived in Rogersville, had been guests at the inn since Thursday night, and the entire weekend had been a flurry of showers, the rehearsal dinner, and now the wedding and reception. And this was a "tiny" wedding, according to Bree. Eloping was looking better all the time.

If he was ever lucky enough to have that decision in front of him.

He shook off the thought and opened the back door where Shayla and her crew stood at the ready, arms loaded with boxes and bags.

"Can I help?" he asked, hoping for a chance to talk with Shayla alone.

She couldn't seem to look him in the eye. "Thanks, but we have a system."

"Okay. I'll just stay out of your way then. Let me know if there's anything you need." He showed her where they could hang their coats.

A plump redhead got out of the car, and she and the guy followed Shayla's lead, setting up drinks and laying out the boxes, apparently in a certain order.

Plates and napkins were arranged just so on the counters, and every surface had been cleared, awaiting the light supper and dessert—including wedding cake—that Coffee's On was providing. Flowers in soft pastel colors sat on every table and as centerpieces on the serving tables. Link wasn't sure where they were going to fit the people. Of the seventy-five guests Drew and Bree had invited, almost sixty of them had RSVP'd that they were coming.

"The inn looks beautiful," Shayla said, still not quite meeting his gaze. "A lot different than last time I was here."

He chuckled. "Brace yourself. All those same kids will be here in half an hour." *Except Portia.* He'd missed that little squirt almost as much as he'd missed Shay. Almost.

He wondered if she was thinking the same thoughts, feeling the same emotions he was. But she laughed and went on setting things up for the reception. He wanted to ask about Portia, but now didn't seem the right time.

While Shayla and her crew of two made numerous trips to and from the delivery van, Link found a butane lighter and went around the house lighting the tapers and votive candles tucked anywhere one would fit.

"The candles look pretty," she said coming in with a stack of boxes.

"Let me know if you see one I missed. I promised my mom they would all be flickering when the guests arrived." He checked his phone. "You sure you don't need any help? People should be getting here in about twenty minutes."

"We're right on schedule." She looked past him to the redhead. "How's that coffee coming, Valerie? Did you get that carafe for the decaf?"

The girl gave Shayla a thumbs up. "I've got it."

Link shook his head. "How can you be so cool, calm, and collected?"

"It's all an act. I'm like a duck. You can't see it, but I'm paddling like crazy under the water."

He smiled. "Well, you make it look like a piece of cake."

One corner of her mouth—her lovely mouth—lifted. "No pun intended, right?" She removed a heart-shaped cake from a box, as if to make her point.

He laughed. "It really wasn't intended. But good one, if I do say so myself."

Now it was her turn to laugh. "If you were serious about your offer to help, you could take these cake boxes back out to the van for me. I want to keep them clean, in case we need them for leftovers later, but they can go on one of the shelves in the back of the van for now."

"Got it." He took them from her and headed outside through the garage.

He tucked the boxes away where she'd told him, and closed the door. Hearing a scuffle behind him, he turned to see Huckleberry dashing for the open garage, a streak of chocolate brown. The Lab was supposed to be locked in Dad's work shed for the day. At least until all the guests were inside. How had Huck escaped?

Valerie came out, leaving the door into the house open.

"Hey, you'd better close that or—"

Too late. In a flash, Huck was inside, barking at the strangers on his turf.

Link made a beeline for the kitchen. "Huckleberry Whitman! Get back here right now. Heel, boy!"

Huck obeyed like always: by doing the exact opposite of what he was told.

The Lab headed toward the front door, his legs—and tail—going ninety miles a minute. Link tried to catch up to him, but four legs always beat two.

Huck let out a bark headed back to the kitchen. Link followed, then heard a crash—and Shayla screaming.

Link rounded the corner in time to see the cake hit the floor. Thankfully still right-side up, but the shock and despair in Shay's eyes were reminiscent of the day he'd almost hit Portia with his truck.

Link froze, trying to decide whether to go for Shayla, Huck, or the cake. He decided taking Huckleberry out of the equation made the most sense. He dispatched Huck to the front porch, then hurried back inside to find Shayla kneeling on the floor, staring wide-eyed at the cake.

"Thank goodness it was only a little one."

Her breath left in a rush. "A little one? Only a little one? Are you insane?" She grasped both sides of her head with her hands.

"Link, it's the top of the wedding cake! It's the one most important thing I had in that delivery van! And now it's ruined!"

He squatted down to inspect the damage. Except for some nicks in the frosting, it was mostly intact. An idea struck. "Hang on. I'll be right back."

He ran to the pantry and rummaged among the utensils. He returned to Shayla, holding up his dad's biggest grilling spatula.

"What are you doing?" Shayla looked at him like he was certifiable.

He knelt beside her and slipped the edge of the spatula beneath the cake.

"Oh." Shayla winced. "What if—"

"Trust me." He centered the cake on the spatula and rose slowly to his feet. Carrying it ever so slowly to the counter, he became aware of Shayla's catering duo looking on.

He could feel Shayla following inches behind him. "You're not doing what I think you're doing?"

He grinned. "Mom always says her floors are clean enough to eat off of. So . . ."

"You're not serious."

"As a heart attack. You have a better idea?"

She looked at the rescued cake. "I guess it's really not *that* bad. And your mom does keep a clean house."

"See? No harm done." He bent to inspect the cake and picked off what could have been a dog hair. "Good as new."

Shayla turned to Derrick and Valerie and wagged a finger between them. "So help me, you two, if I *ever* hear so much as a *hint* of this story going around town, I will hunt you down and you *will* pay."

Convulsing with laughter, the two gave a smart salute and hurried back to finish setting up the buffet tables in the dining room.

Link tried to keep a straight face but couldn't contain a little snort.

Shayla glared at him. "That goes double for you, mister." But the twinkle in her eyes revealed the chuckle she was holding in herself. She carefully lifted the cake onto the stack she'd already assembled, then gave him a sideways glance. "Okay. This is what I'm going to do. And you aren't to breathe a word of it."

"Pinkie swear." He held out a pinkie.

Which she promptly ignored and continued to assemble the cake. "Here's the thing." She pointed to the dropped cake. "This is called the anniversary cake. Traditionally, it's taken off and set aside before the cake is cut at the reception. A lot of couples freeze it and eat it on their first anniversary. Or sometimes after they get back from their honeymoon."

"Okay. And you're telling me this fascinating history because...?" Despite having lived through three sisters' weddings, he'd learned more about the hallowed sacrament of marriage today than he had the entire rest of his life put together.

"I'm telling you this because what I'm going to do after the cake is cut, is put this cake in a box like I always do. Then I will take this cake home, I will toss it in the trash, and I will make a new anniversary cake, which you"—she thumped his chest with her index finger—"will somehow sneak into Drew and Bree's freezer while they're on their honeymoon."

"Oh, I see what you did there. Clever."

"I'm not kidding, Link. Nothing like this has ever happened to me! I'm just sick about it."

"Shay, I guarantee you, my family would find this hilarious. Nobody would care one bit that—"

She stopped frosting, palette knife in hand. "You're not going to tell them? Please, Link. You can't tell *anyone*."

"It'll be our little secret. I promise. But it's not like it was your fault. It was the dumb dog."

"You're right. It was." She stood back and inspected the cake.

Link swiped a dollop of frosting off her palette knife and licked his finger. "Mmm. That's good stuff." He paused, frowned, and pretended to pick a dog hair off his tongue.

She gave a little growl and swatted his arm. "That's not even funny."

But it was. And they both cracked up. He looked at her, only then realizing how much he'd truly missed her. Whatever was yet to happen between them—or wasn't—it was a relief that they'd found their way back to the easy friendship they'd known.

Although, he doubted he could *ever* look at her as merely a friend.

Link heard the front and back doors open at the same time, and through the front windows, he could see a caravan of vehicles streaming up the drive. "In the nick of time. Here they come."

Shayla wiped a microscopic smudge of frosting off the cake stand and untied her apron. "Derrick? Valerie? You guys ready?"

Her crew appeared under the archway between rooms and stood at attention.

"Looks like you have everything under control here," Link said. "I'll go put that dog back in the shed."

Shayla nodded, then winked. "You do that. And while you're at it, the three of you keep that *cat* in the bag."

25

Audrey wove her way through the dwindling crowd of wedding guests and sought out the one face in the crowd that made her heart beat faster. Still, after almost forty years.

Grant stood at the fireplace, a cup of coffee in hand—fully leaded, no doubt. The man would be up all night. But he was in his element this evening, helping her host sweet Bree's wedding reception, and getting to show off his masterpiece, which was this house.

She wished her grandparents could see what the house had become. How much love it held. How well their children were all doing. Audrey didn't for a moment take for granted that they'd been so blessed to have their kids all stay so close to home for all these years.

Grant was always reminding her to hold these blessings with an open hand. And just last week, Landyn had hinted that she and Chase might be moving back to New York. Much as Audrey wanted to pray they would stay right here, she didn't dare. If not for their first apartments in New York, Chase and Landyn might not be raising their sweet twins together. And Audrey held a secret only Grant knew. And of course Chase. Landyn was expecting again. Due in July. Oh, she would have her hands full. But so did a lot of mommies—including her, once upon a time.

She still had her hands full. But now with grandbabies and an ailing—but beloved—mother-in-law. And with the guests this inn brought into their lives each week. She'd allowed it all to get her down too often. But with this wedding behind them—and so much ahead—she was determined to figure out what it would take to scale back a little and make her life manageable. But she would take one day, one moment at a time, and see what God had for her in that moment, and that moment alone.

Grant caught her eye across the room and motioned for her to meet him in the foyer. After weaving his way through a tangle of grandkids and assorted lingering guests, he put an arm around her and kissed her cheek. "I'd say it all came off pretty well, don't you think?"

"It did. Everything was about as perfect as it could be. And oh, they looked so happy."

"They are. Drew loves that girl like crazy."

Audrey looked past him into the kitchen where Link was talking to Shayla. She nudged Grant. "Speaking of loving a girl like crazy..."

"I know. He's got it bad, doesn't he? Do you think they're on again?"

She shrugged. "I don't know. It looks pretty mutual. She's a sweet girl. Did you get to talk to her much?"

"Not much. But I've always thought that... that she was sweet. Just from the bakery. I have half a mind to go have a word with Mike Michaels."

"Ooh, Grant. I'm not sure you should do that. You know how much trouble I got in when I tried to set Link up that one time."

"I'm not trying to get him to turn over a dowry or anything. I just think it might be good for two dads to have a heart-to-heart."

"Would you tell Link first?"

"I don't know. Let me pray about it. I won't do anything stupid."

She reached up to pat his cheek. "I know you won't. I trust you."

He watched the two lovebirds in the kitchen. "I've never seen our son that... besotted. Reminds me of when I met you."

Audrey looked up into eyes that held only love. She could read every nuance of his thoughts and knew no words were needed.

"Thanks, Derrick." Shayla handed him the last box to be loaded in the delivery van. "Couldn't have done it without you guys tonight. Thanks."

"Thank *you* for the extra hours," Valerie said.

"You're sure you don't mind giving Derrick a lift?"

"Not at all. I go right by the dorms to get to my apartment."

"Okay. Thanks." Shayla had been watching the two of them tonight, and she had a sneaking suspicion they were flirting with each other. Or maybe she was just confusing it with all the flirting she and Link had done.

Most of the guests had gone home, and the honeymooners had been sent off with rice and bubbles and balloons an hour ago. But the rest of the Whitman family was gathered in the front room, ties loosened, shoes off, with lots of love flowing through the house.

She sighed. It made her sad. And it made her happy. If Mama were still living, this is what their house would be like. On a smaller scale, yes. But she could so easily picture Mama and Daddy relaxing in stocking feet in the sitting room above the bakery—before it had become Portia's room. Jerry and Tara would be on the floor playing with Portia, and—the next image tugged at Shay's already-tender heartstrings—she would be curled up on the love seat, maybe pregnant with her first baby, a handsome husband at her side. And try as she might, she couldn't picture anyone in that role but Link Whitman.

They'd found their way back to each other so easily. Like these past three weeks had never happened. Like all the crazy issues they faced had evaporated. But it couldn't really be that easy, could it?

Landyn came around the corner carrying a stack of wedding gifts. "Shayla, you're still here? Good grief, woman, go home. You've worked your tail off!" She set the gifts on the end of the island, picked up a dish towel, and started drying one of the serving trays Shayla had washed.

"You don't need to do that. I'm almost finished."

"I don't mind. I've hardly gotten to say a word to you anyway. Everything was perfect, Shayla. Thank you so much. I'm sure Bree will get in touch with you when they get back, but she was so pleased. Everyone was."

"I'm so glad." Shayla dipped her head, but she felt like cheering, despite a twinge of guilt over the near-fiasco with the cake. It was one thing to cater a corporate luncheon or a company picnic, but there was a lot riding on a once-in-a-lifetime wedding. "I'm really glad you're happy with the way things went. And hey, I've been meaning to tell you that I haven't forgotten about saving those coffee bags for you—if you're still interested."

"Oh, I definitely am. I'll stop by sometime next week."

"Um, you might want to give me a couple weeks. I took your and Bree's advice and made curtains from the ones I'd set back for you." Shay cringed. "Sorry. But they turned out really cute."

"Oh, no problem." Landyn waved her off. "I'm in no huge rush." She tilted her head, studying Shayla. "Your hair is so cute like that. I wonder if I could get my crazy curls to do that?"

She laughed, remembering what Link had said about his sisters wishing they had each others' hair. She picked at a bouncy curl falling over her forehead. "I can try to straighten it all I want, but it pretty much has a mind of its own."

Landyn rolled her eyes. "Tell me about it. Since the twins, I usually default to the messy ponytail. At least it's supposedly back in style."

"I hear you. I'm just thankful I can wear a scarf at work. Best 'do ever."

Eyes wide, Landyn snapped her fingers, laughing. "Scarves! Hey, maybe you could hook me up with a couple of those!"

"I'll get you fixed up next time you come in, girl. Just ask for Shayla."

Landyn smiled. "You'll laugh when I really do come in and order a dozen scarves instead of scones." She dried her hands and picked up the gift boxes again. "I'd better get these loaded. Thanks again for everything. See you soon."

She breezed out of the room and Shayla laughed. This had to be a first: a hair discussion where she could commiserate with a white girl.

"You need any help in here?" Link poked his head around the corner. "What's so funny?"

She hadn't realized she was still smiling. She waved him off. "Nothing. And thanks, but Derrick and Valerie got me all loaded. I just want to finish cleaning up the kitchen." She picked up the dish towel Landyn had been using as if she owed him proof.

He came closer. "The place looks great, Shay. You don't have to leave it spotless." He motioned back toward the front room. "It's about time to roll out the snacks, so it's just going to get messed up again."

"I'm almost done." Truth was, she didn't want to leave. She had a nice little fantasy going on in her head, and she wanted to languish in it for a while.

"You did a great job today... tonight. I heard lots of compliments about the food, the presentation... everything. Especially that cake." He gave an exaggerated wink.

She smiled. "That's one for the books, for sure." She gave a little gasp. "And by books, I mean the top-secret, locked-away, never-to-be-read-aloud kind of books."

"I promised, and I'm as good as my word."

Yes, you are, Link Whitman. You're a good man, and your word is the same. "I'll let you know when the anniversary cake is ready. You're sure you don't mind sneaking the right one into their freezer?"

"I consider it my sworn duty on behalf of my crazy dog. And speaking of that cake, where's the damaged goods? Don't you dare throw it out. The top part never touched the floor. We can slice off the bottom and—"

She plopped her hands on her hips, dish towel still in hand. "And just how are you going to explain why you're *eating* the anniversary cake?"

"Oh. Hadn't thought that far ahead yet."

She rolled her eyes. "And that's exactly what scares me." She folded the towel and laid it back on the counter. "Well, I guess I'd better get out of here."

He put a hand on her forearm. "Hey, I wanted to ask . . . How's Portia? I kind of miss Her Prissy Little Highness."

Shayla laughed. "She's spunky as ever. She's all about polishing toes and fingernails these days."

He shook his head. "I think my sisters had to be twenty-two before Dad allowed that."

"Yeah, well, I might spoil her just a little. I *am* making her wait till twenty-two for her first tattoo." She wondered if Link would remember telling her how much his dad hated tats.

His laughter said he did. When it faded, an awkward few seconds passed as he seemed to be grasping for something else to say. "So . . . things are going okay at the bakery?"

She loved the spark his blue eyes held. "Actually business has picked up a little."

"That's good."

"Well, maybe. It's mostly college kids, and Daddy's afraid they'll scare off the regulars."

"Uh-oh."

"Yeah, I know. But hey, those kids order four-dollar lattes instead of ninety-nine cent free-refill black coffee, so I don't see the problem."

He laughed.

She wanted to stay. Listen to that laughter, listen to him talk all night. But what purpose would that serve? It would only send her back to square one with trying to get over him. She looked at the floor. "I really need to go, Link."

"Oh. Okay. I'll walk you out. Hang on, and I'll get your coat."

"Thank you, but I'm fine. You go be with your family. I've stolen you away for too long tonight."

"Well, let me follow you to the door at least and turn on some lights."

He helped her with her coat, then flipped a couple of switches that lit up the driveway.

"Goodnight." She opened the door and walked outside, a cold wind hitting her in the face and a heaviness in her heart that she feared would never go away.

"Shay—"

She turned back to see him standing in the doorway. *So handsome. So... fine.* "Yes?"

"It was really good to see you again. Will you tell Portia hello for me?"

She couldn't honestly assure him she would. Portia had asked about Link—whined to see him—almost daily over the past three weeks. Shayla didn't want to stir that pot, only to have to wean the girl off of him all over again. She sighed, too loud, and tried to cover it with a smile. "It was good to see you too, Link. Goodnight."

She had to get out of here before she said something she'd regret. Before she asked the questions that were eating her alive: "Why did you quit calling? Why didn't you pursue me harder?"

She hurried to the van, searching for her keys, eager to be home—and very aware of Link still watching her from where he stood in the doorway. She climbed in and buckled up, enjoying that satisfied feeling of a job well done. While also being glad it *was* done.

She slipped the key into the ignition and waved to Link as he closed the back door, then smiled to herself as the image of that silly anniversary cake going *splat* on the floor returned. Thank the good Lord Link had come up with a way to salvage—

She turned the key again. Nothing.

No! No... not now! Please, God, let this stupid *van start.*

She tried a third time. But the engine didn't even attempt to turn over. Daddy had said it was fixed. And it ran fine all the way out here. *Why* was this happening?

She tried turning the headlights off and on. She tried pumping the gas pedal. She'd learned a lot of tricks over the years they'd owned this temperamental vehicle. But none of them were working now. Including prayer.

Finally, she grabbed her phone and started to dial her dad to come and get her. It was late. He'd have to wake Portia and bring her with him—and waking Portia in the middle of her night was never a pretty proposition.

But before the call could go through, she realized—she'd parked, at Link's insistence, directly in front of the garage. To make it easier to load the delivery van. She couldn't just leave the van here. She'd need to have it towed. Tonight. Or at least roll it out of the way so the Whitmans could get their vehicles out tomorrow.

She growled with frustration. This was beyond embarrassing—and such an inconvenience to Link's family when they were trying to celebrate a wedding. She dialed her dad. Maybe he could at least tell her what was wrong with this bucket of rusty bolts. Maybe there was some new trick he knew since his latest repairs to get it running—at least long enough to get her home.

He answered on the first ring. "Hey, baby. Everything okay?"

"No! This stupid van won't start."

"You're kidding. It was running fine this morning."

"Well it's not now. It won't even turn over."

"Did you try giving it some gas while you hold the key?"

"I tried everything that ever worked before, Daddy. I've got lights, but nothing happens when I turn the key."

"That makes no sense. It was running fine." He blew a frustrated sigh into the phone. "I'll have to get the girlie up, but I'll be there as soon as I can."

She pictured her father pulling into the inn's driveway, likely causing the entire Whitman family to come out and see what was wrong—not to mention Daddy and Link face to face again. And Portia no doubt howling in her booster seat.

Another image came. Link, under the hood of his pickup out at the pond, that night his truck wouldn't start. "You know what, Daddy? Don't wake Portia just yet. I know one more thing to try. I'll call you right back."

Steeling herself, she climbed out of the van and picked her way around to the front door in the dark. She rang the bell and the door opened almost immediately.

Link's mother stood there, smiling, no doubt with the remains of some family joke that had just been told. "Shayla! Come in. Is everything okay?"

Before she could answer, Audrey called over her shoulder. "Link? Come here, honey."

Audrey held the door wider. "Come in out of the cold."

Link appeared, saving her from having to face the whole family. "Hey." His smile held concern—and curiosity. "What's up?"

Audrey slipped away, perhaps thinking this was something personal. She wouldn't blame Link if he thought it was just a ploy to talk to him a while longer. "I'm so sorry to bother you, but the van won't start."

He chuckled, then stopped abruptly. "Sorry. I promise I'm not laughing at your troubles. Just remembering when the shoe was on *my* foot. Let me grab my coat and we'll take a look. Come on through and we can go out the back way."

A rush of laughter from the inn's front room made her hesitate. "I don't want to intrude. I'll just meet you around by the van, okay?"

"Suit yourself." He bent to look out past her. "Can you see okay out here? Let me turn some more lights on." He flipped a couple of switches and the spots at the side of the house lit up.

"I can see fine. Thanks." She followed the sidewalk around to the back where her van sat like a giant, unbudging elephant in front of the garage.

Link came out of the house carrying a flashlight and met her at the driver's door. "Is there a hood latch inside?"

"I don't think so. I'm pretty sure this was one of Henry Ford's originals."

Laughing, he held up the flashlight. "If you'll aim this for me, I'll see if I can get the hood open." He tinkered with the latch.

She concentrated on pointing the light where he was working, hoping this was a quick fix so she could get out of here.

He fumbled some more, squatting down to peer beneath the lip of the hood. "Man, there must be some secret to this I'm not getting. You're sure there's not a latch inside?"

Link went around to the driver's side and groped blindly beneath the dashboard. "Let's see what we've got here."

The longer he worked, the worse she felt for taking him away from his family on this night they were supposed to be celebrating together. "Link, I'm so sorry. I called my dad to come and get me, but then I realized if we left the van here overnight no one would be able to get out of your parents' garage in the morning and—" Her voice wavered with embarrassment.

He regarded her in the dark, but she quickly let the flashlight dangle, and turned her face away so he wouldn't see how close to tears she was.

He paused and held up a hand. "Hey. It's okay. I don't mind at all. I truly don't, Shay."

The kindness in his voice, the way he said her name, broke the dam. The tears came, silently, but in a flood. She turned away, trying to keep holding the flashlight and wipe her cheeks dry at the same time.

"Hey." An arm encircled her, and she let him pull her closer, her back against his chest. She imagined she could feel the beating of his heart, even through the heavy layers of their coats. His warm breath brushed her ear with tender words. "Please don't cry. We can fix this."

Oh, if only they *could* fix it. Fix everything that had gone wrong between them. But that was just it. Everything was right between *them*. It was the rest of the world that had issues. And she was afraid, so afraid, they were beyond repair.

26

It destroyed Link to see Shayla's tears, and he suspected they were for so much more than a "bag of rusty bolts" that wouldn't start. And yet, he had to admit he was glad for an excuse to hold her. To feel the familiar warmth of her body pressed against his. To feel her hair tickle his cheek. To breathe in the familiar scent of her perfume.

He missed everything about her. Her voice, her laughter, the feel of her hand in his. Missed her more than he'd even realized until tonight.

And he realized something else. Losing Shayla was more than a mere "breakup" with a girlfriend. It felt so much bigger than that. Like a defeat in a battle they'd been forced to fight against their wills, simply because of the color of their skin.

They'd done nothing wrong, yet they'd let a messed-up world tear them apart. To make them rivals. And it made him question if things could ever be better. If the wall dividing them—and so many others—could ever really be torn down.

Before he'd met Shayla, he'd often thought the solution to this great divide was merely a matter of time. Let one more generation pass away, and with that passing, their ignorant, hateful, prejudiced ways would disappear. But it seemed those hateful ways lived on in yet a new generation, in jerks like Mohawk. And if nothing changed, men like Mohawk would teach their children to hate and belittle and kill. And they would teach their children, and so it would go.

But it had never been so personal before. Until now, that wall had never kept him from someone he loved. *For no good reason.*

He thought of Portia, and his heart ached for the world she was growing up in. There had to be a better way. There had to be answers.

Shayla stirred against him, cradled in the crook of his arm. "I'm okay. I'm sorry." She pulled away.

But he drew her back, leaning against the van. "There's nothing to be sorry for." But he *was* sorry. For so much.

She looked up at him over her shoulder, her face only inches from his. Her lips . . .

He turned her in his arms and took her face in his hands. Brushed a mass of those beautiful ringlets off her cheek. "I've missed you so much," he whispered. And he did what he'd been wanting to do all night. He bent and pressed his lips to hers, savoring the softness of her skin beneath his fingers, the taste of her.

She kissed him back, as if she'd been wanting the same thing he had the whole evening long.

Yet, a moment later, she pushed away from him. "Link . . . No . . . I can't." She took a stumbling step backward. "Please. I'm sorry if I—" But just as quickly, she was back in his arms of her own will, kissing him, cradling his head, drawing him even closer, if that were possible.

Now it was him who needed to take a step back. Gently, but firmly, he put some space between them, still gripping the sleeves of her coat, not willing to let her go. Yet knowing he must. "I'm sorry if . . . if that was too soon." Catching his breath, he offered a smile, hoping it conveyed even half of what was in his heart. "But I'm not sorry I kissed you."

She looked up at him, her expression serious. But he thought he detected that spark in her eyes that he loved so.

Her shoulders slumped. "Great. Now I'll *never* get over you." The sarcasm was thick in her voice, but a soft smile bathed her face in light, and held a very different tone.

And Link felt as if he'd just won the lottery.

He turned away now, went back to work on the latch as if nothing had happened. But very aware of her watching him as he worked, he couldn't quit thinking how she'd felt in his arms. How it'd felt to kiss her.

The latch finally gave way and he lifted the hood. "Okay, let's see what we've got."

She shined the light over his shoulder.

"Oh, I think I see what's wrong. It looks like one of the battery cables came loose." He tugged gently on the cable and the connection came completely apart. "I don't know how that could have happened. If it was that loose, it surely would have jiggled off before you got too far down the road."

"You've got to be kidding!" She looked horror-stricken. "If that had happened on the way to set up the reception . . . I can't even imagine!" She looked at the sky. "Thank you, Lord."

He couldn't help but laugh. "Let me go get something to clean this connection. I think I can fix it—at least long enough to get you home."

"All I know is Daddy came as close to cussing as I've ever heard, trying to figure out what was wrong with it. But I don't know what he fixed exactly."

"I have a feeling this will do it. Be right back." He jogged to the garage and came back with a wire brush. He cleaned off the connectors and the terminal, neither of which appeared to be corroded. But it was hard to tell in the dim light of the flashlight Shayla held.

When he was finished, he hooked the cable back to the battery and climbed in behind the wheel to try it out.

The van sputtered, but the engine caught and started on the first try.

Shayla let out a little whoop. "My hero," she said when he came around to close the hood.

"Ask your dad, but you probably ought to let the car run for a while after you get home. Make sure the battery is good and charged before you turn it off."

"Okay. Thank you so much, Link."

They stood facing each other in front of the purring van. There was nothing to keep her here now. And nothing to bring her back.

Feeling a sort of desperation, he reached for her again, cradling her face between his hands and kissing her softly, briefly. She didn't resist. "I meant what I said, Shay. I'm not sorry."

"I know. Neither am I."

"I don't want this to be it. I don't want *us* to be over. Why . . . why didn't you answer my calls?"

"Why did you quit calling?"

"That's not fair." But he was the one being unfair. He was stalling. Because he wasn't sure of the answer to her question. And after tonight, he wished he could turn back time. Do things differently.

She breathed out a long sigh and closed her eyes. But she shook her head. "I need to go, Link." Without waiting for a response, she climbed into the van and backed out.

He stood in the driveway watching until her taillights disappeared into the night.

"Is everything okay?" His mom looked up from the sink as soon as he stepped into the kitchen.

His eyes adjusted to the light while he tried to shake off the emotions of what had just happened with Shay. "Yeah. Her car just wouldn't start. I got it running."

"Oh, good. She's a sweet girl." His mom studied him, fishing, he knew, for details.

But even if he'd been in the mood to offer any, he had nothing. He didn't know if he'd ever see Shayla Michaels again. Unless he pursued her. And she'd probably had enough of stalkers for a while.

"You need any help here?"

"No, I was just getting ready to set some sandwich stuff out. You hungry?"

"Maybe." He wasn't, not really. But Mom was never happy if she couldn't offer to fill someone's belly. "You need some help?"

A burst of laughter came from the front room. His mom smiled. "No, you go on. Go hang out with the family. I'll let you know when the spread is on."

"If you're sure."

He stepped into the front room to another outburst of laughter. It made him smile just to hear it, even though he didn't have a clue what they were talking about. He sat listening, trying to catch up on the conversation before diving in like usual.

Panning the room, it struck him that everyone had someone. Corinne and Jesse sat with their two littlest girls between them. Danae sat on Dallas's lap, and Chase and Landyn cuddled on the loveseat. Bree and Drew were on their honeymoon. Even Dad had headed in to help Mom in the kitchen. It was hard to be in this house when his heart was in a van, driving away from here.

He sat on a folding chair, fending off the nieces and nephews' pleas to come play with them. Trying—and failing—to get into the lively discussion.

Half an hour crawled by and—much as he loved his family—he'd had enough of the noise and commotion. He just wanted to be alone, needed time to think about everything that had happened. To think about how good it had been to see Shayla again today. And how hard it was to let her go. Maybe he could call her under the guise of making sure she got home okay.

Of course, she'd see through that in a heartbeat. Her dad was expecting her, and she knew that. There was no reason for him to call. Except that he was in love with the woman. Wasn't that enough? Why did he have to have a guise?

He waited until the noisy crew was involved in another conversation before he slipped out to the kitchen. Dad had his head in the fridge, while his Mom sliced something on the cutting board. Apparently an onion judging by the tears.

He couldn't help but think of Shay's tears of embarrassment and frustration this evening. And his wanting to comfort her. He shook off the thought and went to give his mom a quick hug. "Hey, don't cry," he teased. "I'll be back."

Mom laughed. "I always cry at weddings. Wait. You're leaving?"

"Yeah, I think I'm going to head home. I've had about all the festivities I can take for one day."

"Are you sure, honey? You don't want to eat something first? It's almost ready."

Dad popped out of the refrigerator. "There's leftovers out the wazoo in here. Why don't you fix a plate to take home."

"Yeah, I might take a sandwich or something, if that's okay."

"Of course. But, you're sure you don't want to stay? Everything's okay?" He hated that too-familiar worried look her eyes held. Especially knowing it was on his account.

"I'm fine. Just tired." He sighed. He didn't have the energy to convince her he was okay. Especially when he wasn't sure whether he really was.

He built a sandwich from the fixings they'd laid out and wrapped it in a paper towel. "Are we on for Tuesday night this week?"

"We are." Mom rinsed her hands under the gooseneck faucet. "But don't be disappointed if supper is this same spread."

"Looks good to me." He gave a little wave. "Okay, I'm outta here. See you Tuesday. Love you guys."

"You too, bud," they said in unison behind him.

His throat constricted. He'd never really thought what it would be like to lose one of his parents the way Shay had. But he could imagine how losing Mom might change his father. And vice versa. He hadn't shown enough empathy for Shayla's situation, not to mention the way things had snowballed with Jerry and Portia's mother, and then taking the little girl on.

He had to ask himself if he was truly aware of what it meant to love Shayla Michaels. For the long haul.

Outside, the wind had picked up, and the temperature had dropped. Link buttoned his jacket as he walked to his truck. At least he didn't have to work tomorrow. He just might skip church and sleep in. After all, he'd been to church already today. He hoped God saw the humor in his little joke. Shayla would have.

He started the truck, grateful it hadn't stalled out on him since that night out at the pond with Shayla. As he backed around and headed out the driveway, his cell chirped in his pocket. He braked at the end of the drive and pulled out his phone.

The name that displayed in the Caller ID window lifted his spirits: Coffee's On.

He couldn't keep the smile from his voice as he answered. "Hello?"

"Is this Link Whitman?"

"Yes. This is Link."

"This is Mike Michaels. Shayla's dad." His voice sounded gruffer than usual.

Link hesitated. "Hi, Mr. Michaels. How are you?" How had Michaels gotten his phone number?

"Is Shayla still there? She said she was having trouble getting the van started, but she never got back to me. I was kind of expecting her home by now."

His concern edged up a notch. "She's not home yet?"

"No. Like I said, her van wouldn't start. She was out at the inn where the wedding reception was. At least I thought that's where she was when she called."

"Yes. I mean, she was here. And we got it started. But she left here"—he glanced at the clock on the dash—"close to an hour ago now."

"Okay. Well, she must have had to take one of her crew home. Sorry to bother you."

"No. Wait, Mr. Michaels. Valerie took Derrick home. Shayla was going straight home as far as I know. She should have been there long before now."

"Well, she's not. And she's not answering her phone."

"That doesn't sound right. I hope she didn't get stranded again."

"How'd she get the car running again anyway?"

"One of the battery cables was loose. We connected it again and the van started right—"

"Loose? Why would the cables be loose? I put those on myself, and there's no way they coulda come loose."

"I saw it myself." He hadn't meant for that to come out sounding like an argument. "I mean, I'm the one who opened the hood. The cable was just barely hanging on. Not even connected really. I thought maybe it was corroded so I—"

"No. It *wasn't* corroded. I cleaned those cables and the terminals myself not three days ago. They were in good condition. *Good* condition. Somebody must've messed with them."

Link wasn't sure if Michaels was accusing *him* or just making an observation. But if what he said was true, then that was about the only conclusion that made sense. Somebody *had* messed with the van.

"You said she's not answering her phone?" Link's grip tightened on the steering wheel.

"No. I've been trying for the last half hour at least."

"I don't like the sound of that. I was just leaving the inn. I'll head that way and watch for her. See if maybe she had more trouble."

"Okay, I'll head your direction from here. Call me if you find her."

"Of course. You'll do the same?"

Michaels grunted and hung up.

Link's mind kept taking him to a place he did not want to go. Why would that cable have been disconnected? He wanted to think it was a prank. Maybe Derrick and Valerie were just messing with Shay. But they wouldn't have left her stranded. They would have stuck around to see her reaction.

He'd seen a group of teenagers—wedding guests—hanging out by the garage during the reception. But they'd been too busy flirting with each other to vandalize the caterer's van. Besides, they were good kids. Friends of Dallas and Drew.

And somehow Link knew it was neither of those.

And if it wasn't... *Oh, dear God. Please, no...*

Link dialed Shayla's father again. He answered on the first ring.

"Mr. Michaels, we need to go find her. We need to find her *now*."

27

Link drove as close to the speed limit as he could and still search the ditches. He drove in a zigzag with his headlights aimed first on one side of the road, then the other. Less than twelve minutes out, he saw headlights approaching. Shayla's father, no doubt.

If Mike Michaels reamed him out for not following Shayla home, for not insisting that she let him know when she'd arrived safely, Link couldn't blame him.

He *should* have followed her. He should have taken her home himself and worried about the van tomorrow. What if he hadn't gotten the cable connected right, and it'd slipped loose again?

It chilled him to realize that, at this point, that was the best news he could hope for.

But it seemed almost impossible that cable could have come undone, given the way it was connected. Still, how had it happened the first time? It almost had to be deliberate. But why would anyone—

His breath caught, remembering how the door to the shed had been open when he'd gone to put Huck back inside after the cake incident. Dad would never have left it unlatched, especially on a day like today.

He pulled over to the side of the road, and the oncoming vehicle—a smaller Toyota—did the same on the opposite side. Link realized he didn't know what kind of car Shayla's father drove. He'd only ever seen him in the delivery van.

He breathed a sigh of relief when it was Michaels who got out of the car.

Link jogged across the road and shook hands with him.

"You didn't see her?" Her dad's voice held a world of worry.

"No. Nothing." Spotting Portia awake in her booster seat in the back, Link leaned in through the open driver's door. "Hey, sweetie. You're up awfully late, aren't you?"

She shook her head, watching him with wide eyes. "No. Big Daddy said I'm up early."

He grinned. "Well, Big Daddy is right. But if you want to sleep a little longer, you can just lay your head down there, okay?"

She put a thumb in her mouth and listed to one side. He'd never seen her suck her thumb before, and it tugged at his heart. He didn't know what Michaels had told her, but it seemed Portia knew something was up. *Oh, God, please don't make us have to break this little girl's heart.*

Michaels shook his head, staring into the distance as if he might see Shayla's car off somewhere. "It makes no sense that we wouldn't have come upon her if she broke down."

"She didn't ever take a different way home?"

Michaels gave him a look. "You know well as I do, there *is* no different way." He pulled out his phone and pressed a button. Seconds later, he grimaced and returned the cell to his pocket. "Straight to voice mail. I'm going to drive the route between here and there one more time. Just in case we missed something. I've been checking the roadsides and ditches, but some of 'em are too dense to see."

Too dense, and too far down. "Yeah. Me too." Link scuffed his shoe on the pavement, eager to get going. "You want to meet back here in about ten, fifteen minutes."

"Okay. You have my cell number?"

"Not your cell." He pulled out his phone and input Michaels's cell number.

Michaels shook his head. "I don't like the way this is looking."

Link heard the discouragement and frustration in his voice. If they didn't find Shay soon, he was going to call 9-1-1. He didn't care what her father said.

He hopped in his truck and eased back onto the roadway, but as his headlights shot across to the opposite ditch, a flash of light caught his eye. He maneuvered the truck to position the lights where they'd catch the reflection again.

There! Something shiny lay among the gravel lining the road. He tooted his horn, trying to catch Michaels before he got too far down the road.

The Toyota's brake lights flashed, and Michaels backed up to where Link was parked. Link grabbed a flashlight from his glove compartment and climbed out.

Michaels got out of his car. A vehicle was coming from the opposite direction, and he waited for it to pass before crossing the road.

Link pointed to where the rays from his headlights shone. "See that?"

He led the way to where he'd seen the light turn the gravel to glitter. Their breaths hovered and mingled in the cold night air.

"Is Portia okay? She won't be scared?"

"She fell back asleep."

Link prayed she'd stay that way. The glimmer in the gravel caught his eye again.

Michaels saw it too and ran ahead, squatted down to inspect it. "Look at this." He held up a shard of red plastic.

"From a taillight?"

"Looks like it. Or a driveway reflector."

But there were no driveways nearby.

Michaels studied the jagged piece. "One of Shay's taillights was busted. I don't know if this is the same type. But I never got around to fixing it. I should've."

"You think it might have fallen out while she was driving?"

"I don't know why it would. It wasn't jagged. Just cracked."

"Where's the rest of it?" Link knew Mike Michaels had to be thinking the same thing he was. And it wasn't good. But neither of them mentioned Mohawk—as if they could keep the worst from being true if they didn't talk about it.

Michaels shook his head, then rose. He walked back and forth, kicking at the gravel, hoping, Link knew, to find another clue.

Link dialed Shayla's phone again. And again, it rang three times and went to voice mail. "I don't like this at all. I think we need to call the police, Mr. Michaels. Or my dad knows the sheriff. He's a good guy. Are you okay with calling him?"

"Yes." For once, he didn't hesitate. "Something ain't right. I just know it. We need help."

"I'm going to drive up to the next crossroad, drive down some of these side roads and see if maybe she took a wrong turn or something." There were no wrong turns to take. But Michaels didn't argue with him.

Link started to get in his truck, then turned back to Shay's dad. "Listen, let me call my parents to come and get Portia. She can sleep at their house so you can help me search."

"I don't want to interfere—"

"She'll be in good hands with them. Two of us can cover more territory."

"All right. Call them. I'll wait here until they can come and get her. If they can."

"They will. Don't worry."

Link called his dad and explained what was going on.

"You go find her," his dad said. "I'll get the sheriff out there. And Mom and I will come and get Portia. We're praying, son."

"Thanks, Dad." Link relayed the message to Michaels. "Do you mind staying here until my Dad arrives? He can wait and tell the sheriff what's going on. Unless Sheriff Peterson beats him here."

"I'll stay." Michaels pointed back toward his car. "I don't want to be driving on any back roads with her this late."

"I understand." Link understood what the man *wasn't* saying.

They agreed Link would take the east-west roads and Shay's father would start traveling the north-south crossroads, covering a four-mile grid—not that Southeast Missouri had anything resembling a square grid, but they'd cover as much territory as possible this way.

"I'll call you if I find anything at all." Link gave the man's shoulder an awkward clap.

"You do that. I'll let you know when your parents get here and I get started. You call me when you find her. *When*, son. I don't want any other answer."

"Yes, sir. We'll find her."

"And Link?"

"Yes sir?"

"Pray. Pray like you've never prayed before."

He tried to smile—and failed. "I'm already on it." He climbed in the truck and revved the engine, backing around as quickly as he could, trying to think how Shayla might have been thinking if she'd had car trouble. Or if she'd run into some kind of trouble. *Please, Lord…*

He never thought he'd pray that it was only his lousy mechanical skills that had caused her trouble. But it didn't make sense that she wouldn't be on this road. It didn't make sense at all.

Link drove with the radio off and the heater on. Still, he felt chilled to the bone. The night had suddenly turned ominous, every tree sporting claws, every shadow a demon. His eyes started playing tricks on him, seeing light where there was none, and turning every wisp of steam rising off the creeks into smoke.

Michaels called him less than ten minutes out. "Your dad let the authorities know what's going on, then he and your mom took Portia back with them."

"Good."

"I'm gonna head south a mile, then backtrack. You seeing anything out there? Anything at all?"

"Not yet. I'll call you when I do."

They exchanged location information and Link drove on. They talked twice more, about three minutes apart. Three of the longest minutes of Link's life.

He and Michaels should converge about a mile up the road. He slowed down, now watching the side roads for Michaels, as well as scouring the ditches for Shay.

His phone chirped again. "Yes?"

"I found the van!" Michaels sounded out of breath. "It's not good, Link. You need to get here. We need an ambulance."

His blood ran cold. "How bad is she hurt?"

"I don't see her yet, Link. I can't get to the car, but if she's in there, it's serious."

"Where are you?" He leaned over the steering wheel panning the horizon. Trying to get his bearings.

"I think I see your headlights through the trees. Come on about a half mile east on Pritchell Trail."

"On my way." His gut sank. He punched the accelerator, no longer needing to check the ditches. He dialed 9-1-1 and told the dispatcher to send an ambulance. He could only approximate the location, but surely they'd see the lights from their vehicles out here. Hopefully the sheriff would arrive about the same time.

Link saw Michaels's vehicle in the road and slowed. He wasn't inside the car. Link scanned the pitch black horizon, listening. But the man was nowhere in sight.

"Michaels?" he called out.

Then he saw it—a hazy glow below road level. Way below. He looked over the side of the embankment into a deep ravine. Two beams of light shot into the woods at odd angles, eerily illuminating the lower foot of pines and poplars. A hushed, steady hiss rose up from the ravine. He hoped it was nothing more than the radiator leaking coolant.

Still, if Shayla was in there, they had to get her out. "Shayla! Mike?"

He stopped to listen, then hollered again. "Shayla! Michaels? You down there?" He shined the flashlight into the ravine. He wasn't sure how he was going to get down into it in the dark when he needed both hands to climb. He hoped Shay's father hadn't fallen. He yelled for him again. "Mike?"

Nothing. What was going on?

28

Shayla!" Link shouted into the night, inching his way down the steep embankment, the flashlight mostly worthless since he'd threaded it through a belt loop to free his hands.

"Michaels?" It was muddy and slick in the freezing December temps and his breath formed a cloud in front of his face. Shayla had to be freezing.

"Link? You down there?" The voice came from above him.

Michaels. Link turned, grappling for something to hang on to. "You on the road still?"

"Over here!"

Link turned toward the voice. He could barely make out Michaels's silhouette in the dark.

"I don't think I can get down there." Michaels's breath came hard. "You don't need two of us hurt. I'll direct the ambulance. Get her out of there!"

Link slid down a few more feet, praying he didn't fall.

"Wait! Wait, Link! Come back! She's here!" Michaels was struggling to breathe.

What? He scrambled back up the incline and jogged to where Michaels stood, pointing.

Link saw her then, stumbling along the edge of the road. He took off running.

"Shayla! Shay!" She didn't seem to hear him at first, looking dazed. But when she saw him she started running toward him. Or trying to. She was limping badly and gasping for air.

The second he reached her, she crumpled against him. He held her upright. "She's okay!" he shouted to Michaels. He didn't know that, but she was alive, and he knew the man needed to hear it.

"Shayla? Are you okay?" He took a step back, trying to assess her injuries.

Her face was covered with blood, and she was favoring her left leg—foot?—severely. He thought she was in shock. "Shayla? Are you okay? Talk to me."

"It was him!" Her voice shook. "Link, it was him!"

"Do you mean that guy? Mohawk?"

She nodded, trembling violently. "His name is Billy Waverton."

"What? How do you know that? What happened?"

She started crying, hysterical sobs that wracked her entire body.

"You're in shock, Shay. We need to get you to the hospital." Where was the ambulance?

"Shay? Baby?" Michaels reached them and helped Link hold Shayla up. She slumped against her father much as she had on the day he'd almost run over Portia.

"Can you hold her while I get my truck?"

Michaels nodded. "I've got her."

"It was him, Daddy! It was him!"

Link explained what she'd said earlier and about her calling the guy Billy Waverton.

"What do you mean? You know who did this? Did he hurt you, baby?" Anger grew in Michaels's voice.

She gulped in air. "He hit me. The van, I mean. He just kept ramming me! I couldn't get away from him." She paused as if trying to process what had happened. "He cut me off on the highway. I couldn't get around him. I couldn't do anything but turn off. But the road was so narrow and he just kept ramming me again and again."

Link felt sick, thinking of that monster playing with her like a cat with a mouse—right before it kills.

Shayla fell quiet, the effort of living through it all again in the retelling apparently taking its toll. Link looked around, watching for the EMS crews, not seeing the strobing lights he so desperately wanted to see. He watched the edges of the darkness too, wondering if Waverton might be watching from a distance, taking some sick satisfaction in the damage he'd inflicted.

Michaels held up a hand, cocking his head to listen.

Link stilled too. The distant wail of sirens sent a rush of relief through him.

"The ambulance is on the way, Shay." He pushed the hair off her face, and aimed the flashlight, trying to determine the extent of her injuries. "Hang in there a few more minutes, okay?" The blood was already congealing around the wounds he could see. They didn't appear to be deep, but there was a lot of blood.

"Here." Her dad moved closer, pressed a handkerchief to her forehead. "It's gonna be okay, baby. You hear that? The ambulance is on the way."

The sirens grew louder and they could see the lights getting closer. Shay held her head. "I'm sorry… I'm so sorry. I should have told you. I should have said something."

Michaels pulled her closer. "What's wrong, baby? What are you talking about?" He gave Link a look that said he thought maybe she was delirious.

Link wondered the same thing. He moved to her other side and bent to look into her eyes. Check her pupils. It was likely she had a concussion judging by the wounds on her head. "Shay? What happened? What did you need to tell us?"

"He followed me."

"We know, baby. But he's gone now. You're going to be all right." Mike looked at Link again, and shook his head, looking beyond worried.

"No. I don't mean tonight. On Thanksgiving. He followed me… from the shelter. He was just—" She closed her eyes and leaned harder against Link.

He braced his knees and tightened his arm around her, feeling a new wave of gratitude that they'd found her, and she was going to be okay.

"You rest now, baby. You can tell us when you're ready."

"No." Her eyes opened, and she seemed to be more alert. "He was just toying with me that day. I don't know why, but he backed off. He never did anything. But this time...He ran me off the road. Is the van okay?"

"Don't you worry about the van." Michaels looked at Link over her head. "You're the one I'm worried about. Hey, look, the ambulance is here now. Let's get you checked over." Michaels strode to where the EMS vehicle was parking.

"No. I'm fine." She reached out as if to stop him. "Link? I'm fine. I don't need an ambulance."

"Shay." He worked to keep his tone calm. "Just let them look you over here, okay? Then you can decide. After we know what's going on with you."

That seemed to quiet her, and she let the paramedics assist her onto a gurney and tend to her wounds. Link and Shay's father stood close enough that she could see them but far enough away to not interfere.

When the techs were finished, one of them came over to Shay's father. "She's refusing transport. It doesn't appear she has any broken bones or internal injuries—and we can't take her if she doesn't want to go—but you might want to have her checked over tomorrow. Just to be sure. And watch her through the night."

Link listened in as the tech told Michaels what to watch for. "If she's up to it, the sheriff's en route. Since it sounds like a case of stalking and aggression, they're going to want to take a statement."

"You think she's up to it?" Michaels asked the paramedic.

"As long as they keep it short. Probably easier to do it here than to have to go in later."

Michaels nodded. "If it was your daughter—would you make her go to the ER?"

He shrugged. "It's always best to be on the safe side. But she's pretty adamant about not going."

"Link, can you talk some sense into her?"

"I'll try, sir. But you, of all people, know how stubborn she is."

That got a smile from the man. "Give it your best shot."

Sheriff Peterson stepped from his SUV, leaving the emergency lights flashing. "Sorry to keep you waiting folks, but we've got some good news for you. We have our suspect in custody."

"That was quick," Link hadn't meant it to sound so doubtful.

Michaels glared at him. "Is his name Billy Waverton?"

"Yes, sir. One of my deputies found the suspect sitting in a thicket, shaking in his boots." He sneered, an undercurrent of sarcasm in his tone. "Says he didn't mean for her to get hurt."

Michaels straightened like he was ready for a fight. "He sure has a funny way of showing it."

Saying nothing, the sheriff offered a parting nod, then went to speak with Shayla. Link and Michaels followed him, standing a short distance away.

Link strained to listen over the squawking of the police radios and the rescue vehicles' idling engines.

Sheriff Peterson was gentle, if professional, with Shay, having her repeat everything she'd already told them. She included the encounter at the theater. And more details—things she hadn't told anyone else—came out as she recounted the altercation at the homeless shelter on Thanksgiving Day.

Link shook his head. How could she have kept that in all this time? She must have been terrified. And that night could easily have ended the same as this one. Or worse.

Shayla bowed her head. "I should have said something. I should have told you, Daddy. I'm sorry." She turned her gaze on Link. "I'm so sorry."

He moved close enough to put a reassuring hand on her shoulder, but backed away again when the sheriff cleared his throat.

"Is there anything else you can remember?" Peterson looked stern. "We'll need names of any witnesses who saw what happened at the shelter." He turned to Link. "I assume you'll be willing to testify about the altercation at the theater?"

"Of course."

The sheriff told Shayla, "If we can prove he was stalking you over a period of time, it will help our case. But I think you've got a solid one. Felony charges some of them. We've got this thug on harassment, vandalism, aggravated stalking, assault with a deadly weapon . . ." He counted the offenses off on his fingers. "And that's just for starters. I think we've got enough to put him away long enough to maybe do some good."

Peterson turned to Shayla's father. "I'm gonna let you get your daughter home. I think we've all had enough for one night. But I'll need some information from you, sir, so we can arrange to get your van towed. The deputies are down there now, looking for evidence, and securing your personal effects. I hate to say it, but from what little I could see, I don't think you're going to be driving that van any time soon."

29

Link, can I have a bandage on my head?"

Moving his hand from the light switch he'd been about to turn off, Link went back to Portia's bed. "You mean like Shayla's bandage?"

She nodded, looking solemn.

"You don't want a bandage, honey. That means you have an owie."

"But Shay's not cryin'."

"No, not now. But she cried tonight, when it happened."

They'd told Portia only that Shayla had been in a car accident. But she'd seen her aunt's bandages, which were pretty impressive.

Shay's dad had insisted she go to the ER in Cape. They'd waited three hours to be seen, but were back now, at two a.m., and Shay seemed to quickly be returning to her old self.

While she and Mike were at the ER, Link had gone to get Portia from his parents'—who seemed reluctant to let her go. Apparently the girl hadn't slept a minute but had kept them entertained until the wee hours of morning. Dad was still chuckling when he'd walked Link and Portia to the door of the inn.

Link tucked the blankets around Portia's shoulders—for the third time. "That's enough talking for one night. You go to sleep now."

She yawned as if she couldn't help but obey.

"And will you do me a big favor?"

"What?" she whispered, matching his tone.

"Will you play really quietly in the morning so Shay can sleep?" He had a feeling Portia would be zonked until noon too, but you never knew about this girl.

"Big Daddy said it was church tomorrow."

"Oh, you're right. It is. Well, you might be going to late service."

"What's late service?"

He laughed. "No more questions tonight. Go to sleep."

He chucked her under the chin and quickly turned out the light before she could stall any longer.

He went past Shayla's room and paused at her door. But he resisted the temptation to bother her again, since he'd already told her goodnight when they'd returned from the ER.

He went downstairs to the bakery, expecting to let himself out, but Shay's dad was still up, sitting at a table with a cup of coffee—decaf, Link hoped. Michaels looked up at him.

Link risked putting a hand on the man's shoulder. "She still doing okay?"

He nodded. "For all she's been through, I'd say yes. I know you must be tired, but she wanted you to step in again for a minute before you go. Do you mind?"

"Of course not. I'll go up now." He was glad for permission.

Michaels scraped his chair back. "And I think I'll call it a night. The door should lock behind you. Check it though. Please."

Link climbed the stairs again—his second time tonight, which had given him his first glimpse of where Shayla lived. Her door was halfway ajar, but he knocked lightly before stepping into her room.

"Hey, you. You still awake?"

"Hi." She smiled and started to sit up in the bed.

"Don't get up." He went to kneel beside her bed. In the dim light from the hallway and a tiny nightlight near the floor, her complexion appeared a worrisome gray. But with the cuts on her forehead bandaged, and the blood cleaned up, she didn't look so battered. He found her hand atop the covers. "How're you doing?"

"I'm a little afraid to close my eyes."

"Don't be afraid. You're safe now." He squeezed her hand. "You're safe."

"Stay with me for a while?" she whispered.

He nodded, and prayed he was telling her the truth.

Shayla opened her eyes to see Link sitting on the edge of her bed. "You're still here?" Was she dreaming? She reached to touch his arm. No, he was the real deal.

He laughed. "You've been asleep for about three minutes. Don't give out any Florence Nightingale awards yet."

She swatted weakly at him. "Go home. It's late. You don't have to stay."

"I *want* to stay. At least for a few minutes or until your dad kicks me out." He looked behind him as if he expected to see Daddy standing in the doorway.

"Did they get him? Billy Waverton? Did they get him for sure?"

Link looked puzzled. "You didn't hear the sheriff say they did?"

"I thought I did, but I just want to be sure. My head was pretty mixed up."

"They have him, Shay. He's in jail. The sheriff said even if somebody tried to post bail, they'd be watching him like a hawk. And given his homeless shelter address, I don't think anybody is going to spring him. Besides, half the law enforcement in the county is going to be driving by here every half hour making sure you're okay, and the other half is watching every road that leads here."

She knew he was exaggerating, but she loved him for it.

"Sheriff Peterson told my dad if he has anything to say about it, Billy Waverton will be punished to the fullest extent of the law."

She hoped that was true. But she suspected Daddy would be skeptical.

She closed her eyes, her mind a whirl of images. She wondered if they'd gotten her purse out of the van. And her phone. Would any of the catering equipment be salvageable? And—Oh! A little giggle escaped.

"What?" Link studied her like she might be having a breakdown.

"I just thought of something." She giggled harder.

"What's so funny?"

"We have our cover story now," she whispered.

He looked askance at her. "Cover story?"

"The cake. It was in the van. Bree and Drew's cake. We'll have to break the news to them. But I'm sure that cake was completely destroyed."

Her meaning dawned on him, and they dissolved into laughter.

"Shh! We'll wake Portia," Link said, his shoulders still shaking.

"Oh!" She gave a little gasp and tried to sit up. "Where is Portia?" Her head pounded and she winced. "She's here, right? Everything's such a blur."

"Portia's fine. She's in bed, Shay. I tucked her in myself, just a few minutes ago. *Shh.*" He put a hand under her head and leaned across her to plump her pillow before easing her head back onto the bed. He smelled like wood smoke and pine, and she breathed him in.

"Where was she? While you were looking for me?"

"Your dad woke her up and brought her with him. But my parents met him out on the highway and took her back to the inn while we searched."

"Oh, Link." She winced again, but from humiliation. "I've ruined this whole night for your family."

"Stop it. They were glad to do it. And apparently she was quite the little entertainer while she was there."

"Oh, no." She closed her eyes. "I don't even want to know what she might have said. Oh, Link..."

He laughed, and she took comfort in the sound. "I'm so sorry."

He patted her hand. "Shh. Enough of that. None of this is your fault. It's all on him. Your dad is fairly certain they'll discover Waverton is the one who loosened the battery cable."

She shivered, thinking of that monster out there at the Whitmans' while she worked, oblivious, inside. "But can they prove that? And why would he do that? If he wanted to get me on the road, why would he try to disable my vehicle? That makes no sense."

"You expect a man like that to make sense?" He shook his head. "It was about revenge. He made you his target and he wasn't going to rest until he felt like he had the upper hand."

"Well, he has it."

Link frowned. "No, he doesn't, Shay. He hasn't won. He's caught. And he's going to pay for what he did."

She didn't argue with him but instead closed her eyes. When she opened them again, Link was still there.

He smiled. "I should go so you can really sleep."

"How long was I asleep?"

He laughed. "That time? About four minutes."

"Oh." She memorized the feel of her hand in his. Tried to remember if the kiss had been real. The whole night was a swirl of confusion. But she didn't think she'd dreamt it.

As if he'd read her mind, Link cupped her cheek like he had out by her van at the inn. He leaned in, his voice barely a whisper. "I'm going home now. I'll check on you tomorrow."

"Thank you."

He started to rise but squatted down beside her bed instead, his words coming in a rush. "All I could think, Shay, all I could think when we were searching—" He stroked her face tenderly, and she could feel every nuance of emotion in his feather-light touch. "And when I started to know deep inside that something was wrong. That it was foul play... it was that creep. All I could think was how glad I was that I kissed you tonight. If things had turned out... different. If—" He shook his head. "At least I'd have the memory of that kiss. And"—his words breathed against her cheek—"that you kissed me back."

Her throat full, she couldn't find words. She only hoped the tears that rolled onto her pillow spoke of all that was in her heart.

30

Leave your jacket on, baby." Shay hollered across the playground where half a dozen kids scrambled for real estate.

Portia defied her with her eyes—and let the jacket fall to the ground.

Beside Shay, Link snickered.

"Don't laugh at her." Shayla slapped his knee and gave a low growl. "Portia Beth!"

Sighing, she started to rise, but Link ruffled the hair at the back of her neck, holding her back. "It's really not that cold, babe. And she's running around."

"It's February. And besides, it's the principle of the thing now. Didn't you see the defiant look that little imp gave me?"

"Here." He pushed up from his spot beside her on the picnic table bench. "I'll take this one."

"Good! She listens to you better anyway."

Tucking his chin, he spoke in a baritone. "It's because of my low voice."

She laughed, watching as he strode toward the jungle gym. That man would make a good daddy some day.

"Portia!" His stern voice carried across the park. "Did you hear what Shay said?"

The girl turned long enough to see that Link was gaining on her, then took off running.

"You go put your jacket back on." Link trotted after her. "Right now."

Shayla smiled. Link would catch her, but given Portia's head start, it would be a race to watch.

A middle-aged woman, pushing a stroller with one hand and half-dragging a towheaded toddler by the other, parked at the picnic table beside theirs. "Is this taken?"

"No, it's all yours."

The woman plopped down with a sigh. Shayla guessed her to be the grandmother, but you never knew these days.

The woman looked up at the bright winter sun. "Nice to be able to get the kids out on a rare day like this, isn't it?"

Shayla smiled. "It sure is. I was going a little stir crazy." She leaned to peer into the stroller. "She's darling. How old?"

"Let's see. I guess she's five months now." The woman laughed. "I should probably know that. She's my daughter's. Her second. And this little guy is two. *That's* not hard to remember."

Shayla frowned. "Terrible two?"

"You got it."

She looked up to see Link carrying a squirming Portia across the playground toward them. He hadn't yet succeeded in getting her jacket on her.

Link acknowledged the woman with a brief hello, then sat beside Shay and secured Portia between his knees while he helped her back into the jacket. "Okay, all set," he said when he'd zipped her up.

Portia strained to get loose, but Link held her shoulders and spoke quietly but sternly. "You take that jacket off again, and we will get in the car and go home, you understand?"

She nodded.

"Portia, answer me. Do you understand?"

Silence.

He lifted her to the seat between them. "When you're ready to answer me like a big girl then you can go play."

The grandmother at the table next to them chuckled. "That age can be a challenge, can't it?"

Shayla laughed. "Terrible five?"

"She's beautiful," the woman said, ostensibly low enough so Portia couldn't hear. She glanced at Link, then back at Portia. "There's no question where she gets those pretty blue eyes."

Before Shay could think how to answer, Portia jumped up and tapped Link on the shoulder. "I'm ready to be good."

Link winked at the woman, then turned his full attention to Portia. "And you'll leave your coat on?"

"Yes." Portia bobbed her head.

Link looked at her.

"Yes, *sir*."

"Okay." He patted her behind. "Go play."

"They listen to their daddies, don't they?" The woman looked on in awe.

Shayla hesitated, feeling like she needed to set the record straight. Thankfully, Terrible Two chose that moment to throw a handful of gravel at the baby in the stroller.

Jumping up, the grandmother apologized and packed the toddler into the stroller with the screaming baby and headed across the park.

"Way to go, Daddy." Shayla teased, when the woman was out of earshot.

He batted his eyes at her. "It's the blue eyes."

She cracked up. But what the woman had said was true. Portia's eyes were an exact match to Link's. And as much as her niece looked like *her*, Portia could have been their daughter.

Shayla thought about the incident long after they left the park. That simple exchange somehow filled her with *hope*. A stranger in the park had mistaken them for a family. A multiracial family. And the exchange had been so matter-of-fact. Talking about what they had in common. Not the things that might divide them.

She supposed that woman would have been surprised to learn how profoundly their little exchange moved her. But it had served as a reminder to her that there were still good people in the world. People who, if she and Link continued together, wouldn't instantly judge them by the color of their skin, but…*by the content of their character.*

It scared Shay a little that she'd begun to *think* of them as a family—Link and her and Portia.

These last six weeks since the "accident"—as they called it in Portia's presence—Shayla saw things—no, *everything*—in a different light.

Instead of making her bitter, though, the incident had somehow made her stronger. Helped her begin to see how bright the kindnesses were compared to the hate. News had traveled about the attack, and people had showered her and Daddy with kindness and concern. People of all colors.

Even Daddy seemed to have softened a little over these weeks, though she suspected his transformation had more to do with Jerry's change of heart, which seemed to be sticking—knock on wood.

But Daddy hadn't offered one word of protest when she and Link spent time together nearly every day—if not in person, then on the phone.

She and Portia had been to Tuesday family dinners with Link twice now—with her father's knowledge, if not his blessing. Audrey had even invited Daddy to come along, though he'd used his Bible study as an excuse not to go.

Still, it wouldn't surprise her if one of these Tuesdays he up and said yes.

And the thought of that happening made her heart sing for reasons she didn't quite understand.

31

Grant swirled the ice in his glass and stared at his son, not sure how to even process his own emotions, let alone Link's. "You sound like you've thought this through."

"I have, Dad. I know Shay and I are going to face some challenges that most couples don't. But now that I know her—and Portia—I can't imagine not having them in my life."

Beside him, Audrey sighed. "We love them too, Link. Both of them. And I can't imagine you without them either."

"But?" Link narrowed his eyes. "You sound like you have reservations, Mom." He got up from the kitchen table and carried his glass to the fridge, filling it with ice and water from the dispenser in the door. "Anybody want a refill?"

Grant and Audrey both waved him off.

"The main thing that worries me is Jerry." Audrey took a nervous sip from her glass. "What will happen when he gets out?"

"And what if he gets out early?" Grant had thought about that plenty. It could happen. And it would devastate Shayla. And Link.

"I don't think he'll get out early. And even if he did, I don't think he'd try to make trouble for Portia or for us—Shay and me. Mike seems to think he's really turned his life around."

"Yes," Audrey said. "But that's all the more reason to think he might want Portia when he gets out."

Link nodded. "Maybe. But I can't just walk away from Shay and Portia because of what *might* happen in the future."

"You're right about that." Grant knew it was true. But that didn't keep him from worrying about what his son's future might hold.

"It just seems a little soon, honey." Audrey's voice wavered. "We just don't want you to rush into anything."

"Honestly, Mom, right now Portia is growing up so fast we don't want to waste another minute. We want to be the family she needs. And Shay and I . . . we'd like to have a family of our own. I . . . I want to make it official. I haven't proposed yet or anything," he added quickly.

"You sound pretty sure about all this," Grant said.

"Well, I want to get Mike's blessing first. But when you're our age, Pops, you don't have time to waste."

Grant and Audrey cracked up at that.

"Oh, my sweet son, you have all the time in the world," Audrey said, still laughing. "But it sounds like you're going into this with your eyes wide open." She eyed Grant, sending him a silent question, and he knew they were in agreement.

It was time.

Link's quizzical expression said he saw what had passed between them.

Audrey nodded and cleared her throat. "We've been talking about something, bud, and wanted to run this by you."

Link's eyes held intense curiosity. Grant wasn't sure how their son might respond to their proposition, but he was beginning to think God's hand might be in this even more than they'd first known.

"Your mom and I have been talking about making some changes." He reached for Audrey's hand. Tears welled in her eyes, but Grant knew they were happy tears. Or maybe tears of relief was more like it.

But now Link looked worried, so Grant hurried on. "The inn is doing well, but it's frankly more work than we ever anticipated. We've come up with some things we think will lighten the load a little and help us keep the inn going without burning us out. But we might be able to lighten *your* load a little at the same time. If you agree, that is."

"And no obligation," Audrey said. "None at all."

"That's right." Grant cleared his throat. "We don't want you to feel obligated at all. But it could be a win-win for everybody."

"What in the world are you talking about?" Link shook his head, looking completely bewildered.

Audrey laughed and took up where Grant had left off. "Dad and I are going to move into the cottage."

"CeeCee's cottage?" Link pointed toward the meadow. "Seriously?"

"Yes." Grant said. "With CeeCee's blessing. She's quite happy at the assisted living center."

"Wow." Link blew out a breath. "I didn't see that one coming."

Grant caught Audrey's eye. "You called it, babe."

She laughed, looking happier—and younger—than Grant could remember in a while.

They hadn't told the other kids yet, but Audrey had predicted they'd all be a little shocked about the plans. And yet, he and Audrey were practically giddy at the thought, despite how skeptical Audrey had been when he'd first presented the possibility to her.

"So... what?" Link's brow knit. "You'll rent out your master suite instead of the cottage?"

"Yes," Grant said. "And except for the fact it's on the third story and not handicap accessible, we can get nearly as much for the suite as we could the cottage. But the real game-changer is that we can have our Tuesday dinners at the cottage and rent all the rooms out nightly, so we'll generate significantly more income."

"I think that's great, but—"

"It's beyond great," Audrey said. "It's on the verge of brilliant." She looked up at Grant with something close to adoration. He patted her hand before letting go.

"Your mom was feeling a little stressed, and we—"

"More than a little." She rolled her eyes. "But this will give me a place to retreat to, yet I still can walk to work."

Link still looked a little dazed by the news. "It's really great. But I don't get what this has to do with me."

"Well, our original plan was to see if you might want to move back to the inn. Live in your old room in the basement. I know you're not crazy about your apartment in Cape, and this way you'd save the rent."

"And it wouldn't be like living with your parents," Audrey added quickly, "because we won't be here."

"But you would be here in case a guest needed anything. Or was checking in really late."

"Or checking out really early."

"Wow. Sounds like you've really thought this through." Link looked around the house, and Grant could almost read his mind. He was thinking of all the memories this old house held. The entire substance of Link's childhood memories were in this house. And if it was hard for their son to think of them not living here anymore—even though they'd still be on the property—Grant knew it would be that much harder for their sentimental daughters.

"You don't have to decide right now," he said. "We've got time."

"When were you planning to move?"

Audrey winked at him. "Tomorrow, if your dad would let me."

Grant went around behind her and put his hands on her shoulders. "*Not* tomorrow. But soon. Hopefully by the first of May. There won't be that much to move."

Audrey looked up at him over her shoulder. "And I might even get some new furniture out of the deal."

"But you're welcome to move back in any time. Even before we move out, if you can stand living with us for a few weeks."

"Dad, my lease is up next month." Link's jaw went slack. "And they were going to raise the rent on me. This is huge. I could save so much money. And I'm going to need money."

Grant looked at Audrey again, and she was grinning from ear to ear. "Well, speaking of that, there's something else we want to run by you."

Link cocked his head, and it struck Grant that they were all possibly watching God's provision—for all of them—unfurl before their eyes in ways that left little room to doubt the Almighty was caring for them.

"I think this is the last of mine." With a heavy apple box hoisted on one shoulder, Link stood at the top of the stairs looking down at his mom. Now that Mom and Dad were preparing to move to the cottage, his mother had declared that the Whitman kids had until tax day, April 15, to remove their remaining possessions from the inn. He thought he'd be exempt since he'd moved back to his old bedroom in the basement, but Mom had other ideas, and cleaning out the storage room was at the top of her itinerary.

Link didn't mind. Since he'd been able to go back to working only one shift, he felt like he had a life again. He lived for the weekends, but he didn't mind his job so much now that it was only nine to five, Monday through Friday. It didn't hurt that he was watching his savings account grow now that he was earning his rent by helping out at the inn.

His mom's voice floated up the stairs. "Did you check those white storage boxes in the northwest corner of the basement storage room? I'm sure some of those are yours."

Link sighed. "I seriously doubt there's anything in there I'd want, Mom." If he hadn't used it for a dozen years, he probably wasn't going to miss it.

But he humored his mother and ran down two flights of stairs and flipped on the light to the storage room. He lifted the lids of half a dozen boxes, not recognizing any of the contents as his. But the next box he opened made him smile.

He pulled it down from the shelf and sat cross-legged on the floor. Mostly old school papers and cheap sports trophies. Probably nothing he wanted to keep, but he'd leaf through things for old times' sake before he took them to the burn pile.

For a few minutes, he went through each paper and folder one by one, but when they all started looking the same—and making him feel a little too nostalgic—he picked up a stack and riffled through them. Lifting an old high school yearbook out, a sloppily folded sheet of paper fell out and fluttered to the floor.

He knew what it was before he'd even finished unfolding it. That old list they'd made at youth group that night. What had he been? sixteen years old? maybe seventeen? Strange he still remembered that after all these years. He smoothed out the now-brittle paper and read down the list.

The Woman I Want to Marry

1. She loves God.
2. She cares about other people.
3. She's pretty but not conceited or self-centered.
4. She has blue eyes and blonde hair.
5. She's not fat.
6. She's a good cook.
7. She will make a good mom.
8. She makes me laugh.
9. She ??
10.

He read the list, chuckling. He must have run out of steam at the end. Or maybe out of time.

He folded the paper and stuck it in his shirt pocket. Shayla would get a kick out of it. She would think it—

He took out the list again and unfolded it. He read it once more, this time with a particular woman in mind. Shayla Michaels fulfilled every single attribute on his list, except for one: #4. Her eyes were not blue and her hair wasn't blonde.

He smiled. He thought that was negotiable.

And maybe those last two, maybe the years had filled those blanks in for him too.

He took out a pen and started writing.

32

Grant pulled up to the curb in front of the bakery, relieved to see the lights were still on inside. He strode to the door, but it was locked for the day. He checked his phone. Almost six-thirty.

He knocked on the glass and resisted the urge to cup his hands and peer in the window, knowing the Michaels family lived here. He looked away when he detected movement inside.

The door opened and a smile lit Shayla's face when she recognized him. "Grant." She opened the door wider. "Come in. How are you?"

"I'm good, how about yourself?"

"Good. But"—she grimaced—"I hope you're not looking for a doughnut. Daddy already took the extras to the shelter." Her gaze went briefly to the floor, and Grant recognized that some fear must still linger there. Billy Waverton hadn't yet been sentenced, but he was in jail. In St. Louis, according to the sheriff. They'd all breathe easier when he'd been put away for a good long while.

"A doughnut is the last thing I need, Shay. Actually, I was hoping to talk to your dad, but if he's gone, I'll catch him another time."

"Oh, no. He's already back from Cape. He's just out in the garage. Let me go get him."

"I'll just go talk to him out there, if that's okay." This would be perfect. He would be out of earshot of Shay and Portia.

"Sure. Here . . ." She motioned for him to follow her through the bakery to the back door.

The place was tidy as ever, floors freshly mopped and countertops shining. There were little vases of flowers in the center of each table. He didn't remember that from before, but the effect was warm and homey. Grant was pretty sure that was Shayla's touch.

The door to the garage across the back alley was open, and when they rounded the corner, Mike Michaels looked up from under the hood of a van—a new vehicle that had replaced the totaled one, Grant assumed.

Shayla gave a little wave, said good-bye, and went back inside the bakery.

"Well, good evening, Mr. Whitman." Michaels came to greet him, wiping his hands on a shop rag. "What brings you here this fine evening?"

Grant put out a hand. "Call me Grant, please."

"I will if you'll call me Mike." They shook hands.

"That's a nice vehicle." Grant gestured toward the van. "Bigger than the last one, isn't it?"

"It is. Don't know that it runs any better though." He shook his head, looking disgusted.

Grant laughed and took a step back. "Well, don't look at me. I'm worthless when it comes to being a mechanic."

"Apparently that makes two of us." Mike went back to the van, closed the hood, and wiped his hands again. "Can I offer you something to drink?"

"No. Thank you though. I won't stay long. And I may be in big trouble after tonight." He was only halfway kidding. He swallowed hard and shot up a prayer that this didn't backfire. "Mike, I'll get right to the point. I'm here as one father to another. My son does not know I've come—and he probably wouldn't be too happy with me if he knew."

Mike frowned. "How so?"

"You probably won't be surprised to know that Link is going to be coming to see you one of these days. Soon. He's going to ask—*beg*—for your blessing to ask Shayla to marry him. And your blessing on his being a part of your granddaughter's life. I've watched these kids together, Mike. They've overcome what so many can't seem to. They've managed to love each other, and all of us"—he gestured between them—"despite all the barriers, despite the world's hate. I just . . . I want to put in a good word for my boy. Believe me, I know from experience there's never a man on this earth who's good enough when it comes to our precious daughters. But I'm begging you as Link's father, Mike to just at least consider his request. Give him a chance. I promise you won't find any man—of any color—on this earth who will love your daughter the way my son will. The way he *does*. And Portia too."

Michaels had stood, listening, seeming intent the whole time Grant poured out his spiel, but now he looked at Grant with a hard-set jaw. "You finished?"

He nodded. "I suppose I'd better be. And forgive me if I overstepped my bounds. I just see that—" He swallowed the lump of nerves that had made its way into his throat. "I think our kids are better at this—all this racial stuff—than our generation was. Better than our parents' generation, for sure. I just hope we can give them a chance to show the world that we *can* love each other, despite our differences, despite our humanness. I don't know about you, but I can't think of a legacy I'd be prouder of." He blew out a breath, harder than he intended. But he'd said his piece, and he believed every word he'd uttered. That was all he could do. The rest was in God's hands.

"*Now* you finished?"

Grant nodded, unable to read the look on the man's face.

Mike shook his head. "I'm sorry I couldn't save you from having to go through that. You kind of got to ramblin' there, and there wasn't any place I could jump in."

"Sorry. I just wanted to get it all said before—"

Mike held up a hand. "Before you stick your foot in any further"—he gave a low chuckle—"I'm sorry to say, your son beat you to the punch. He pretty much gave me the same flowery speech two days ago."

Grant's jaw dropped. "Are you kidding me?"

"I would not kid a man about something like that."

"Son of a gun." Grant threw back his head and roared, and Michaels did the same. Then he clasped Grant's shoulder and shook his hand again.

The flowering dogwood and redbud trees all along Chicory Lane were in full bloom, and it was only the first week in April. Link thought God had chosen a good year to send them an early spring.

He patted Shayla's knee in the passenger seat beside him, then caught Portia's eye in the rearview mirror. "Are you warm enough back there, kiddo?"

"I'm *hot*!" She tugged at the turtleneck of her little pink sweater.

"Okay, okay. Cool air coming your way." He turned up the fan and adjusted the vent.

"Portia. Be nice." Shay peered out the windshield, shading her eyes from the fast-setting sun. "It is so gorgeous out there."

"It's pretty gorgeous in here too." He reached across the console to stroke her face with the back of his hand, meaning every word. Even now, with her torn jeans and mud-splattered T-shirt, she grew more beautiful in his eyes every time he looked at her.

She shook her head, dismissing his compliment, but the grin she wore said she didn't mind.

They'd spent the day out at the inn helping his parents get the flower beds ready for planting. He'd told her he wanted to talk to her alone, and he knew she'd been dying of curiosity all day. And no doubt suspecting what was coming.

But he'd refused to give her even a hint. He'd been keeping a secret for weeks now—a couple of them, actually—and it was about killing him. But tonight the cats would be out of the bag.

When they got into Langhorne, he drove around behind the bakery and waited outside while Shayla took her niece in through the back door. Ever since Link had gone to talk to Mike, "Big Daddy" had become more willing to watch Portia while he and Shay spent time together. He wondered if Shay had noticed.

A few minutes later, she came out. She'd changed into a clean shirt, and was zipping up a hoodie over it.

"You still want to go for a walk?"

She shrugged. "Sure, if you do. It's such a pretty night."

Ever since the weather had turned nice, they'd taken to walking the quaint streets of Langhorne, talking and dreaming, and learning to know each other almost as well as they knew themselves.

Link had planned their routes carefully, steering her by CeeCee's house each time they walked, telling Shay stories about his childhood growing up there. But his goal had been to make her fall in love with the place. It had worked. She'd lamented the Realtor's sign in the yard and wished aloud that she could afford to buy the house herself. "Doesn't it make you sad to see your grandmother's house for sale?"

"I guess it would if CeeCee had died or something. But she's happier at the center than I've seen her in a long time."

He'd all but promised Shay a tour of the house some day before it sold, but the renters hadn't moved out yet the last time they'd walked by.

CeeCee's house was only a few blocks from the bakery but Link steered Shayla the long way around. They were deep in conversation when they crossed the street to the block where the house sat, but Shay stopped talking immediately and pointed. "Link. Look. The sign's gone."

"Sign?" His heart was beating a mile a minute.

"The Realtor's sign. It's gone. Did the house sell?"

"Oh, yeah. I didn't tell you?"

"No! It was here just the other night. It sold already?" She sounded near tears.

"Yeah, it did."

She frowned. "I never got to see it."

"You want to see it now?" He fished in his pocket and brought out a key on a plastic keychain.

"What? You have the keys? But if it sold, that would be trespassing."

"I don't think they'll care." He started confidently up the sidewalk to the front porch.

"Link." Shay lagged behind then jogged to catch up with him. "You can't just go in somebody's house without permission."

He stopped and looked at her, his heart about to explode. "What if I told you I have permission?"

"You do? You know who bought it?"

"I do." He put the key in the door and turned it. The door swung open. "Come on. I'll give you the tour."

33

Shayla stepped inside the front room of CeeCee's old house, excitement rising in her. She didn't know what it was about looking at houses, but she loved it. Maybe it was because she'd never really had a house. They'd gone from the apartment in Cape when she was young to living over the bakery.

"Wow! This looks really good. I was kind of expecting it to be run down, since it's been a rental for a while."

"It does look good, doesn't it?"

She inhaled. "Smell that? I think they've painted it."

"It does look like it has fresh paint."

"I love this color." The living room walls were her favorite barely-there shade of aqua. "This is exactly the color I would have painted it."

"It looks nice."

She turned back to Link. "Are you sure we should be here? Who was it that bought the house? How do you know them?"

A strange smile came to Link's face.

"What?" Something was up. He was acting weird.

"We have permission, Shay." Link drew her into his arms, tipped her chin up and kissed her. Sweetly, but insistently, too. "We have permission. I promise."

She wriggled free. What was wrong with him? "Well, I bet we don't have permission to be *making out* in their house. Link! That better not be why you brought me here!"

She trusted the man completely, and it was important to both of them to wait for marriage. But she knew Link was frustrated they so rarely had time alone together. It seemed like either Portia or one of their parents were always around. Which was probably a good thing, because on the rare occasions they *could* steal a moment alone, Link was all about kissing.

This—here in this house, alone—was pushing it though. Especially... She felt her face heat. She wasn't sure Link realized what it did to her when he kissed her like that. She headed for what looked like the kitchen. "Aren't you going to show me the house?"

She heard him behind her and hurried ahead before he could grab her again. *Oh, Lord. How long will you make me wait for this man?*

She let the kitchen distract her. "Look at this, Link! Just look. Is this what it looked like when your grandmother lived here? This is perfect. Oh! Those open shelves. I couldn't have designed it better myself."

She turned to see him beaming at her. "You like it?"

"It's amazing. So who bought it? Do I know them?"

"You know them." He pulled her into his arms again. And kissed her in that wonderfully disturbing way. "You know them," he whispered. "And you're kissing them."

She pulled away and stared at him. "What? *What?* Are you serious? *You* bought it?"

"Well, I'm buying it. The bank owns a pretty big chunk of it right now."

"Link!" She covered her mouth with her hands. "You're going to live here?"

"Shay." He took her hand and dropped to one knee. "I hope *we're* going to live here."

And suddenly she knew exactly what this was all about. Tears sprang to her eyes and she went to her knees in front of him. "Link. Really? *Really?*"

He looked suddenly nervous, and like a little boy. The sweetest little boy she'd ever known. He reached into his shirt pocket and pulled out a folded paper. He handed it to her, still grinning.

"What's this?"

"It's not a ring, Shay. I wish it was, but the down payment on the house pretty much wiped out my savings, so it might be a while before—"

She shook her head adamantly. "I don't care about a ring, Link. I'd probably just lose it in the dough anyway. I don't care about that at all. I'd rather have you. And this house. Oh, Link!" She must have said it fifty times, but she couldn't help it.

He touched the folded paper in her hand. "Aren't you going to read it?"

She looked at the paper, turned it over.

"I found it when I was helping my parents pack." Link looked like the proverbial kid in a candy store.

"What is it?"

He sat cross-legged on the floor, patting the spot in front of him. "Here. Sit."

She looked around the room, dying to explore. "This can't wait until after the tour?"

"Nope. You have to read it first."

"What is it?" she said again.

"It's a list I made in youth group. About the perfect woman." He patted her cheek, his voice tender. "Just read it." The paper was folded in quarters. He unfolded it once, leaving it folded in half.

She took the paper from him and started to read.

The Woman I Want to Marry

1. She loves God.

2. She cares about other people.

3. She's pretty but not conceited or self-centered.

~~4. She has blue eyes and blonde hair.~~

5. She's not fat.

She looked up at him. “Well, one out of five isn’t bad. I do love God.”

He laughed. “You nut. You’re all of those things. Except fat. You’re *not* fat, I mean.”

She giggled.

He unfolded the sheet so the rest of the list was visible.

She read it.

6. She’s a good cook.
7. She will make a good mom.
8. She makes me laugh.
9. She ?? looks exactly like Shayla Jean Michaels.
10. She comes with a bonus little girl named Portia Beth Michaels.

“Will you marry me, Shayla Michaels?”

She started to cry. “Yes. Of course I will. Oh, Link, I—I thought you’d never ask.”

“I thought I’d never get permission.”

“What do you mean? About the house?”

“No, silly. From your dad.”

She gasped. “Daddy *knows*?”

Link beamed. “He knows and approves.”

“He does? He gave his blessing?”

“It was like pulling teeth, but he finally did.” The way he grinned, she thought he was exaggerating.

But then, knowing her father, maybe not. “Does Daddy know about the house?”

Link nodded. “I invited him to live here with us, Shay. I hope that was okay. He said no, but maybe you can talk him into it.”

“Oh, Link. This can’t be happening.” She truly felt like she might disintegrate from joy. She wanted to kiss Link—her husband-to-be! She wanted to run and tell Daddy—even though he already knew. She wanted to tell Portia. Oh! That child would be so happy!

And she wanted to finish the tour of the house. Her house. *Their* house. *Oh dear God. Is it possible to die of pure joy? Thank you, Jesus. Thank you.*

Sitting cross-legged on the floor across from each other, Link took her hands. "So . . . you're happy?"

The tears came again. "You just don't know. You just don't know, Link."

He leaned and touched his nose to hers. "I think I might know. Because I think I might be about the same amount of happy."

She laughed, then cradled his face between her hands. "I love you." She'd never spoken those words to a man before Link. But she knew she'd never be sorry she had.

"I love you too, Shayla Jean. Now, you want to go see the rest of your house?" Without waiting for an answer, he jumped up and pulled her after him. "You have no idea how hard it was to keep this secret. We've been painting and putting in new flooring for three weeks now. We just finished the shelves in the kitchen last night."

"We? Who all knows about this?"

"My parents, your dad, my sisters. Chase and Drew hung the shelves."

"What? Are you serious?"

He nodded. "Nobody knew I was going to propose tonight. That was my secret. But they all know about the house, obviously. I was so afraid you'd see my truck down here. I parked in the garage when I could. We even talked the Realtor into leaving the sign up, so you wouldn't get suspicious."

"You're kidding. How did it all come about? I still can't believe you bought it."

"That day my parents offered for me to move home and help out at the inn; they also told me the renters were moving out of CeeCee's house and they were going to put it on the market. Dad thought that I might be interested. For an investment. But that day—before they told me about the house—I told them I wanted to marry you. And raise Portia."

"Link—" She whispered his name, in awe at how everything had unfolded.

"It just kind of seemed like God was setting everything up."

"And Daddy said yes? I still can't believe it."

He swaggered. "I think I'm growing on the man."

She laughed. "You must be living right."

His expression turned serious. "I feel like I've been living right ever since I met you."

This time, she didn't argue when he pulled her into his arms and kissed her again. And again.

Epilogue

Ohhh, Shayla!" Audrey folded her hands in front of her chin as if she were praying. "Honey, you look stunning!"

Shayla twirled in front of the mirror in a guest room at the Chicory Inn that had been converted to a dressing room for today. She looked back over her shoulder to see the full effect. That winter wedding she'd always wanted was overrated. At least if it meant waiting even one more day to marry Link Whitman.

But even for a June wedding, she *had* figured out a way to pull off the "fur" trimmed wedding gown she'd always dreamed of. She ran her hand lightly over the downy feather trim that lined the graceful neckline and the scooped cowl back of her gown.

Chicken fur, Link had dubbed it when he saw it on the hanger. The very thought made her laugh. But then her husband-to-be was good at doing that. And making her heart glad every day. So if he wanted to tell the world she got married in chicken fur, let him.

Audrey frowned and inspected the shoulder seam of the gown, picking at a thread. "There. The *perfect* June bride."

The way she said it sounded so much like Mama, Shayla felt tears threaten. She would probably always wish that her mother could have met Link. Could have known all the people who were most important in her life now. And yet, it made her connection to Daddy—and Jerry—all the more precious. Her dad would bring pictures to show Jerry when he went to visit next. And maybe, just maybe, she would go with him. And take Link. Introduce her brother to her husband.

"Have you seen my dad yet?" she asked Audrey.

"I have, and he's looking quite dapper!"

She giggled. "I've never seen him in a tux before."

"Shayla!" Portia flew into the room and pirouetted across the carpet in a blur of lavender tulle, which they were calling "purple" for the occasion.

Shay held out her arms. "Come here! Let me see you, birthday girl." She knelt, taking care with the hem of her gown. "You look so pretty, Portia!"

"You do too, Shay." She touched the feathers at Shay's neck, then blew on them. "I like your chicken fur." The gleam in her eyes told Shayla where that remark had come from.

"Link told you to say that, didn't he?"

Portia put her hands on her hips, in tattletale mode. "He told me to say chicken *poop*. But that's not nice."

Shayla stifled a laugh. "No, it's not. And good for you for not saying it."

Something caught Portia's attention, and she tiptoed to the window overlooking the meadow where the wedding tent was set up. "People are here already!"

"No!" Shayla squealed. "I'm not ready!" She picked at her hair. These stupid curls that were bound to be frizz by the time the night was over. But that was the way Link liked it. She'd make that concession on *his* wedding day.

Corinne popped her head in the door. "Your groom is waiting—Oh, Shay, how beautiful!"

Portia stepped in front of Shayla. "I'm beautiful too."

Corinne laughed. "Yes, you are, birthday girl."

"I'm six."

"I know. And since you're six"—she winked at Shayla—"why don't you come with me and we'll get your basket of flower petals ready to go." She took Portia's hand, then turned back to Shay. "Link is out by the climbing tree. The photographer wants to take a few pictures after you guys . . . have a moment. But go let your groom see you first! He is going to *flip*!"

Her heart warmed at this family she'd gained. But it warmed at the family she had to offer too. They were a good mix.

She crept down the stairs, afraid some of the guests might have come inside, but the coast was clear. She held up the hem of her gown as she hurried to the back door. Stepping outside, she looked down toward the meadow and—

There he stood, beside the Whitmans' "climbing tree," looking a little nervous, but handsome as all get out. A man in a tux…it didn't get much finer than that.

Closing the door behind her, she picked her way down the steps of the deck. She'd changed into white tennis shoes for this part of the day. But she wasn't about to run and risk falling down—and ruining her chicken fur gown.

Link looked up and smiled when he saw her. She was pretty sure by the look on his face that he liked what he saw.

As she came closer, he held out his hand. She took it, and he pulled her into his arms. Just as quickly, he held her at arms' length. "Let me look at you." He shook his head. "I'm not sure I can take it."

"You're looking pretty fine yourself, Whitman."

He leaned to kiss her. "I know, I know…don't mess up your lipstick."

"You can mess it up all you want tonight."

"Mmm." He pulled her close again, his voice husky. "I love you, Shayla Michaels. And that's the last time I'll be saying that."

"What?"

"After today, it'll be I love you, Shayla *Whitman*."

Some guy with a huge camera came traipsing down to spoil their moment.

"Is my makeup okay?"

"You couldn't look more beautiful. I mean it, Shay. Except for maybe—" He reached up and picked something out of her hair.

She leaned back to see him grasping a fat June bug between his fingers. She squealed. "Get that thing away from me!"

Link clowned around with the bug and made chicken fur jokes while the photographer snapped away.

All the nerves of the day drained away. And, except for missing Mama, Shayla couldn't imagine feeling any happier than she did in this moment. By the time they were finished with pictures, guests were beginning to find their seats under the tent.

Link slipped away to round up his groomsmen—his three brothers-in-law. And Shayla went to find her dad and Portia.

Daddy spotted her and instantly teared up.

"Daddy, don't! You'll ruin my makeup."

He pulled her into a hug. "You couldn't look more beautiful, baby. Your mama would have been so proud. So happy for you."

"I love you, Daddy."

"That goes both ways, baby." He offered the crook of his arm and she took it.

She and Link had both tried to convince her father to move into CeeCee's house with them, but he remained adamant. "I'll be fine. You and Portia deserve a real home. It's not good, you livin' in a bakery."

But she'd chided him. "We have a real home. Some of my happiest memories are in that bakery, Daddy. You and Mama made it a home for us. And we'll be back there every day to help with the bakery. It's only a five-minute walk from the house, you know."

"Six minutes, actually. I timed it. And I gotta say, I'm kind of pumped to turn Portia's room into that man cave I've always wanted."

Shayla knew better. Her dad was not a man cave kind of guy. But she loved him for putting that spin on it. It made it easier to think about him alone at the bakery.

"Okay, baby, wipe those tears. It's time to give my little girl away."

Shayla peered into the mirror of the powder room at the inn. "Shayla Jean Whitman," she whispered at the reflection staring back at her. If it weren't for the diamond sparkling on her left hand, she would think it was all a beautiful dream.

She held her hand up to admire the ring, splaying her manicured fingers. The ring was CeeCee's that Bree had worn while she was married to Link's brother and that had now been passed on to Link—and her.

She'd sneaked away from her wedding reception to check her hair before the dancing started. It was its usual frizzy mess, but Link was teaching her to tolerate, if not love the curls God had given her.

Unable to keep from smiling, she turned off the light and went outside to rejoin the rowdy celebration that was going on in honor of her and Link.

Picking her way back down to the meadow, she stopped at the top of the ridge and took in the amazing scene. A mass of stars winked at her in the deep blue, cloudless summer sky overhead. And beneath the canopy of their wedding tent, a dozen strings of twinkle lights made a valiant effort to echo God's starry night.

She stood perfectly still, listening to the quiet chatter of family and friends gathered under their wedding tent.

Daddy's friends from Bible study were all here, most of them gathered to themselves at a table in the corner—with CeeCee, who, judging by the men's laughter, seemed to be as entertaining as she was entertained.

Derrick and Valerie—who were an item now—had volunteered to cater with a few friends from college, as their gift to the newlyweds.

Portia held hands in a circle with Link's nieces, while his sisters rocked their babies on their hips and their husband's stood outside the tent shooting the breeze.

Shayla thought of that children's song CeeCee had quoted the first time Shay'd met her. "Red and yellow, black and white, they are precious in His sight." She'd scoffed that day, thinking CeeCee was being condescending. But that didn't keep her words from being true. They *were* precious in His sight. Each one of them. Maybe even Billy Waverton. He just didn't know it yet.

A gentle breeze ruffled the soft feathers at her neck and shoulders and made her shiver.

"Hey, Mrs. Whitman."

She turned to see Link—*her husband!*—striding across the ridge toward her.

His smile matched hers. "It's almost time for our first dance."

Shayla laughed. It really would be their first time to dance together. He'd tried to talk her into practicing a simple waltz step, but she wanted their wedding night to hold many firsts, including that sweet dance. "You're not going to step on my toes, are you?"

"I make no promises. Especially with you looking so beautiful."

She tipped her head to receive his feather-light kisses. "What does that have to do with anything?"

"You'll be distracting me."

She laughed. And let him mess up the hair she'd just worked so hard to put in place. "You're not nervous?"

He studied her, a gleam in his gorgeous blue eyes. "About the dance?"

"About . . . everything . . ."

Smiling softly, he took her hand and knit their fingers together, then pressed his cheek against hers and pulled her into their own private dance. "Nervous? Not even a little," he whispered against her cheek, rocking her to the music that wafted up to them—the music of laughter and chatter of the ones they loved, who'd come to celebrate this night with them.

She wove her fingers through his hair. "Me neither. I think we're gonna hit it out of the park."

Group Discussion Guide

SPOILER ALERT: These discussion questions contain spoilers that may give away elements of the plot.

1. In *Home at Last*, the final book in the Chicory Inn Novels series, Link Whitman is the "last man standing" in his family—the last one to get married—and he has his entire family eager to get that crossed off his list for him. How do you feel about matchmaking in the twenty-first century? Is it ever a good idea? Do you know anyone who's ever successfully made a match that lasted?
2. *Home at Last* deals with some difficult issues, especially in the area of racial unity. The characters in *Home at Last* discuss their belief that racial divides are deeper in some parts of the country than others. Have you found that to be true? And if so, how would you evaluate the community where you live? Are people of all races and economic situations generally given respect and fair treatment?
3. When Link and Shayla start dating, their families both have some reservations. Did you agree with and understand the reasons for Mike Michaels's reservations about his daughter dating someone of a different race? for Grant Whitman's reservations for the same reasons? Do you think either or both of them were revealing their own prejudices by expressing concern for Link and Shayla's future together?
4. What are interracial relationships like in the part of the country where you live? Are your neighborhoods, schools, and churches integrated, or are there sharp dividing lines? Have you ever lived in a town like (fictional) Langhorne, where only a few ethnic families resided? Were those families accepted and welcomed in the community?
5. The characters in *Home at Last* had a range of experiences when it came to the way they were raised and taught about racial issues. Talk about some ideas you may have grown

up with or learned in school or in the workplace that might actually be "racist" (defined as having or showing the belief that a particular race is superior to another).

6. What do you think are some of the challenges Link and Shayla might face as a married interracial couple? What about Portia? The issues are complicated enough for adults, but how can Link and Shayla help Portia understand issues of racial division. And how can we help our children learn what is needed for racial unity?
7. Another related issue this novel dealt with is that of stereotypes. Shayla was angry with her brother for going "down the list of bad stereotypes people have of black people." (Jerry was involved in gangs, drugs, fathering an out-of-wedlock child, in prison.) Are those things, in reality, limited to any one ethnic group? Why do you think stereotypes of any group get started? What stereotypes fit you? Do you think any person likes to be fit into a stereotype? Why or why not?
8. What do you think of Link's opinion that he and Shayla can make a difference in promoting racial unity by simply living their lives in a way that demonstrates unity and compassion for all people?
9. What challenges do you think Link and Shayla might have parenting a child who isn't either of theirs by birth or adoption?
10. Discuss the scene between Grant Whitman and Mike Michaels, the fathers of Link and Shayla. Do you think it is ever right for a parent to intervene on behalf of an adult child? How could things have backfired for Grant? Why do you think they didn't?

Want to learn more about Deborah Raney
and check out other great fiction from
Abingdon Press?

Check out our website at
www.AbingdonFiction.com
to read interviews with your favorite authors,
find tips for starting a reading group,
and stay posted on what new titles are on the horizon.

Be sure to visit Deborah online!
www.deborahraney.com

About the Author

DEBORAH RANEY dreamed of writing a book since the summer she read all of Laura Ingalls Wilder's Little House books and discovered that a little Kansas farm girl could, indeed, grow up to be a writer. After a happy twenty-year detour as a stay-at-home wife and mom, Deb began her writing career. Her first novel, *A Vow to Cherish*, was awarded a Silver Angel from Excellence in Media and inspired the acclaimed World Wide Pictures film of the same title. Since then, her books have won the RITA Award, the HOLT Medallion, and the National Readers' Choice Award. Deb is also a three-time Christy Award finalist. She enjoys speaking and teaching at writers' conferences across the country. She and her husband, Ken Raney, make their home in their native Kansas and, until a recent move to the city, enjoyed the small-town life that is the setting for many of Deb's novels. The Raneys enjoy gardening, antiquing, art museums, movies, and traveling to visit four grown children and a growing brood of grandchildren, all of whom live much too far away.

Deborah loves hearing from her readers. To e-mail her or to learn more about her books, please visit www.deborahraney.com.